FIRE HORSE

A Novel by

PAT OLNEY

Karome Publishing

First published in 2024

ISBN (pbk): 979-8-9905495-0-0

ISBN (ebk): 979-8-9905495-1-7

ISBN (audio): 979-8-9905495-2-4

Printed by Karome Publishing

CHAPTER ONE

Don

AUGUST 2019

FOUR YEARS. DON DRAINED the last sour sip of his beer and dropped the bottle onto the porch beside him, resting his hands on the arms of the rocking chair. He felt the rough wood against his palms and he worked his left hand into it until a splinter penetrated his skin. The sun was setting behind the trees, the air had taken on a chill and even though the days were still hot, he could perceive the approach of autumn. The cold air filled his lungs and together with the pinpoint of discomfort in his hand, it was proof of life against the growing numbness he felt.

He was startled by the faint sound of voices, laughter from a nearby cabin—*God, sound carried up here*—and felt a mixture of envy and loathing. He guessed it was the Langdon cottage, two lots over. They rented it out for weekenders now, and his mind crafted the image of a young father with a few days of stubble from 'roughing it', up for a getaway from the stress of the city. There was, perhaps, a beautiful wife and some children too, all attempting to cram family salvation into a few precious days.

He sat like this in silence, and the sour taste of the beer lingered on his tongue. Sometimes, when he drank, he could barely taste the beer as he drained the bottles, he would just pour them out into a seemingly bottomless void. Tonight, though, he savored the beer's familiarity - the bitter of the hops, the hint of sugar and tart, until a stray mosquito buzzed by his ear, stirring him from his reverie.

Four years.

It felt like an eternity. Don swept his bottle up and went inside.

Each evening followed a similar routine. It was a daily death. After some beers or wine on the porch, Don would retreat inside from the vitality of nature, and one by one, would darken the lights of his one-story cabin, until finally only the feeble glow of his bedside lamp remained. Some nights he would lie awake awhile, staring at the shadows on the ceiling, but this night, he had self-medicated sufficiently to ensure that his mind passed into oblivion just as he withdrew into the shroud of the bed. He didn't even bother to turn the lamp off.

As much as the evenings felt like little deaths, Don found the daily rebirth of consciousness worse. It would come through slowly at first; cracks in a breaking dam.

Light.

I exist.

The first trickles of water.

I am a man. Don.

More cracks and a steady flow now.

I'm at the cabin.

I am married. Was married.

The dam would burst, and the full force of his existence would be restored.

It took all his strength to rise from the bed to begin his daily ritual. He stumbled, dressed solely in his underwear, to the ensuite bathroom, his mind filling with a chore list for the day ahead. As he arrived at the sink under his mirrored cabinet, he began with what was becoming a frequent part of his morning routine—two Tylenol and a handful of cold water. Don had never understood how some people could swallow the damn things dry but despite the water he nearly choked anyway.

He stared into the open medicine cabinet as he set the Tylenol back into its place next to several prescription bottles with labels full of indecipherable fine print. Only the medication names and his own jumped out at him: Effexor— Don Rydell, Ambien—Don Rydell, Ativan—Don Rydell. He chased the Tylenol with an Effexor, and as he closed the cabinet he was confronted with his image. He stared intently, as though needing to confirm that his consciousness had reincarnated into the correct body, still not fully feeling it was his.

His mind told him that he was forty-two, and his driver's license would provide the proof, but he felt as though he were staring at an older version of himself, the brother he'd never had maybe. Dark hair with a slight curl tufted up on his roundish head and he had a slight widow's peak, the kind that could be attractive in a younger man, but today it seemed to be in full retreat. Briefly, a vision of himself with a bald pate crossed his mind and he banished it in disgust. He considered the sturdy, Roman nose beneath his brown eyes.

Nothing noteworthy, he thought, but the eyes betrayed the mileage he felt. Dark, puffy bags sagged beneath them, and today he prodded them with his fingertips tentatively, as if questioning their reality.

He stretched his mouth into an oversized grin, confirming that his straight and slightly yellowing teeth were all in place. His tongue carried the film of yesterday's sins, and he decided to brush his teeth straight away.

Next, he shuffled to the toilet, polluting the bowl with a thick, dark yellow liquid, and he found himself assessing yesterday's damage through the color of his urine. This was a daily process, which was often followed by self-recrimination and an affirmation to treat himself with a little more respect. Today, however, he was in no mood for such self-reflection.

After washing his hands, he slipped back into the bedroom and grabbed socks from the drawer. He'd never thought he'd see the day when he would prefer to sit to put his socks on. Faded blue jeans and a plain blue T-shirt completed the ensemble, and he made his way to the kitchen.

The cabin was a small affair, inherited from his father. It had been a source of family pride and although modest, held many memories — memories that no longer felt authentic to Don, but rather more like echoes, or maybe flashes from a film that had been cut and reassembled in some random order. As he made his way to the kitchen, he considered the cabin with fresh eyes. It was a simple one-story layout and was of the construction favored in the first half of the twentieth century, a brief period of frugality when function triumphed over form. His father had purchased it from an elderly Toledo couple some thirty years ago—the Eldridges or Eldritches, he could never remember—and had saved for nearly a decade for the promise of it.

The layout was simple; it was a rectangular building about sixty feet wide and twenty feet deep with a front porch across a large part of its breadth, and a sole door in the center. The door was solid mahogany, stained a dark brown over its smooth surface, with no letterbox or knocker to blemish the wood. Don's father had replaced the latch twenty years ago but had preserved the mid-century modern style in the form of a large, ornate brass handle with a thumb latch on top. Don had held on to that handle for dear life more than once as he reentered the home from an evening drinking alone on the porch. The door itself was aging, but Don couldn't bear the thought of replacing it with some fiberglass imitation. It was a magical portal to Don, and he wouldn't dare to alter it in any way. He would sometimes fantasize that, if he opened it just right, his father, or maybe Julia and Charlie would be waiting to greet him on the other side.

This morning, on his way to the kitchen, Don stopped to stare at the door, imagining himself welcoming a visitor into his solitude. If anyone should ever come, they would, upon entering, immediately perceive the bulk of the building. Coming into the home, to the right, was a small, enclosed laundry room with a door off the entry hall. To the left, over a short half-wall, a sizable kitchen held a black cast-iron stove, an old white fridge, counter and sink, and the usual other necessities.

To the left of the sink was an Italian coffee machine, an anachronism in this place if there ever was one, from which Don now pulled a steaming black coffee. He remembered arguing with Julia about the purchase—as she hadn't been able to understand how anyone could spend a thousand dollars on a coffee maker—and he remembered, too, the feeling of self-importance as he'd explained its various functions to the family and friends that had once visited the place. He had once thought it a marvelous piece of engineering and style. Now, as if succumbing to the forces of its environment, it was reduced in his mind to a functional item only, grinding out coffee day after day. He blushed with the memory of his pride.

To the rear of the cabin, adjacent and open to the kitchen, was a small living room adorned with two off-white linen couches and a brown leather easy chair. The couches and chair all bore the imprints of their prior occupants, and a faint but pleasant smoky odor. The source of their smell was a wood fireplace, located at the rear of the cabin, centered opposite the front door and flanked by large windows on either side. A door just to the right of the fireplace led to a sizable rear patio. The cabin had two bedrooms, each with an adjoining bathroom, located on opposite wings of the central living area, and Don used the bedroom to the left as it was his childhood room and just a few feet closer to his morning coffee. He also didn't feel quite right using his father's bedroom and doubted that he ever would.

Ownership of the cabin had passed to Don eight years ago upon his father's death and oddly he still felt like a child in the house, as though it was not yet completely his somehow, and he sometimes wondered if the labor he put into caring for the property was a way of claiming his rightful ownership of it.

As usual, Don took his first coffee of the day on the front porch. Everything felt different in the morning, and the mental fog of the prior evening cleared in the crisp morning air. The cabin faced southwesterly, and this meant that it sheltered the front porch, leaving Don to enjoy the morning sun by reflection only as it played off the tops of the spruce and pine trees that filled the property.

Although it was cool now, he knew that today was going to be hot, and wanted to get some work done early. His mind continued to forestall the inevitability of the coming weekend, and he filled it with thoughts of his chores instead. He decided that he didn't have time to savor his coffee, so he dumped the remaining half cup onto the gravel driveway. After setting the cup down on the porch, Don walked to his pickup truck and hopped in.

The Ford was about ten years old, another inheritance from his father but unlike the cabin, he had largely neglected it. Don had long since bothered to wash the exterior of the vehicle, and it was difficult to discern its true color amongst the shades of brown and gray. Windows down, he drove away, watching as the cabin receded in the rearview mirror and listening to the soothing, rhythmic crunch of gravel beneath his tires.

Don's cabin was one of many scattered in the woods of Western Michigan, and it was about ten miles from the lake, which suited Don just fine. Today, as he did most days, he started with a quick trip into town, which superficially was a supply run. Why he needed to take these so frequently was best not examined too closely, lest his professed reasoning collapse under the weight of logic. In truth, the rituals he enjoyed most were breakfast at Kay's and his visits with Diane at the hardware store.

The town itself was a small hamlet, nestled on the shores of Lake Michigan south of Traverse City, and there were probably no more than five thousand souls full-time—maybe double this time of year due to vacationers—but it held the necessities of life. There was a grocer, bakery, gas station with attached auto shop, hardware store, liquor store, and various craft and sundry shops clearly geared to the seasonal traveler.

Kay's was a mainstay of the town and could be best described as a classic diner. It was a plain red brick building, save for a large red sign over the front door advertising the restaurant's name, and inside it housed a long lunch counter and a dozen or so tables and booths which had not been updated for as long as Don had been coming here. He entered, and conducted a quick survey of the place, confirming that Linda was working. She had arrived early this summer, from God knew where, and had picked up work as a server at Kay's shortly thereafter. He paused a moment to verify her area of responsibility and casually took a seat at one of her booths.

A brief and redundant examination of the menu did not reveal any new insight; it would be eggs, bacon, and coffee, like most mornings. Linda spotted him from two tables over where she was waiting on some well-dressed vacationers, and flashed a brief smile and nod, indicating she would be right over.

As she approached, he smiled and greeted her as warmly as his mood allowed.

"Morning Linda. Looks like you've got your hands full today."

This was met with a smile that seemed to light up her face, and Don always felt this was genuine with Linda. He'd seen phony before, but when she smiled, her blue eyes would brighten to match her lips. She had a soft complexion without blemish, and her shoulder-length blonde hair framed slightly chubby cheeks that were already flushed with the growing heat of the day and the kitchen.

"Let me guess. Eggs over easy, bacon, brown toast, black coffee," she offered.

His chest quickened at the thought that she deemed him memorable. He nodded and she brushed off to fill his order.

Each visit, he coached himself on how to negotiate the boundaries of the exchange further. His pride ensured that it was a tentative approach —a comment here, a wink there—never staking out a position from which there was no courteous, face-saving retreat. Previous reconnaissance had failed to reveal any sign of a significant other and he wondered at her life outside of work.

Soon, she returned to set down a steaming plate of food and top up his coffee. He decided on a safe pitch.

"Any big plans this weekend? I hear there's a band playing down at the waterfront Saturday night."

As soon as he had blurted it out, he cursed himself. He must have been fifteen years her senior and on reflection, realized that he preferred the comfort and promise that came with not knowing. He hoped he hadn't pushed too far; he had no idea what he would do if she ever expressed any interest, probably run out the door and never return. Fortunately, the question was easily deflected.

"Nothing much. What about you?"

He should have seen this coming.

"Memorial back in the city," he managed thinly, and the mood was gone.

She lightly touched his shoulder. "Let me know if you need anything else."

She attempted a smile, but this time her eyes were flat.

After completing the perfunctory visit to the hardware store—today it was for chainsaw oil and some fertilizer for the garden—he stepped back up into the truck. He was surprised Diane hadn't been working today and hoped she wasn't sick; he decided he would text her later. He paused before turning the ignition, being briefly immobilized by the morning's events, and his face flushed as he thought back on his conversation with Linda. The real root of his discomfort, though, was the growing dread of the weekend ahead. It was less than a week until he would face Julia again.

His memory wasn't what it used to be, but he had no trouble recalling their last encounter.

Why was it so easy to remember the shittiest parts of life with such clarity, while the good memories felt like feeble echoes of their former selves?

Good memories seemed to just fade until they were memories of memories in some unending recursion. Charlie's first step: *was it in the kitchen or the living room?* Losing his first tooth. Don thought he'd put the money under the pillow, but could he swear to it? Flash forward to Charlie's first day, leaving the house nervously to make his way to school, his proud parents in the doorway waving. Or, watching him water ski for the first time. *Had it been Don or his father driving the boat?* That was the last summer Don's dad had been alive. Then, Don and Charlie cutting down their own Christmas tree at the cabin when he was thirteen—their last really good Christmas. *What had they given him that year?* Don wished he'd known at the time what he now knew — wished he'd *focused harder* on enjoying those precious moments, maybe capturing them with higher fidelity.

Sitting now in his truck, with his forehead against the cold leather of the steering wheel, he found that, try as he might, he couldn't bring the images to mind. Sometimes, when it got bad, he had trouble seeing Charlie clearly. He hated himself the most in those moments, when his great weakness was exposed and when he would have to sneak a glance at an old photo to bring his memory back. He'd swear to himself that, this time, it would stay firmly implanted in his mind, only to have it shift and fade and again elude his grasp.

And of course, there was Julia.

Yes, Julia had made it clear in no uncertain terms that she never wanted any contact with Don again. Ever. But this weekend was different. After four years of searching, hoping, waiting and grieving, they would finally bury their son.

CHAPTER TWO

Julia

SEPTEMBER 1998

A WARM BREEZE DRIFTED in through her bedroom window, carrying the sounds of shouting from the street below. The sound woke Julia from a deep sleep, and she lay motionless for a moment, finally deciding the noise was some kids playing down the street. They were probably delinquent from school, not being ready to make the transition back after the long summer break. She risked a look at the clock at her bedside.

Shit. It was two in the afternoon already; *why hadn't her alarm clock gone off?* Kelly was picking her up at seven thirty and she had things to do beforehand.

Adjusting to the schedule at Rick's, where she had been working since her twenty-first birthday, hadn't been too bad, but she was only three months into the job and still felt like a strange animal, neither fully nocturnal nor diurnal. Living *in between*. Sleeping while others played, working while they slept.

She rubbed her eyes and sat up.

Get moving, she told herself, her inner cheerleader taking charge. She bolted out of bed and threw on a T-shirt, exercise shorts, and socks. The first order of business would be a quick run—she still had time—and she left her room to head down the hall to the bathroom. She was careful not to make noise for fear of waking her father, who was definitely nocturnal, and reached the bathroom in silence. Relieving herself at the toilet she waited for her soul to catch up to her body, feeling that it was still back in the bedroom somewhere. Finishing, she got up, and with only the slightest glance at the mirror, washed her hands and face and put her long, brown hair into a ponytail.

She slipped down the stairs quickly to the back door, popped her running shoes on, and stepped out to North River Street. She would cut her run a bit short today, but would still make it around the park to get a couple of miles in. They lived in the Depot Town neighborhood of Ypsilanti, about forty miles from Detroit, and she definitely felt better running by the park in the middle of the afternoon than in the evening. Nobody from around here called it Ypsilanti—it was just "Ypsi" —as if the town and its residents didn't deserve more than two syllables on the tongue. Julia didn't think Ypsi was as dangerous as most people thought, but it wasn't as safe as most people wanted either.

She got to the church past Prospect Park and swung right. The last two weeks had seen a big change in scenery for her run, as the families had abandoned the park for school and work, leaving it an empty patch of green. The air was still warm, though she found herself looking forward to the smells and sights of autumn soon to come.

The run felt hard today, she didn't know why, and she hardly took note of the houses as she ran past. For some reason though, as she approached her own, she stopped and stared at it for a moment while she caught her breath. It was an ordinary two-story like most of the houses around here, built during the brief period of optimism between the First World War and the Great Depression, and like most of the other homes in the neighborhood, it wasn't very large. Cheap white siding around single paned windows all sat on a bed of gray concrete, with charcoal trim and shingles completing the bleak look.

What did make their home stand out were the gardens. They were the nicest on the block, her mother saw to that, with red roses and bright yellow black-eyed susans around neatly trimmed green bushes. The thought of her mother's effort to make a home here, to bring some beauty to this shithole, caused anger to rise like bile in her throat. *How dare he drag us here?* She suppressed the pointless, juvenile thought, and walked the last hundred yards to the house to cool down.

She went back in through the screen door at the side of the house off the driveway, again being careful not to make too much noise, but the effort was in vain as her father was already up and at the kitchen table reading the newspaper.

Who does that anymore? It was nearly the twenty-first century for God's sake.

The main floor of the house was simple. Entering from the side door off of the driveway was the most convenient for Julia, as the staircase heading up to the two bedrooms and shared bath was located just inside the side entrance. The kitchen lay open to her right. It was lined at the front of the house, with dirty white cabinets over a counter containing a single steel sink under the window. The window provided Julia's mother a view to the street, while she cooked and spouted a running commentary on the activities of the neighbors. Immediately to Julia's right, four chairs and a cheap maple veneer table, stained and scuffed in spots, rested under the sole side window that overlooked the driveway.

Unkempt wisps of black and gray hair on a balding head were visible above the *Detroit Free Press*. Her father was seated at the kitchen table, lurking behind his morning read, and she could just see around the newspaper to his white undershirt—a *wifebeater,* as some called it, although she'd never seen him hurt her mother, not once, at least not that way. Old track pants and slippers completed the ensemble and thin trails of smoke rose from behind the news, as though remnants of some foreign conflict were struggling to manifest themselves in front of her father. The smell of his first cigarette of the day quickly dispelled the fantasy. She was used to the smell from the bar, but it seemed worse in the house as she got older, more personal, even invasive. She loved her father but found more and more that she had to fight feelings of anger and disgust when she thought too long about his choices. At least it was coffee in his hand.

"Morning," he muttered without looking up from the paper. The word coming out sounding more like *marnin*. "Get me some more coffee?"

David McCarthy was a first-generation immigrant from Ireland who had come over in the late sixties to ride the wave of American industry with the hope of good work. After arriving in Hamtramck, he'd been unable to get work at any of the "Big Three," lacking any trade experience, and had bounced from odd job to odd job until finally, after two decades of transient work, he was drawn out to the security job at Eastern University in Ypsi for the promise of steady pay and cheaper living. His accent was still as thick as the day he'd arrived.

"Dad, it's three in the afternoon," she replied.

"Figure of speech."

"When'll Mom be back?"

"She's cleaning over at the Davis house. I've no idea how long that'll take her, the size of that place. Now, how's that coffee coming?" A higher-pitched delivery laced with a touch of impatience.

She wanted to say: *Get up off your ass and get your own fucking coffee* but relented and moved past him to the counter. She brought the pot over to the table topping his cup off, and he nodded his head briefly in gratitude.

"Anything in the news?" she asked, hoping to engage him constructively as she poured a glass of water for herself and grabbed a granola bar from the cupboard.

"You mean that's not about Monica Lewinsky?"

He finally looked up at her, a half smirk on his face. He was not an unattractive man: at least, she could see where he would have been attractive before the accumulation of whisky, smoke, and the grind of night shift work got the better of him. He was still fairly slim—remarkable really, with his diet—and had a long face with sharp green eyes. Julia often thought that those green eyes and his sharp wit, his ability to talk his way out of *almost anything,* were the best inheritance he would, he could, ever gift her with.

"They say the Starr report'll be out this week." He returned his attention to the paper. "More bullshit. I really only pay attention to the sports."

"Alright then, what's new in sports?" She said, still standing. She hadn't the slightest interest in sports of any kind, but thought to make a last, half-hearted effort to converse.

"They say that pretty boy McGwire'll beat Maris's record, maybe this week even."

"What does he play?" Deliberately egging him on, as she had heard her father refer to Mark McGwire before.

"Fuck off, girl."

"I'm going to shower and take the truck to get some things for Mom at the store," she called over her shoulder, already halfway up the stairs.

The hot water from the shower felt good on her skin and she lingered even as she was aware of the time. Finally, she stepped out to dry herself. She was not one prone to self-admiration, if anything, she felt overly conscious of her body with breasts too small, knobby knees, and the birthmark on her hip that always caught her eye in the mirror.

She knew people thought she was attractive, but she couldn't see it in herself. She'd had a couple of dates here and there—one ambitious boy had even told her she looked like Salma Hayek—but they had all fizzled for one reason or another.

Maybe she was too particular, or maybe she scared them off with a little too much of the wit and intellect she took from her father; she wished she knew. Anyway, all the good catches were in Ann Arbor, and she seemed to be meeting them at their worst. Half-pissed and acting like assholes. That brought thoughts of the time, and her inner coach prompted her to get it in gear.

Dressed, she returned downstairs and grabbed the key to the Chev from the hook by the door. She muttered a quick "Bye!" over her shoulder.

"Bye," her dad replied, eyes still fixed on the news.

The grocery store was about five miles from the house, across the river in Midtown. It wasn't the closest, but it was the closest with an international foods section where she could get the jicama her mother had asked for. She drove down Cross Street and barely glanced at St. John the Baptist church as she passed by. She had stopped attending Mass there with her mother this summer, and this was the source of some ongoing friction between them, a hard-fought beachhead that had taken her years to achieve. As the church receded behind her, she experienced a flush of pride in her growing independence and felt as though, for the first time in her life, she was in control of something. Finally, she arrived at the store and picked up the things they needed.

Returning to the house around four thirty, she could tell that her mother was home before she went in the door. It was warm enough for the windows to be open, and the smell of garlic, onion, and cilantro drifted out to the driveway. She realized she was hungry and hurried in.

"Julia?" her mother called from the stove across the room without turning to look.

"It's me, mama."

Julia brought the groceries over to the counter just as her mother turned to acknowledge her.

"Did you find the jicama?"

"Of course."

"Just put the stuff on the counter here. I'm gonna make some nice fries with it and some pork." Isabella turned to face her daughter. "Sound good?"

Julia loved her mother's cooking. It felt like love.

"Sounds great. When will it be ready? Kelly's picking me up at seven thirty."

"Don't worry, I know when you have to go to work. I'll have something ready by six thirty."

"Do you need any help?" Julia offered.

"It's all under control, mija."

Briefly, as her mother returned her focus to stirring the contents of the pan, Julia took her in. She was a heavy-set woman, with golden skin like sand. Her hair was long and dark, like Julia's, and Isabella washed and cared for it religiously. She wore it in a ponytail today and to an outside observer it would be obvious the two women were related. Julia took notice, maybe for the first time, of the wrinkles at the corners of her mother's eyes.

When had those arrived? She reflexively brought her fingertips to her cheek, touching her own skin in an act of appreciation.

Julia asked, "Where's Dad?"

Isabella glanced up from her cooking at Julia and nodded toward the living room.

"Watching TV."

This had been a rhetorical question as the routine rarely varied. Her mother would cook dinner and a lunch for him to take to work, all while he watched television. This, after cleaning one or two other peoples' houses and her own. The two McCarthy women exchanged the briefest of glances, the unspoken bond of a burden shared.

In that moment, Julia recalled one Saturday night a few years back, just after the move, when they'd gone to a friend's wedding. It had been a great Mexican occasion, with a live band, dancing, food and refreshments, and although her mother did not normally drink, she'd had several glasses of wine that evening. While her father was off at the bar, or the bathroom, or somewhere drinking, Julia complained again to her mother about the move out to Ypsi. Her mother attempted to placate her.

"Don't be too hard on him.

"He looked everywhere.

"This was a good opportunity for us.

"You know the economy is bad."

Her mother had offered these as gentle explanations for their circumstance, but to Julia they were indictments - indictments of her father's failure of ambition. She had grown up, like most children, with the unshakable belief in the superiority of her parents – they were the best at everything, could do anything. This view began to shift in her teens, but after the move it began to crumble quickly for her. That evening at the wedding she had felt the last of her innocence slipping away, revealing to her the cold truth. She had vowed she would do something with her life; she wasn't going to slowly decompose on a living room couch in some shitty corner of the earth.

"Mija? Julia?" Her mother snapped her back to the present.

"I'm going to go change for work, Ma."

Julia was fluent in multiple terms of affection from her mixed ancestry and used them interchangeably and comfortably. She brushed out of the kitchen and up the staircase to her room.

A while later they sat in silence at dinner, her father again reading the paper - his shield against uncomfortable interaction.

"Great dinner, Ma," Julia said, filling the air.

"Thank you," her mother replied with genuine appreciation, never tiring of compliments about her cooking. "Be safe tonight."

"I will. Kelly will be here soon. I'd better get outside."

She exited out the side door to the driveway and sat on the steps to wait. Soon, she saw the distinctive lights of Kelly's '88 Sunbird coming down Oak Drive.

Kelly lived on her own in an apartment on the east side of the park and they had met, at the park, a year ago while they were both out running.

She'd had some good friends in high school in Mexicantown, but several years on they had faded, and ultimately they were failing to survive the move to Ypsi. Kelly was really one of her only friends now as they spent a lot of time together at work and on weekends, and there was an easy, if not superficial, way about their relationship.

The sun had dropped behind the houses, and as Kelly pulled into the driveway beside the Chev, the lights from the Sunbird briefly blinded Julia. She opened the door and was immediately confronted by Faith Hill singing about "This Kiss" at the top of her lungs. Kelly loved country music but she quickly turned the radio down as Julia plopped into the passenger seat.

"Sweet ride." Julia smirked.

Kelly offered the standard reply: "Yeah, totally bitchin'."

As the Sunbird moved through the early twilight toward the highway, Julia silently considered Kelly, who was staring intently through the windshield, her face intermittently illuminated by the sodium streetlights creating a slow-motion strobe effect. She was a petite blonde with shoulder length hair and bright, blue eyes. A smattering of freckles dotted her high cheekbones, and she had a beautiful smile with a slight crookedness in her top front two teeth, which only added to her charm. Julia thought she was attractive and sometimes wondered at Kelly's love life. Their work schedule certainly made socializing difficult. Kelly never spoke of a boyfriend, and when she talked about the guys she would meet while working or at the gym, it always seemed a little like a caricature of the real thing, overdone. Despite her attractiveness, Julia suspected that, like herself, Kelly's romantic experience was limited and she wondered why.

"Ready to face the screaming hordes?" Kelly asked, breaking the silence. Julia supposed that it was an exaggeration intended to fill the air between them, as it was Wednesday and there wouldn't be any live music tonight; still, the back-to-school crowd might be sizable. It was Friday that Julia really feared as she hadn't worked at Rick's during the school year and didn't know what to expect.

"Ready as I'll ever be. Who's in charge tonight?" Julia asked.

"Ralph." Kelly said the name with a mock-vomiting sound.

Silence hung between them for a moment.

"That guy gives me the creeps," Julia said finally, staring straight through the windshield.

"Yeah. Wait, did he hit on you?" Kelly asked, turning briefly to assess Julia's reaction to the question. "Because

I heard that he followed Michelle after her shift one night wanting to take her out. It bugged her the fuck out."

"No. Nothing like that," Julia replied, "Wait, did that really happen? Is that why Michelle quit?"

Kelly just shrugged her shoulders.

"Ok, well that didn't happen to me, but sometimes I see him just staring. The place'll be busy, I'm slinging drinks like I've got three arms, and out of the corner of my eye, I'll see him over by the office door. Just staring. It gives me the creeps."

"Maybe it's because you can't tell which eye is looking at you," Kelly smirked.

"It's not his lazy eye, okay? I just get a chill in my spine when he looks at me. Anyway, you asked."

They pulled onto I-94 with fifteen minutes to go. They would be on time.

"Got any plans for the weekend?" Julia asked after a time.

"I'm going to meet a friend who's going to Eastern. I think I want to get my GED and try to get in there. She did hers last year and is going to help me with it." Kelly stared straight out the windshield as though the traffic demanded her undivided attention.

"Good for you," Julia managed.

They pulled up to a parking spot on Church Street near Rick's and got out of the car.

Rick's wasn't much to look at from the outside—a red sign above a steel door that was framed on both sides by 1970s opaque glass block. The bar was surrounded by an eclectic collection of buildings that made it look like the zoning board had been through a civil war, but the two women passed through the door oblivious to the visual discord around them and went back to clock in for their shift. It was close to eight o'clock and still a tame dinner crowd, and Kelly waited tables while Julia worked behind the bar.

In the beginning, Julia mostly filled drink orders for the wait staff to take to the tables, but as the evening progressed the place got busier around the bar until she could barely hear herself think. She liked to be busy, but busy or not the tips were always a mixed bag. Most students couldn't afford to be too generous, but some still recognized fellow residents of the lowest rung on the economic ladder and were generous, nonetheless. Then there were the rich kids who loved to throw daddy's money down while they tried to flirt with Julia and the other wait staff; she was still figuring out how to best deal with these types. Her partner behind the bar was Robert, the head barkeep, and he didn't have to deal with that shit. He was ten years her senior and if she ever had real problems with a customer, she turned to him. He had shown her the ropes, teaching her how to do multiple things at the same time to keep the drinks flowing, as there was often no time for idle chatter.

Business was steady that night and the time flew by with no strange looks from Ralph. After the last patrons had stumbled out, they closed out and locked up. It was about two fifteen when they finally counted the tips; the take had been average.

Kelly and Julia made their way quickly back to the car and drove back to Kelly's place. Traffic was a breeze at this hour, and they made it in well under twenty minutes to the apartment complex. This was the worst part for Julia, and she used to joke that they were like a Navy Seal team making their way from the car to the building. She'd watch their six while Kelly cleared the lobby and unlocked the door. It was a joke, but Julia would startle at the slightest shadow on that short walk and resented herself a little for it. Once into the safety of Kelly's apartment, with the door double-bolted, they flopped onto the couch together.

Kelly had helped Julia get the job at Rick's after she had turned twenty-one and they had established a little routine in the three months they had worked together - an arrangement which had only been cemented with the blessing of Julia's mother when she'd been able to size Kelly up over a family dinner. Julia would go back to Kelly's after shift until sunrise, as she didn't want to disturb her mother's sleep by coming in at three in the morning. Often, she and Kelly would then get into a bottle of wine or some coolers and talk—idle chatter about anything, really. Sometimes, they would watch a movie or just sleep.

Tonight, they sat on the couch and talked over a bottle of wine. They had already covered the basics in the car—no issues with Ralph, how busy it was, how nice it was to hear yourself think without live music going on, how mediocre the tips had been, and so on. It was, therefore, a little quiet at first, though this wasn't unusual.

Finally, Julia broke the stalemate.

"Hey, I'm really happy that you're thinking about getting your GED. You should really go for it."

"Thanks."

"Sorry I didn't sound enthusiastic in the car. I was just distracted thinking about Ralph," Julia lied.

"Oh, no worries. I didn't notice," Kelly said in return.

It fell silent again for a time.

"What about you, then?" Kelly asked. "Are you going to tend bar forever like Robert, maybe be the head barkeep someday, or what?" she probed.

Julia considered the question a moment before speaking, feeling anger rising in her chest.

"You know, I really hate this fucking city, if you can call it that, and I guess I don't plan on being here this time next year." The words surprised Julia as they escaped her lips, as though they'd been spoken by an intruder in the apartment.

At first, Kelly wasn't sure how to respond.

"Wow. Okay. Sorry I asked." Then, "Where's this coming from?"

How could Julia explain it to her when she couldn't understand it fully herself? That if she stayed any longer, she'd be accepting a life sentence, consigned to mediocrity or worse. How could she tell her that she felt herself becoming the worst parts of her father and hated him for it? Or that the thought of leaving her mother filled her with guilt, but she would do it in a heartbeat if she could? It was too much and she couldn't. She didn't even want to think about those things in the privacy of her own mind.

"I've been saving all my tip money," Julia said, looking across the couch at Kelly. "I have close to three thousand dollars already."

"You're a lot better with money than I am, I guess," Kelly replied, taking a sip of her wine.

"Well, you have rent and food to pay for."

"I guess. Don't know where the rest of it goes," Kelly remarked without any note of concern.

"By next year, I should have enough for at least the first year of college. Then I can work my way through."

"Why didn't you go last year?" Kelly asked. "Money?"

"That," Julia replied, looking down into her glass for a moment. "That, and I didn't know if I was ready. Now I am."

There was a momentary pause as Kelly took this new information in. Finally, she looked back over at Julia.

"Do you know where you want to go?" she asked.

"I just want to go somewhere, anywhere but here, get my degree and make some money. You know, *have a life*."

"Well, here's to having a life," Kelly replied, slightly slurring her words as she raised her glass towards Julia. They clinked glasses and drank in silence.

Julia glanced at her watch. "It's almost six. I should get going."

They rose in unison and hugged goodbye, continuing the well-worn routine.

Julia left the apartment and walked east into the rising light of the new day. The air was cool and fresh, and the walk felt good. As usual, she arrived home to the smell of her mother's cinnamon coffee, and after a brief hug and some superficial conversation, her mother left to go to work and Julia went up to bed.

The pattern repeated itself over the coming days and weeks, and soon September was reaching its end and Julia would have to start thinking about taking a taxi home from Kelly's or extending her stays longer. They were discussing this on the way to Rick's on the last Tuesday of the month.

"Look, why don't you just live with me?" Kelly offered. "We could split the rent, and both save some money."

"It's a one-bedroom apartment," Julia countered.

"We could take turns on the couch."

Julia wondered at Kelly's anxiety.

Was she afraid of a change in their routine?

Julia thought again about breaking free from her parents, a fantasy cherished as a salve she applied on every point of friction between them; a fresh start. She feared the uncertainty that came with these thoughts and pushed them, once again, from her mind. They had arrived at Rick's, and it was time to head in for work. Julia wondered if Kelly even noticed that she had not answered the question.

Like most Tuesdays, it was a quiet shift. There were three students down at the end of the bar wearing their Michigan letterman jackets and becoming a little too exuberant for Julia's taste. They were talking about Michigan's win over State on Saturday, and each seemed to want to outshout the other over how badly State sucked, which was not uncommon around here. Occasionally, a member from a religion other than the maize and blue would be at the bar and not have the good sense to leave well enough alone. Julia had feared a fight earlier in the week over this very topic, and she simply did not understand the fascination. It was like a cult in this town; you were either with us or against us.

She now worried these three at the bar would be trouble.

She turned to grab Robert's attention, but he had gone to the back to fetch something. Just then, she heard the sound of shattered glass and she feared, inexplicably, that one of the boys had smashed a bottle over another one's head. It turned out to be a more straightforward case of the drunken clumsies, and she confronted them.

"Alright, fellas. Time to settle up and be on your way."

The one furthest to her left was the most far gone. He pulled his pock-marked face up into an ugly sneer and said, "We were just having fun."

His head was still tilted slightly downward as if too heavy to pull fully upright. His half-closed eyes angled up to glare at her and she felt the hair at the nape of her neck stand on end. She took an almost imperceptible step back behind the bar and opened her mouth to shout for Robert or the bouncer.

Before calling out, she decided to hazard a quick glance to her right at the other two, who were looking like lost puppies and sobering up quickly. Maybe she wouldn't need help after all.

"Come on, Jim, let's get outta here. This place sucks anyway," the middle one said. They dropped forty bucks on the bar, and the three of them negotiated their way to the door in the least efficient manner possible just as Robert returned. He sized up the situation quickly and asked if everything was alright.

"Piece of cake," Julia insisted, almost believing it herself. Maybe she was getting the hang of this.

The next night, before eight, Julia looked up and saw a young man approaching the bar. He had a familiar look which she placed quickly.

"How's your clumsy friend feeling today? Not too good I'll wager." She unconsciously applied a slight bit of her father's Irish twang to the phrase.

"Look," the young man said, "I just came in to apologize. Jim was being a —excuse me—rude, and it wasn't right. Plus, we left so quickly, we forgot to tip you." He dropped a twenty in front of her on the bar and could barely look up to meet her eyes. "Anyway, so I just wanted to apologize. Sorry again..." He looked at her chest, and for a minute, she thought she might have to slap him.

"...Julia."

Julia followed his gaze down to her chest.

Fucking name badge.

CHAPTER THREE

Don

AUGUST 2019

DON WOKE WITH A start, lifting his cheek from a sticky pool of drool. No gradual return to consciousness this time; today it was a full-force explosion. He remained frozen on his side, his eyes glancing around the room, confirming that he was in bed at the cabin. He felt like he had a hangover, but he had held himself to two beers the night before.

Maybe that was the problem.

He'd had a fitful sleep, and after a few seconds of blissful ignorance, memories of last night's dreams, *nightmares*, came flooding back.

Don had divided his view of time into *before the event*, and *after*. *Before* was a life he could hardly recognize or remember now. A life of love, work, friends, and vacations with marshmallows by the fire. *After*, well, that was this. Last night's dream was a scene from the end of the *before* time, when things weren't as happy, but Don would go back there in a heartbeat if he could. How Don wished he'd known it was his last goodbye with Charlie; *fuck*, he hadn't even looked up at him as he'd said it, too consumed with writing an article for some virtual rag he couldn't even recall at the moment.

Don held an undergraduate degree in political science from the University of Michigan, and since working in the dirty cesspool of politics offered no appeal, he had chosen to write about politics. He had eventually become a political observer of modest renown, writing opinion columns for local papers and publishing the occasional article in a more broadly circulated magazine, but he had managed the shift to online work poorly and had really been struggling to stay busy at the end of the *before* time. He simply couldn't compress his thoughts into 140 character blurbs, and he had become angry at the world, at people in general, for being too stupid or lazy to take the time to learn anything. Everybody wanted micro-information: pre-chewed, bite-sized garbage. He couldn't bring himself to do it, at least not well.

The week before Charlie went missing, Don had been given an assignment for a major publication. They had wanted his take on the announcement by Donald Trump that he would be running for president in the 2016 election. Initially, Don had struggled to even compose a serious thought about it, but after a time he had thrown himself into it with vigor. Maybe he'd seen it as his chance to enlighten the masses, to sound the alarm about the disintegration of rational thought and discourse and the rise of the cult of personality.

Or perhaps it was just vanity. Whatever his true motivations were, they were long since lost in the void, never to be known again. Erased from his memory, like so many other things that now seemed trivial; erased, while the things he wished he *could* forget remained.

After, he had tried to continue working. He would write occasional pieces from the house in Birmingham, or up at the cabin. After Julia left for Europe, and when it had become clear to Don that she wasn't coming back, they had sold the house, sorting things out amicably without a lawyer as neither of them had the energy for a drawn-out process. He moved up to the cabin full time, living modestly off what remained of the six-figure inheritance from his father, and his half of the house proceeds.

Don and Julia had never formalized a separation agreement. He had volunteered her share of the house, and she accepted, but she'd rejected, however, Don's offers to split the money that had come from his father's estate, and he now just mentally held half of it in reserve for her; for *someday*. Despite that, Don had enough money to support his frugal lifestyle, and so the laptop he had previously used for work sat on a desk in the other bedroom of the house, collecting dust.

As he lay in bed, the echoes of his dream worked through his brain like acid, burning down barriers he had carefully erected against his memories and freshly revealing them before he could fill his mind with the usual clutter. He was forced to relive the initial worry he and Julia had felt four years earlier.

"Charlie didn't come home last night," Julia had said, prompting Don to check her fear.

"He's probably staying at Geoff's house," he'd replied, needing to keep her anxieties from spiraling. This wouldn't have been the first run-away threat.

Then Julia had added, "Maybe he went to Dad's again."

Her father, David, had moved farther west after her mother's death and taken up working odd jobs at a marina in Saint Joseph, on the shore of Lake Michigan. Charlie had given them a couple of scares by secretly hitching a ride with his close friend Geoff out to his grandfather's place. Julia's father would let Don and Julia know and would chide Charlie, but the hours in between Charlie's absence and the call always caused heartburn.

That night, four years ago, was indelibly burned into Don's mind. Don remembered calling David multiple times after being unable to reach Charlie, but to no avail. Finally, they had received the callback from her father. Julia had pressed the phone so tightly to her ear that Don could barely hear David's voice even though he had his head pressed to Julia's.

"Charlie showed up here again, I think he may have taken *Fire Horse*."

Fire Horse was David's boat, a twenty-seven-foot bowrider that had originally belonged to Don's father.

"What? When?" Julia had replied, growing anxious.

"I'm not sure. I wasn't totally with it when he got here last night. When I woke up this morning, he was gone. So was the boat."

This had brought Julia fully to DEFCON 1.

The police had been alerted, and preliminary searches conducted. Charlie did not own the kind of cell phone with which family members could track each other, but eventually, with the encouragement of the police, the phone company had shared the last known location of his signal. Worry had turned to full-throated panic when they learned the final location: three miles west of Saint Joseph, deep in Lake Michigan.

The ensuing days were pandemonium. Search and rescue teams were organized and dispatched, and state police questioned residents up and down the coast. Finally, after two more days, *Fire Horse* was found, washed ashore, ten miles up the coast.

Empty.

The realization had hit them in waves. They had been at the State Police office in Bridgman, just south of Saint Joseph, when they had received that piece of news, and Julia had turned to Don and whispered, "My baby."

Then her face had scrunched in the oddest contortion he had ever seen, and for a moment, he didn't recognize her. He also had thought his hearing had gone out in shock, as there was no sound – just the image of Julia's twisted face, her mouth and eyes gaping open in recognition. Finally, Don had perceived a hiss, like the air leaving a balloon, which transformed into a high-pitched squeal before building in a crescendo to a full-throated howl. He would never forget that sound, the cry of a wounded animal, and the look of accusation that burned from those green eyes, deep into his guts.

Don shook the memory away and pulled himself up from his pillow to find his eyes were wet. Puzzled, he forced his body upright, removed his underwear, and went straight into the shower in a futile attempt to wash away the imprint of that horrible day. He stood there under the shower for at least twenty minutes, staring at the drain in the floor, wishing he could follow the water down into it. Finally, through sheer force of will, he grabbed the shampoo and set to washing himself.

After his shower he surveyed the world through the rear window to the right of the fireplace. The flagstone patio behind the cabin was decorated with a basic picnic table and was accessible via a small rear door at the far right of the living room. The patio was framed by the wilderness surrounding the cabin and the skies above it were filled with rain—nature, today, being in sync with Don's mood. He decided there would be no trip into town today just as he took note of his garbage pail, which had been upended, leaving trash strewn about the patio.

Bears? he wondered to himself.

They were fearsome to many, but to the seasoned residents up here, they were just big rats; a pain in the ass. He might have to dig his bear trap, a giant white tube, out of the shed even though it had never trapped anything but leaves. He grabbed the last garbage bag from the box in the laundry room and went out to clean up the litter.

Spending the seasons he had up here, he'd found his view on nature had shifted dramatically in the time *after the event*. He used to see nature as a benign thing of beauty, to be observed, appreciated, and respected. These had been the right words. This had made sense.

It was different now.

He had installed Wi-Fi at the cabin some years ago for work, and he'd used it to watch a strange film online last night, a Lars von Trier masterpiece from the Depression series: Antichrist, starring Willem Dafoe. Don had known it dealt with a couple's grief over the loss of a child, a toddler, and he'd *made* himself watch it in some exercise of self-torment. He had vomited on his shirt partway through, but had forced himself to watch it to the end.

He regretted the stupidity of it and blamed it, and by extension himself, for the visceral nightmares. Although he had not enjoyed the movie, one thing did resonate with him and that was von Trier's thesis on nature: it was evil, a thing not to be trusted. Now Don understood that he loved, hated, and feared it in equal measure. He had forced himself to stay at the cabin these past four years, engaging in daily warfare with nature, for reasons he could barely discern himself.

He frittered the day away with inside jobs and finished it with two bottles of wine. He wasn't going to make the same mistake tonight; tonight he would sleep.

****

The rain had broken, and the next morning dawned clear and fresh. Don awoke, dry mouthed, after a dreamless sleep to the sound of birds outside his window. He went through his ritual rerun of the five stages of grief—he was an expert at it by now, or at least at the first four—and performed his morning routine.

It was just four days until the memorial.

Two months prior, just days before what would have been Charlie's twentieth birthday, they had received the news, or more precisely *he* had received the news, that remains had been found washed ashore at Grand Haven, about seventy-five miles north of Saint Joseph and a hundred and forty miles or so south from the cabin.

In order to perform the DNA test for a match the police needed a sample from Don or Julia, or both ideally. Don had no means of directly contacting Julia but knew she had fled to Europe a couple of years ago with someone, a banker or lawyer, she had met.

During the time *before the event,* they had been good friends with a couple, Dave and Lisa Wight, who both worked in the real estate business in Birmingham, and whom they had met while buying their home there. Don had reached out via e-mail to Lisa, and it turned out that she did have contact information for Julia, although she explained that she had been asked not to share it with *anyone.*

In the end, Don had entrusted her with a message for Julia:

Dear Julia,

I know that you asked me not to contact you, but I may have news about Charlie. The police found remains on the coast of the lake and want to perform a DNA test to be sure. I don't need or want anything from you, only to say that I will provide a sample so that I can know for sure. When I hear any news, I will share it with Lisa, and you can decide for yourself if you want to know.

I miss him every day and I know you do too.

I truly hope you are doing alright and can be happy. That's all I ever wanted.   Don

He didn't know if Lisa had sent the message, but he hadn't heard back from her by the time the authorities had contacted him with the results. Ultimately, science told him what his heart had already known.

Charlie was gone.

He had then sent a subsequent note via Lisa:

Julia,

They've found Charlie. We can finally bring him home and lay him to rest. I would like to have his remains cremated. I hope you can be with me for this. If not, I understand, and I will take care of him.   Don

The next day, a reply came via Lisa:

Don,

Thank you for letting me know. I want to bury his ashes at Holy Cross Cemetery where he can lay beside mi abuela and my mother. It would mean a lot to me.

I will take care of the arrangements if that's okay with you.

Hope you are well too.

JC

When he had received the message it had sent his mind into spirals of endless analysis. Julia was being considerate in asking about the burial, given his views on the Catholic Church, views he thought she'd shared. She had said she hoped he was well. She had signed off with *JC*; she never liked to share her middle name—Carmen—with anyone. Only he had been able to jokingly call her *JC*, in a gentle mockery of her family's religion. He had considered every nuance of the message over and over for days until snapping himself back to reality. They would never be together again. She had moved on, he on the other hand, had not. He'd ultimately agreed to Julia's wishes via Lisa, and Julia had been handling the arrangements. That had been just over a week ago.

Since then, he had thought he would have time to prepare himself mentally, to rehearse what he wanted to say to his wife of twenty years. But the days continued to tick mercilessly away, and he still didn't feel ready. All he needed to do was get his suit out and show up in four days. It was just four days until he—*they*—put Charlie in the ground for good.

He finished his coffee and decided he would head into town today.

He had things to do.

CHAPTER FOUR

Julia

SEPTEMBER 1998

"I SAW YOU CHATTING with Mr. Clumsy, at the bar tonight," Kelly prodded in a singsong tone as they rode I-94 back to Ypsi.

"He wasn't the one who spilled the beer, Kell," Julia shot back, deliberately opaque.

"Okay, then. Nothing to *tell*, I guess," Kelly continued with an upward lilt on the word "guess," converting the statement into one more attempt to extract information.

Julia turned her head toward Kelly and cocked it disapprovingly to the left as if to say, *Give me a break here.* She held the pose until Kelly glanced her way.

"Okaaaay, okaaaay." These last words from Kelly were drawn out, like the pouting of a spoiled toddler. "Nothing to see here."

Julia wondered if Kelly would notice the flushing of her cheeks. She hoped it was dark enough in the car. She imagined she could feel the napkin in her pocket, bearing the first phone number she'd ever gotten from a man.

In truth, it had been the other way around. *He* had finally asked for *her* number. After reading her name badge, he had excused himself, and she'd found herself watching him until he reached the door, trying to pretend to busy herself with cleaning glasses and putting things in order. Out of the corner of her eye, she saw him stop at the exit, shrug his shoulders slightly, and turn around. She watched as he marched purposefully back toward her, and when he got back to the bar, they stared at each other in silence for what seemed like an eternity. He finally made his move and asked politely for her phone number.

She was not one to succumb to notions of chivalry, not that she didn't mind a man opening a door for her or being polite, she just possessed the view that everyone was out for what was best for themselves. Survival of the fittest. She knew better than to trust the noble intentions of a man but she didn't care. He was cute and she hadn't been on a date for nearly a year; her limited social circle and homebound lifestyle saw to that.

"Why don't you give *me your* number? *I'll* call *you*," she had finally said.

He had written it on a cocktail napkin with a hastily borrowed pen, so cliché, and handed it to her.

"Looking forward to it," he had mumbled, or something like that. Then, apparently sensing the time had come to leave for real, he had made his exit, and she wondered if he thought it had been a rejection, a way of letting him down easy. The truth was far more practical; she had to ask for his number because she didn't have her own phone. They had one shared line at the house, and she was not ready to have Don converse with either of her parents. She had also noticed that Don had his own cell phone, a new Motorola, and wondered if he had a rich daddy like half the other kids in here. She ultimately decided he wasn't one of *them* with their big egos and bigger mouths. No, he was the quietest thing she'd seen in here in a long time.

Julia and Kelly got back to the apartment. Neither of them smoked, except for an occasional joint, but Kelly's place always carried the faint odor of tobacco, an afterimage of the bar. She always kept a change of clothes at Kelly's so she could shed her skin quickly and be comfortable when they got in, and after they both had changed, Kelly suggested they just go straight to sleep, so Julia lay on the couch as Kelly retreated to her bedroom. Julia found herself unable to sleep and she just tossed and turned for a long three hours.

She spent the duration of her run the next day lost in fantasy.

Should I call?

What if he's an asshole who just managed to put on a good show? She'd only seen a ten-minute performance.

Nothing ventured, nothing gained, she resolved.

Okay, when should I call? She didn't want to seem too eager, nor did she want to miss the chance. Her only nights off were Sunday and Monday, so that made the answer to the question easier; she would give it a day and then call Friday.

What if he expects sex on the first date? She was still inexperienced, being a late bloomer with an overprotective mother.

How and when should I tell my parents? I'm twenty-one, for Christ's sake. Get a grip. This mental ping-pong occupied her throughout her run, and she hardly noticed the chill.

She did feel the after-effect of it when she went inside and her sweat broke loose in the heat of the house. Her father liked to keep it about seventy-five degrees, which was too hot in her view. It was ten past one, the kitchen was empty, and she thought he must still be sleeping. Her spirits were so high, she found that she missed the chance for a little banter and relegated herself to a banana and Gatorade in silence.

****

Later that night, as the three of them sat down to a dinner of pork chops, beans, and rice, Julia considered when to bring up the topic of meeting Don. She didn't want to blurt it out as her opening volley in the conversation, lest she lose control of the topic and have no plan of escape. No, dinner needed to be nearly complete. She cursed her own cowardice. She was an adult and her parents had never really objected to her dating before, but upon closer examination, she realized the problem as she role-played the conversation in her mind:

Oh, how nice, her mother would say, *where did you meet him?*

Like it could be anywhere other than the bar.

I see. What does he do?

Such a vital question. *Umm. I think he goes to U of M, but I didn't ask.*

Oh. What do you know about him?

This was going to be tough.

"Julia?" Her mother and father were both looking at her.

"You all right, mija?" her mother asked. "You aren't eating your food."

Outside of taking the Lord's name in vain, this was the quickest way to get her mother's attention. The living room could be on fire, but if Julia wasn't hungry for her pork chops, something was *really* wrong.

"Sorry, Mama. Just daydreaming."

"Well, it'll get cold." The second deadly sin.

Julia obligingly forked a piece of pork. David went back to his paper, seeing that the crisis had passed.

"There's a gay pride parade coming through town Friday. All the streets'll be blocked. That's when I'm glad I work nights."

Why the fuck did he have to bring that up? Julia wondered. She secretly suspected her father of being a professional shit-stirrer and mentally convicted him of the crime. He had just thrown off her plans to bring up the subject of Don, possibly by an entire day. She attempted to glare right through the center of his newspaper to no effect.

"I don't understand *those people*." Isabella sighed, eyes still on her plate.

This was one of several points of friction on social issues that she had with her mother. Her mother had been raised in a strict Mexican-Catholic household and had retained much of her upbringing in this regard. When Julia was young, Isabella had insisted on the family going to church every Sunday. Over the years, David had made his excuses, until he would only go at Christmas and Easter with them, but Julia had continued to go to mass with Isabella, increasingly against her developing will, until her job at Rick's gave her an excuse to skip the Sunday morning ritual.

Julia thought about how often she and her mother had conducted numerous proxy wars on these taboo subjects, through indirect commentary on the actions of others, always careful to avoid full-out warfare. Her mother was stubborn and would not even entertain the notion that *she* should reconsider her views. Anti-abortion, anti-gay rights, *she was even anti-divorce, for God's sake.* Julia made a brief mental pause on that last one, wondering if that was the only fragile thread holding Isabella to her father, then passed it over as implausible, though not impossible. No, for her mother, these views were traits she had inherited from *her* mother, no different than her green eyes or her large nose, and as such, were not subject to alteration.

After taking a moment to collect her thoughts and swallow her pork, Julia decided to wade in.

"Why do you care what they do with their lives? They're not hurting you or anyone else for that matter."

"That was not God's plan for them. You cannot experience the joy of children like this." Isabella was patient but firm in her reply. "You know this, Julia." *Julia, not mija.*

"Well, why would God *make* them that way if it's wrong?" she asked, deciding to conduct the skirmish on her mother's turf.

"They were not *made* that way. They have made bad choices. God gives us freedom even if it is used to stray from his teaching."

Say what you like about Isabella's convictions, she was a firm believer in free will. You made your bed. Her grandfather had brought his wife and two daughters up from Guadalajara in the thirties and had made a life in Detroit for them through sheer force of will and hard work.

Julia was beginning to consider the best avenue of retreat, when her father surprised them both by quietly and deliberately folding his newspaper and setting it down softly.

"When I was twelve, growing up in Cork," he said quietly, his eyes fixing on the center of the table, somewhere between the plate of pork and the beans, "I used to walk ten blocks to school every day."

Isabella and Julia had both stopped chewing and stared at the source of the unexpected intrusion into their conversation.

He raised his eyes to meet theirs. "There were a couple of men—uh, confirmed bachelors—who were living in a little house two blocks up from us," he continued, so softly they had to lean ever so slightly into the conversation. "My mother told me not to go by their house on the way to school. It was the most direct way, so sometimes, not understanding her reasons, I would walk by anyway." David worked some pork from his teeth with his tongue and replaced it with a new piece from his fork.

"Often, when I'd go by, one of the men, Jonathan, I think his name was, would be out tending the garden. They had such a lovely garden." Her father paused, drawing the story out.

"One night, in the spring, Jimmy O'Connor and his friend, Stephen something or other—I don't remember—well, they thought it would be funny to take my lunchbox from me on the way home. My mother had bought me that lunchbox, and I wasn't going to give it up. So, they had to beat the shit out of me to get it."

Julia couldn't imagine *anyone* beating the shit out of that man. She'd wanted to herself at times, but the thought of someone else doing it brought blood to her cheeks.

"Jonathan saw what was going on from his garden," her father continued. "At least, I guess he did, because before I knew it, he had Jimmy and Stephen by the scruffs of their necks and booted them both in the arse on down the street. He never said a word, just booted them in the arse, quick as you please, and then bent to help me up."

Her father managed a small chuckle at the memory before continuing. "He was strong like an ox, that man. He asked if I was okay, and then went back to his garden."

Julia wondered if the story was finished. Isabella had returned to her rice, perhaps having heard one too many stories from David McCarthy over the years.

"I told my mother and father that I'd got into a scuffle at school, but everything was fine. I didn't say anything about Jonathan. About a month later, I started to notice weeds in the garden as I walked past, and no sign of him."

"What happened?" Julia felt self-conscious interrupting.

"Jimmy's dad had turned them in as queer. It was illegal then," her father said, staring straight at her with an intensity she hadn't seen in him in years. "I don't know what happened to them, but the house went up for sale before the end of the school year."

He returned to his food.

Julia stared at her father. "Wow, that's terrible," she said.

"I pulled the weeds from those gardens every day on my way home from school—just fifteen minutes a day so my mother wouldn't notice," her father said. "I don't know if Jonathan ever knew. I never thanked him."

"What is the point of this, David?" Isabella asked, studying her rice.

"Point, what point?" he said with exaggerated surprise. "I thought we were just talking about gay people."

He glanced toward Julia and winked. She loved those rare occasions when his wit was on her side.

Dinner concluded largely in silence with her father returning to the sanctuary of his paper and her mother clearing the dishes quickly so that everyone could move on to safer ground.

In the end, Julia decided she would wait until she actually had a date to tell her parents about Don and she decided that she would call Don that Friday. When Friday came, she had set her alarm for noon, an hour earlier than usual, so she could take advantage of some privacy before her father woke and her mother returned from cleaning houses. She felt her pulse quicken as she grabbed the phone and dialed Don's number.

"Hello?"

"Um. Hey, it's me, uh, Julia. From Rick's." She mentally face-palmed. So much for playing it cool.

"Oh, hi, glad you called," he said sounding sincere, maybe even eager.

"Well, how do you feel about, maybe, grabbing a bite sometime or something?"

"That would be great," he replied, almost before the word 'something' had left her lips.

"Cool." A brief pause and then she waded back in. "Uh, would Sunday night work for you?"

She groaned inwardly, wishing she was the one with the cell phone and he was having to step his way through this minefield.

"Yeah, sure. That sounds great! I know a great place downtown we could go," Don suggested.

"Well, actually," she hesitated, "could we go out in Ypsi? I don't have any wheels, and I know a cool place called The Sidetrack. It's just a few blocks from my—" she caught herself, "—house." She chose to omit "parent's'" from the equation for now.

"Sounds great. When should I pick you up?"

"I'll just meet you there, say seven?" she said, and then dictated the address.

They sputtered out their goodbyes, and she hung up the phone.

The Sidetrack would be the safest option for her, and it was good. She found herself excited at the prospect of introducing one of her favorite places to Don.

Over dinner that evening, she worked up the nerve to tell her parents and it turned out to be much worry over nothing. Her father, ever the practical man, hammered out the factual details.

Who is he? Where did you meet him? Where are you going? And so on. She almost laughed to herself at the way he tried to smoothly work the questions into the conversation, so as to not appear the intrusive father-figure.

Her mother was surprisingly keen.

Oh, how exciting. Just be yourself, mija. I'm sure it will go well. What will you wear? This, laced with the caution to make sure that her attire was appropriate for a first date, causing Julia to recall her past battles with her mother on this topic.

As to the question of clothing, she ultimately opted for a balanced approach. She would wear her best pair of black Diesel jeans—one of her rare indulgences with her earned money—and a red blouse that came off her shoulders. While she was generally humble concerning her appearance, she knew that her smooth, petite shoulders and slim neck were among her strongest features. She also knew that this outfit would pass her mother's silent inspection. Finally, she picked a pair of two-inch red heels that would be feminine but walkable for the few blocks to the restaurant. Now she just had to wait for Sunday.

Friday and Saturday shifts at Rick's helped to pass the time. Julia could not believe how busy it was and the tips were great. She had shared the news with Kelly on Friday after work, prompting her to offer to make herself scarce and stay at another friend's if Julia wanted the apartment Sunday night, but Julia was inwardly taken aback by the suggestion. It was a reminder to her of just how much they still didn't know about each other. She laughed the suggestion off and promised to share details afterward. This segued into Kelly talking about the latest macho blond she'd caught eyeing her at the gym and how, maybe, she would ask for his number.

Sunday finally came. Julia was up at one, even though she didn't set her alarm on her days off. Not wanting to expose herself to a fresh round of interrogation from her father, or helpful suggestions from her mother, she borrowed the truck and left the house to run errands and do some shopping. She returned empty handed just after three in the afternoon and immediately excused herself for a run.

The air was cool and crisp, the leaves were beginning to turn, and it looked like it might rain later. Prospect Park looked beautiful this time of year and as she ran past, she couldn't help but grin - at the weather, at the thought of heading to school next year, at the *idea* of Don, at life.

She managed four miles and collapsed in the side door, aiming straight for the sink to pour herself a glass of water. Her father was enjoying a cigarette and doing a crossword puzzle at the kitchen table, and his eyes followed her wordlessly as she passed him on her way to the sink. When she moved out of his peripheral vision, his head turned like an owl to continue to track her.

"Should I call 9-1-1?" he teased.

"Hi," she panted between gulps of water.

"Good run?" he asked, bemused.

"Great," she replied, still gasping.

"Yeah, sure sounds great. Do you need CPR 'cause I don't know how to do it. Let me see if your mother does. Isabella?" he called into the living room. For one day each week, Isabella could put her feet up and watch her telenovelas for a few hours.

"You're going to be the one who needs CPR if you keep smoking like that, Dad," Julia chided.

He held his hands up in surrender.

"What?" came her mother's voice from across the house.

"Nothing, dear. We solved it." Her father returned to his crossword and Julia went upstairs for a long shower.

She took extra care with flossing and brushing her teeth.

Julia had not lived long enough to pollute her teeth from their pure white shade, and she felt a small twinge of pride at her smile. She retreated to her room, wrapped in a towel, and picked out her best bra and underwear, for her own peace of mind, and pulled her jeans on. Then she slipped into her blouse, shoes, and a jacket. She went downstairs and found her mother and father at the kitchen table, eating dinner.

"You look nice. Sit. Join us," her mother insisted.

"I've got to get going, Ma."

"It's only six. You have time. I know you can't eat, just sit."

So, she sat while they ate.

There was an unspoken recognition that this was a disturbance in the routine, a break in the pattern they'd hammered out in their existence as a family here in Ypsi, sometimes painful, but mostly comfortable. Everyone normally had their speaking part and knew their lines but this felt like an awkward improv, so in the end her mother simply returned to the subject of food and the tacos Julia was missing out on; she would save her two in the fridge for later.

They kissed goodbye, and Julia waved as she went to the door. Her mother smiled but her father bore a strange expression, as though he wasn't quite sure what he felt. He was smiling, but the rest of his face seemed a little sad. Before Julia could leave he hustled over and embraced her. She didn't know he could move that quickly.

"Have a good time, love." His rough, tobacco-stained hand tentatively held out a twenty-dollar bill for her. "Here," he said. "In case you need a cab."

She was about to remind him it was only a few blocks away, but not wanting to deny him the gesture, she simply said, "Thanks, Dad," and lightly kissed his cheek. She could smell the tobacco on him, together with his aftershave, and in that moment, for Julia, it was not an unpleasant smell. She grabbed an umbrella and closed the door behind her.

When Julia was about halfway to The Sidetrack, the clouds burst. The wind had picked up and the rain was blowing sideways, rendering her umbrella nearly futile. She could only trot gently in her heels, and she finally came up to the restaurant exactly at seven.

The Sidetrack Bar and Grill was an art deco-styled restaurant with an eclectic, turn-of-the-century railway theme. At the entrance was a small alcove with a single suspended globe of light under its intimate arch, and sheltered there, out of the rain, Don's wet face shone in the light. He broke into a grin as she crossed the street and ran to meet him.

CHAPTER FIVE

Julia

AUGUST 2019

JULIA RAN HER FINGERS over Gerrard's naked back as he lay on the white linen beside her. She gently folded the sheets back into a triangle over his legs to extricate herself from the bed undetected, revealing his upper half, and twisted back to touch him as she sat up, her legs draping off the bedside. He continued to snore, undisturbed by the intrusion, and she closed her eyes briefly.

She had been living the past eighteen months with Gerrard at his flat in Chelsea, in London's West End along the north side of the river Thames. It was a gorgeous home that had probably set him back a couple of million pounds or more, and was one of the row house "walk-ups" that had survived the tidal wave of gentrification in the borough; gentrification which, while beautifying the neighborhood, had also pressed the artists and students outwards from the river in favor of lawyers, bankers, doctors, and other fine citizens. Gerrard's home was one of many connected houses lining the street – narrow and five stories tall, with a pastel yellow stucco exterior and large white trim around double hung windows. A bright, red door greeted visitors eight steps up from the sidewalk and welcomed them into the well-appointed modern home.

As Julia and Gerrard had walked the neighborhood together on her first visit, he had pointed out that he lived less than two blocks from the former home of Mick Jagger, impressing her at the time. She had heard him use that boast at least a dozen times since, at dinner parties with executives and their spouses he wished to impress, making it sound each time as though he had only just realized the fact himself. They would all suitably cluck and fawn at his scripted charm, thus reinforcing the cycle. This had apparently lost its appeal for Gerrard's ex-wife, Theresa, who had made her exit three years prior.

Following Charlie's disappearance Julia had lived in a trance; she hadn't felt like herself anymore. His disappearance and presumed death had killed her inside. Her heart had ceased to beat, her lungs had ceased to breathe. For over a year she had been a specter, wandering the earth and immune to all but the deepest human sensations.

Outwardly, she appeared functional. She ate, she shopped. She even smiled occasionally. So clever was her disguise that a year after her separation from Don, her friends had thought she was well enough for an introduction. She demurred, laying the blame on the *healing process*. It was chaff however, a deflection as she knew that she would never heal, not from this. She thought of Charlie at some point, many points, most points every day. There was no escaping it and the triggers would vary—a woman with a child, teenagers gathered at a coffee shop, the river. Once, she'd found herself crying while staring at a poster for the musical *Charlie and the Chocolate Factory*. There was no telling.

She had met Gerrard in Detroit nearly two years ago, when unexpectedly introduced by a mutual friend, Jen Knowles. Julia had been Jen's guest at a charity dinner for the local food bank, and Gerrard had come with other colleagues from the Detroit office of the London investment bank where he worked. Jen knew Gerrard from some work he had done for the corporation where she served as treasurer. He had clients all over the globe, and this aspect of his life appealed to Julia as she listened with genuine interest to his travel tales over dinner that evening. He had cut a handsome figure in his Armani suit with his straight teeth, his thick blond hair, and his charming British accent. Despite having been through two years of hell, Julia had found herself, in some remote corner of her psyche, surprisingly interested in a man again.

They had agreed to have coffee before he flew out the morning after the dinner party, then subsequently maintained a fragile connection via e-mail and text. Eventually, he had enticed her to come to England by assisting in her application for college in London, along with the necessary student visa, to study graphic design. She had initially taken a separate room in his house and insisted on paying rent, until her resistance to his charm crumbled and they began dating in earnest about a year ago.

She pulled her hand back from Gerrard's flesh and rose from the bed. She didn't think what they had was love, not yet, probably not ever, but he was funny, kind, and a good lover. It didn't hurt that he was wealthy either, but she wasn't sure what she wanted from life anymore. Once, in a prior life, she had wanted to be an architect, to guide the act of *creation*, to translate her thoughts, her will, to paper and watch as they took form in the real world. This ambition had been put to the side abruptly as she'd been sidetracked, first staying home to care for an infant, and then as Charlie grew, taking low wage work to help with the bills as things were tight. Later, when Don's father passed away and they'd finally had some financial stability, the troubles began with Charlie.

Now that she was free to pursue her own path, she found that those dreams no longer held any interest for her. Her greatest act of creation had been laid to waste, exposing for her the futility of the effort. She pursued her college courses stubbornly now, simply determined to show the world, or herself, that she wasn't completely defeated.

Even in her grief, she had been enthralled in the beginning of her relationship with Gerrard. He would take her to the nicest restaurants, and they would enjoy romantic walks after dinner down King's Road, window shopping hand in hand, eyeing all of the precious treasures mankind had on offer. Julia found her desires muted, but still, in some selfish corner of her mind, she coveted these shiny things. When they weren't shopping or dining, they would wander through the parks, and Gerrard was thoughtful enough to avoid the river being mindful of Julia's sensitivities.

He once had taken her on an exotic weekend trip to Paris, a city she never dreamed she'd see, where she had observed Gerrard practicing his three or four memorized phrases "en français" for the shopkeepers and waiters. She knew that he was just showing his feathers, but she didn't care; her exposure to a city she'd only imagined going to was reward enough for tolerating his occasional machismo.

Julia had found that in this new environment her familiar anchors had, one by one, been cast away. She had not made the time for running outside, preferring to go to the gym for yoga or some spin classes. Contact with her father had dwindled quickly and deliberately after Charlie's disappearance. Being in Europe, immersed in its old-world charm, was still not potent enough to rekindle her love of architecture.

And of course, there was Don. She would have no contact with him and being an ocean away just made this simpler.

Then, abruptly, this fledgling new world of hers had been torn apart by the e-mail that had come from Lisa a couple of months earlier, leaving Julia stranded between two realities. She moved to the bathroom and looked at the mirror, her green eyes staring back, as if challenging her to state her business. She wore one of Gerrard's T-shirts as a nightgown; it was soaked in last night's sweat and she felt vaguely nauseated.

The second e-mail had come from Don a week ago. She had replied to Don via Lisa, contacted the priest, ordered a casket for the remains, booked the funeral, scheduled the cremation and burial, and reached out to some friends to make arrangements for a luncheon after the service. Now she had to prepare *herself*. She could do this. Tomorrow, she would board the plane that would take her to Charlie, and Don. She wiped a stray tear from her cheek and stepped into the shower.

CHAPTER SIX

Don

AUGUST 2019

DON SHOOK OFF THE reminder of Julia's e-mail and readied himself for his trip into town. He arrived at Kay's to the realization that Linda was not working today, filling him with relief. He had a simple breakfast of toast and coffee before driving over to the hardware store. Coffee and toast—no eggs—his attempt to change something in his routine as though to prove to himself the existence of free will.

He grabbed bait for his bear trap, some garbage bags, and after a moment's hesitation a box of nine millimeter ammunition, and approached the counter where Diane was working. She was a forty-something divorcee who had come to town five years ago after finding her husband in bed with another woman, and she had one daughter, now in her mid-twenties, who Don thought had moved out to

Oregon. Diane wore her long, thick brunette hair loosely up in a clip at the back, and brown eyes over a petite nose sat in perfect balance on her oval face. She was quiet when Don had met her five years ago, but through the course of his grief and eventual move up here full time, he had discovered that she had a hell of a wit.

"That's an interesting purchase today, Don." She smirked as she scanned the items into the computer.

Don looked up at her, a puzzled look playing across his face.

"Well, bear bait and ammo seem redundant, don't you think?" she clarified. He provided an obligatory chuckle.

Diane was a friend. She had been there for him in the early part of the time *after*, consoling him when it had all become too much. Sometimes, they would get a bottle of whisky or a six pack and sit down at the park in town when she finished work. Don now recalled the first such evening, almost a year after his separation from Julia, not long after he'd moved here permanently. He'd been at the store in the mid-afternoon, and when he'd approached the counter, Diane had been weeping through a fragile smile. "Hey, Diane, everything okay?" he'd asked.

"Darryl and Jess just got married," she'd sobbed gently, inhaling on the name *Jess*. He'd turned his mouth into a slight downward frown of sympathy just as she looked up into his eyes.

"I feel like such a failure," she had said, simply.

The store had been mercifully empty, and he'd gone around the cashier stand to give her a hug and hand her a tissue from a box beside her.

"You're not a failure," he had reassured her. After a moment, he released her, and she looked up at him, her eyes still dewy, despite the Kleenex.

"I'm sorry, I shouldn't dump this on you," she'd said, still sniffling a bit. "What can I help you with?"

"It's no trouble," Don had replied, feeling genuine empathy for a kindred spirit in mourning. "I know what it's like. My son went missing two years ago and my wife, well, my wife couldn't live with me any longer, I guess. She left."

He couldn't believe he had felt the urge to blurt this out so plainly at the time but done was done.

"Oh, I'm so sorry," Diane had said, looking back at the counter as though sharing for a moment in Don's shame. "Here I am feeling sorry for myself, and I forgot that other people have troubles too." She looked back up at him before continuing, "What happened?"

So, Don had entrusted Diane with the story of Charlie's disappearance, at least the short version of it.

How do you summarize the most significant thing to ever happen in your short, miserable existence, the one fork in the road that changed everything about your life: who you were, who you could love, what you thought you cared for in this world? He had found himself apologizing for talking too much about it despite the gravity of the subject.

"Don't ever apologize for remembering your son," Diane had replied, with a gentle admonishment that had stuck with Don to this day. The way she supported him and scolded him all at the same time, like an old friend. Finally, Diane had asked, "Hey, I clock out in an hour, wanna grab a drink with me in the park, compare nightmares?" as she wiped some fresh tears away with the damp tissue.

They had bought a bottle of Johnnie and found a picnic table in the park, where they could savor the warm, dying glow of a beautiful May evening. The spring flies buzzed around them in the rapidly cooling air as the sun set over the trees at the west end of the park, and she'd turned to him after taking a deep pull from the bottle, "I guess no one gets a guarantee for happiness."

He had thought it an odd remark in its simplicity.

"I did everything I was supposed to," she had continued absently, gazing at the grass and then turning to look at him directly. "Went to school, followed the rules, looked after my husband, paid my taxes. And for what?"

He had put his hand reassuringly on her shoulder.

"Look who I'm talking to. I have no right to complain to you," she'd exclaimed, before he could reply. "I'm sorry for what you've been through, Don. Really, I am. You seem like a good man." Then, after a brief silence, "I guess I just wonder why we bother following somebody else's rules. Just do what feels right, that's my new motto - Carpe fuckin' diem." She took one more long pull from the bottle and passed it to Don. She had a slight Southern accent that seemed to intensify as the whisky went to work and Don found himself wondering where she was from originally.

They had continued that way for another hour, sharing superficial details of their respective burdens; comparing philosophies on life and happiness, while passing the nearly empty fifth back and forth until it was obvious that Don should not be driving back to the cabin that night.

"You should crash at my place tonight," Diane had offered, and Don agreed.

Diane's place was three blocks off the park, and they had stumbled to it around ten, propping each other up on the way, and the contact between them was becoming incrementally intimate. Inside, they sat on the couch together, and the conversation, which had flowed freely in the park, was weighed down by the tension in the air. They kissed clumsily in a whisky fog, and Don felt *wrong*. The memory of Charlie, and Julia, was too raw but he didn't want to hurt Diane, so he had just said, "I can't—it's too soon. I'll just sleep here on the couch." She hadn't pressed the matter and they were both keen to reframe the friendship back onto its natural footing in the sober light of day.

"Don?" Diane said, snapping him back to the present.

He considered her, as though for the first time, as he handed over his credit card to complete the transaction. He knew that most women did not like to be referred to as handsome—*where did that term come from anyway?*—but for him, it was the best fit with her. Smile lines creased the ends of her small mouth, almost shaping into dimples, and at the corners of her eyes were subtle crow's feet. She was a slender woman, and to Don, she had a very attractive figure. Her real asset was her smile, though, which was warm and almost always contagious for him.

As he gathered up his purchases and made his way to the door, she called out to him,

"Drink tonight?"

"Rain check? I've got some things I need to do at home." He flashed a smile and hoped that would placate her enough for now. "I'll see you later in the week."

He could still feel her adopting a flirtatious way with him from time to time, implying that she hadn't found anyone to keep her company, not even for the long, lonely winter nights after the vacationers had left and only the diehards remained. He felt for her loneliness, and often entertained the idea of latching on to one of her flirtatious comments, but he told himself that he hadn't yet out of respect for Diane, that he didn't want to grab on to her as a lifeline, the two of them sinking beneath the surface under the weight of their shared baggage.

When he got back to the cabin, he spent the last hours of daylight cleaning up a bit of remaining garbage at the back of the house and setting up the bear trap. He put some bait in the middle of it and went inside to wash his hands.

He fried himself two eggs for dinner, a grim smile crossing his face as he considered the idea of inevitability.

Free will be damned, he thought. After putting his dish in the sink, he grabbed a beer from the fridge and settled into his easy chair for a bit, feeling restless. Finally, at about nine, he went to the cellar.

The root cellar was accessed via a trap door in the floor of the laundry room, immediately to the right of the entrance to the cabin. He grasped a handle in the flooring and pulled up a four-by-three section, hinged at one end, revealing a gaping black hole. He crouched down, feeling inside the hole, and flipped a switch, illuminating rough wooden steps that descended steeply into the darkness. A single bare bulb hung about six feet in the air above the rough concrete floor at the bottom of the stairs, and cobwebs caressed Don's face as he carefully made his way down.

The root cellar only existed under the central section of the home, making it about twenty feet by thirty feet in dimension. There were old, dusty floor-to-ceiling shelves lining the wall near the landing, and Don recalled when his father had made these himself from scrap wood lying about the place. The single bulb only had enough power to illuminate the shelving, almost ineffectually at that, and Don had to move his head to avoid hitting it as he reached the base of the staircase.

Somewhere to the left, in the darkness beyond, were the scattered remains of life *before:* an old Christmas tree, boxes of knickknacks Don couldn't bear to part with, old dishes, and some worn books. *A child's sled.* Mercifully, the lightbulb was too impotent to confront Don with these images directly, although they persisted in some unforgiving corner of his mind. They were phantoms, grasping at his waking mind, threatening to pull him down into the darkness with them.

After scanning the shelves for a moment, he found the object of his search—a small, hard case about twelve inches across by eight inches deep and about four inches thick. Don grabbed it from the shelf and his arm dropped quickly with the weight of it.

Upstairs, he stared at the box in front of him on the kitchen table and thought of his father.

Don Rydell Senior had died of a heart attack just over eight years ago, unexpectedly and in his sleep. There had been no bedside handholding or expressions of affection possible, no last-minute dispensing of final words of wisdom from father to son that Don Junior could cling to in his time of greatest need. No, death had been merciful, if premature, for his father, and when he wasn't feeling sorry for himself, Don could be glad for that.

Don's mother had died after a lengthy battle with pancreatic cancer when Don was almost five. He knew that some people claimed to have memories from as far back as their toddler years, and he had always questioned this, as he suspected their minds just pieced together stories from fragments of dreams and memories instead. For him, he had no direct memories of his mother whatsoever, although his father had told him stories, and he had expressed interest. But for him, they were just that: stories of someone else, stories that had created his memory of a memory of his mother, an entirely fictional character to Don. He knew that his father's tales of her were not objective, and that he would never know the real her.

Don Sr. had worked as a sales executive for an automotive supply company in Auburn Hills, Michigan, and they had lived in nearby Lake Orion, making it possible for his father to usually be home when Don got back from school. His father was a kind man and Don had never heard him raise his voice, not once. He now thought it surprising that he had the *impression* that his father had never missed an important milestone for him. Not a birthday, not a school play, not a soccer game. He knew that couldn't actually be true, but his father had made such an effort to juggle work and parenting that it had left an imprint, and Don could feel it now like a warm embrace. Don had known many childhood friends with two parents who would search the auditorium or the stands in vain, because neither parent could make it to cheer them on, while he would nearly always see his dad there, smiling and waving. Later in life, his dad had also been great with Charlie and Julia. They had enjoyed some great times together at the cabin, walking in the woods, celebrating Christmases, singing folk songs by the fire.

God, how I miss you, Dad, Don thought, exhaling heavily.

He was truly thankful for the fact that his father's untimely death at the age of sixty-eight meant that he hadn't had to live through the teenage years with Charlie or the time *after*.

Don unlocked the case with a key he'd fetched from the kitchen drawer. He took a deep breath, and gently extracted his father's Smith & Wesson from the tight, foamy embrace of its case.

Chapter Seven

Julia

August 2019

Julia woke suddenly and bolted from the bed. She barely made the bathroom before vomiting violently into the toilet.

"Everything alright, love?" Gerrard called from the bedroom. She knew he was expressing concern, but he was not concerned enough to get up and rush to her side.

Gerrard is a helpful gentleman but a man on his own timetable, she thought as she retched again in reply. Finally, Gerrard appeared in the doorway. He came to her and pulled her hair back.

"Nerves?" he asked. "I know this is going to be hard. I wish I could go with you. I want to. If it wasn't for this pitch tomorrow to Blackburn, I would. You know that."

She wiped her mouth on her nightshirt and stood weakly.

"It's okay. I know, Ger," she said, consoling him. She went to the sink and brushed her teeth. In reality, she had not wanted him to go, and was relieved to provide him the out when the news of Gerrard's meeting came up. It was going to be difficult enough seeing Don again and she didn't want Gerrard to be part of the equation. She didn't feel it would be fair to Don, and she didn't like unnecessary complications.

Julia went to her nightstand and checked her phone. It was seven thirty in the morning. She had booked a flight to Detroit via Newark that left at four forty-five in the afternoon, and she didn't need to be at the airport until two thirty or so. Gerrard had purchased his absolution with first-class fare and a promise to take her to the airport himself, rather than hire a chauffeur.

She showered, quickly dressed, and joined him for coffee downstairs.

"I've got to go up the street for a few things. Do you need anything from the chemist?" she asked, adopting the local vernacular to accommodate Gerrard.

"No, thanks love. I'm fine."

He had his nose buried in his laptop, working from home today to ensure he was at her side before she left.

Julia decided to walk to the pharmacy, which was only five blocks or so, as the weather was cold but dry. She passed a gaggle of teenagers in their neat blue and gray uniforms, rushing to class. *The future of the nation,* she thought.

She tried hard to fight the wave, but it came as usual, uncontrollably. Over the last four years, Julia had grieved all the things she'd lost: Christmas, the cabin, dinners with her father, with Don's father, laughing and swimming at the pool behind their rental in Ferndale. She had worked these memories of Charlie over and over in her mind until they were deeply etched, grooves in a record she could play, had to play, over and over again. With the arrival of the news that he would never return—was *gone for good*—she found that she grieved the loss of all the things that *would never be.* Graduation, the joy of Charlie's first job, a wedding, a child—her *grandchild.*

She had become expert at riding these waves, sometimes crying, sometimes not. Today her eyes stayed mercifully dry, so her mascara did not need a touch up before she entered the shop, and she quickly grabbed the things she needed, returning uneventfully to the flat.

There, she packed the last of her things and grabbed her phone. Gerrard carried everything to the car for her, and they rode mostly in silence to the airport, occasionally punctuated by awkward conversation about the weather, or Gerrard's pending deal.

The worst was whenever he attempted to console her. He had always been smart enough to know that this was a potential minefield with her, and that he had no new revelations to bring to her grief, no miracle remedies to offer. His safest and preferred approach had always been to focus on their lives in the here and now, and this intrusion of her past grief into the present had clearly challenged him, but he knew better than to dig in. Mercifully they finally arrived at the airport, where he kissed her goodbye at the curb. She promised to text when she arrived.

First-class check-in was light, and she was drinking mineral water and savoring canapés in the lounge in no time. Finally, they called her flight, and she went to board.

She found her seat, took the hot towel the flight attendant offered, and braced herself for the long journey ahead. There was a time she had found the prospect of flying thrilling, *exotic* even. Now, she just hoped she could keep her food down.

Today, she had learned that somewhere, somehow, in that barren wasteland of her body, Gerrard's seed had found fertile ground.

Chapter Eight

Don and Julia

September 1998

Don watched bemused as Julia moved to close the distance between them, throwing herself into the alcove and nearly bumping into him.

"Trouble finding the place?" she asked.

"No, it was easy."

Just then, a group of young women about their age squeezed quickly past and spilled into the restaurant to escape the rain, their laughter fading into the warm glow of the building. Don suggested they follow the women inside and get out of the weather.

Julia had been the one to make the reservation and the hostess led them to a table in the Fireplace Room. It was not as exotic as it sounded, being the larger of the restaurant's dining areas, but it seemed cozy. The place was about three-quarters full tonight, and they were fortunate to be placed at a table near the fireplace with only one adjacent table occupied. The fireplace was a wall-mounted gas insert with dark wood trim surrounding it, and the walls on either side were covered in a red-brick veneer. Oddly, a moose head hung above the fireplace. It was a railroad-themed restaurant, and Don amused himself by wondering if the moose had been hit by a train.

The seating was bar-style with small, square tables, similar to those found in half the bars in the state. A glossy lacquer covered the dark wood.

They chose to sit opposite each other.

"Your server will be right with you," the hostess informed them.

"Thanks," Julia responded. She removed her small jacket, revealing her red blouse and bare shoulders.

"You look great." Don again found himself awestruck. He hoped he hadn't already committed some kind of faux pas by commenting on her appearance; he still didn't understand why or how he was here. He had been almost surprised to see Julia approach in the rain, certainly *relieved*. Although he had mentally rehearsed for this, he still hadn't expected, deep down, to actually have to conduct a conversation. Somewhere in his psyche, a small voice was whispering, *Just wait. You'll see. The trap hasn't sprung yet. Don't get your hopes up.*

Maybe this was because he had been picked on relentlessly as a young boy, losing various possessions and a little blood to bullies throughout his schooling. At least, until sometime in high school when he figured out how to use his wit to deflect them.

"So, Don, I never caught your last name."

"Rydell," he replied.

Names. He could do this. "With a 'why' and two 'ell's."

"So, Don Rydell, with a 'why' and two 'ell's," she continued in a playful tone, "do you actually go to U of M, or are you just an imposter?"

He quickly attempted to decode her mischievous challenge, settling on the letterman jacket he had worn to the bar.

"My jacket? Yeah, I actually go to U of M; want to see my student card?" He made a show of reaching for his pocket and grinning.

She pressed on with a brief smile of acknowledgement.

"What do you study?"

"I'm a POLISCI senior. Sorry, political science. U of M is pretty well known for the program."

Damn, there must have been a better way to say that. He flushed slightly at the thought that he was sounding brash, arrogant, overcompensating for the nerves he felt twitching in his intestines.

"Cool," Julia replied.

They'd had no props to fiddle with yet, being seated at a barren table, and thankfully a young blonde server quickly approached them.

"Hi, and welcome to The Sidetrack Bar and Grill. I'm Kelsey and I'll be your server tonight. Can I get you both something to drink?"

Don wondered if there was a pool of a dozen or so names you had to choose from if you wanted to be a server: *Brittany, Ashley, Tiffany, Kelsey. Observational bias*, he decided.

"Um, could we get a couple of menus, please?" he asked. This drew a look from Kelsey which seemed to imply, *We have all the drinks a bar has, and this isn't your first time, so why don't you just use that pretty little memory of yours and order something already*, but she adopted a helpful protocol and smiled.

"Sure, I'll be right back."

Don had always found social interaction to be fraught with so many pitfalls, traps, and misdirection. People who said one thing and meant another. *Why couldn't people just say what they meant and listen to the words they were told?*

In the intervening period—it seemed to take longer than it should to get menus—Don had learned Julia's last name, her work schedule, and a few standard details.

When Kelsey finally returned, they settled on a light beer for Don as he had to drive, and a glass of chardonnay for Julia, before glancing at the menus. Kelsey gave them a polite look as if to say, *See? I knew you could do it* and then claimed the upper hand by asking for ID, one area where she didn't have to be deferential. Thus, Don ultimately did have to produce his wallet, and this had the effect of deflating the mood slightly—having to prove that they were grown up.

****

Don was charming, certainly handsome, and Julia found herself focusing on the details of his face as he spoke. Those deep brown eyes, a perfect match for his thick, dark hair. The little freckle on his left cheek, his dimples when he smiled, the stubble on his face. Perhaps she feared he would be like the others—pretty on the outside, but growing increasingly tiresome as they rambled on, or irritating her sensibilities by behaving like strutting peacocks. It was usually all too obvious for her and she wondered if this was why she had so few dates; she had set the bar so high that there may not be a man alive who could clear it.

She asked him to tell her more about his college program, and despite his obvious nervousness Julia could see that she had found a topic he could safely navigate. He talked passionately about his Democracy course, the professors, and how fourth year was easier as most of the weeding out had already been accomplished. He talked about his house and his roommates, again apologizing and offering a spirited defense of their moral character, attempting to paint a positive, three-dimensional image for her. While relaying a story about Jim volunteering his time as a Big Brother on weekends, he stopped mid-sentence and said, "Julia, I don't know anything about you, and I really want to. I know you work at Rick's, a lot. What do you like to do in your spare time?"

She looked up from her glass. She had chosen chardonnay because she liked it, but also because she felt it made her look mature. She held the glass, palm up between her index and middle fingers, cradling the liquid like precious, golden treasure. She had known the attention would turn to her sooner or later, but she continued to be economical in her replies.

"Run," she offered simply.

They continued through appetizers of fries and wings. Don had insisted on ordering them, and she wondered if he was trying to be the gentleman, or just prolonging the evening as much as possible.

"You know," Don said with a mischievous grin between bites of his French fry, "I think you would make a good secret agent, or maybe an FBI agent."

She pulled her head back on a level plane, like a bird. A slight frown on her brow added to the look of surprise.

"No really," he continued, "It's so hard to get information out of you. This all could be a set up," he said in an exaggerated whisper, "I'll bet there's a microphone in that moose's mouth." He tilted his head slightly to the left and cast his eyes in the direction of the fireplace. She laughed, abruptly and fully, like a sneeze. She could not have held it back even if she wanted to. It was as if all of her apprehension and anticipation for the evening was finally released.

They spoke more easily after that, covering current events, the pros and cons of Ypsi versus Ann Arbor, Don's ideas for work after college, and other small but comfortable topics. Julia still held her college plans in reserve.

They got their main courses and continued their conversation. Julia ultimately shared the facts of her living situation with Don, and they exchanged brief bios of their parents without color-commentary, just the basics.

"It must be interesting at home sometimes, with an Irish father and a Mexican mother," Don offered as he chewed the last of his burger.

"Sometimes I think I got the best of both worlds," she said, pushing her half-eaten plate to the side, not wanting to reveal the voracious appetite she was capable of.

"I got my father's wit—the gift of the gab—and my mother's hot blood, her passion. And her love of cooking," Julia added, worrying that it sounded weak and a little old fashioned.

Don smiled and nodded, encouraging her to continue talking.

"Sometimes, though, I think I may have gotten the worst of both," she groaned, smiling wryly. "I have my father's sarcasm and my mother's temper."

"Well, I'm sure you got the best of both of them," he asserted, smiling politely.

She shifted the conversation to Don's backstory. The absence of his mother, and his father's balancing act of working and raising him.

Before Julia was ready for the evening to end, Kelsey arrived bearing the check. Julia's first thought was that this was a premature intrusion and wondered at the increased velocity of Kelsey's attentions as the evening progressed.

It had certainly taken much longer to get the menus. Just then, Don reached for the bill.

"I'll get it," Julia directed. "After all, *I* asked *you* out."

Don looked like he had been zapped with a stun gun. Momentarily, she feared that she had emasculated him somehow.

Why do men need to think with so much testosterone?

"How 'bout we split it, fifty-fifty?" he said, apparently regaining muscle control.

"Deal," she said, cutting him a little slack.

They debated the size of Kelsey's tip, with Julia's empathy toward a fellow server prevailing over Don's procedural calculation. Fortunately, thanks to the twenty contributed by her father, Julia had enough cash to avoid needing separate bills as that might have spoiled the mood.

They rose from the table and made their way to the door, seeing that the rain had passed.

"Can I drop you at your house?" Don suggested.

Julia paused, not sure if she was ready for Don to know where she lived. To see *how* she lived.

"Sure," she said, hoping her hesitation had not betrayed her.

He dropped her at the house without any commentary on the neighborhood.

"When can I see you again?" Don asked through his open car window.

"Don't worry," Julia replied, her body shining in the misty glow of the headlights from the Corolla as she playfully stepped backwards.

"*I'll* call *you*."

And for the first time in a long time, she meant it.

Chapter Nine

Julia

August 2019

After a light meal only half-eaten, Julia reclined her seat back into its flat bed-style position. A helpful flight attendant had brought her some pajamas and a thin mattress pad for the bed. She marveled bitterly at the achievements of mankind, and lay herself down, pulling a poor imitation of a duvet across the length of her body.

She took every step prescribed to ensure sleep: the earplugs, the mask for her eyes, even some British equivalent of Dramamine from her purse, that being the more benign of her pharmacy purchases. These were largely in vain, as the news from the day, although suspected, had driven a spike into her guts. She did not feel as though she wanted a child, certainly not with Gerrard and perhaps not at all; she was too old. She had reached the point where the price—in anguish, sorrow, fear, and simple *effort*—was just too high. Too high when the reward was so uncertain and fragile.

Should she tell Gerrard? A mini courtroom drama played out in her mind:

He was the one who said he was infertile, Your Honor. He swore it. My client should not have to bear this burden.

She is a grown woman, milord, capable of making her own decisions and protecting herself, came the counter from the prosecution. *She knew the risk. The father has a right to know, at the very least!* he blared.

No, she did not feel she owed Gerrard that. She already knew what he would think; this child would be a nuisance for him. He loved and cherished his career.

And me?

That was for another trial. She banished the judge to oblivion before he could render a verdict. As usual, she was her own arbiter, and she resolved to get an abortion upon her return to England without telling Gerrard. That would be the simplest.

She tossed and turned on the plane, torturing herself with fantasies of raising a child with Gerrard. She imagined a girl, as no one could replace Charlie, enjoying faux tea parties, playing hide and seek in an imagined garden, taking walks to the river hand in hand and feeding the ducklings. In her daydream, she had conquered her hatred of the water, and she even imagined herself in a pool, teaching her daughter to swim. She visualized her child with golden hair and bright blue eyes, like her father. She would have her mother's fortitude and they would call her Isabella, after Julia's mother. Julia imagined Isabella hugging her, comforting *her*. She wept silently in the confines of her pod, already grieving Isabella until finally, through sheer force of will and self-distraction, she succumbed to the monotonous roar of the Airbus's engines and drifted into a dream.

The plane was hurtling toward a clouded mountain at four hundred miles an hour, and she wanted to scream, but no sound came out. She pointed wildly, running up and down the aisles, but her fellow passengers continued to drink their wine, watch their movies, and sleep. No one was heeding her warnings. She set off running for the cockpit and tried to reach it, but her feet felt stuck in concrete. No matter how hard she tried, the door remained off in the distance. She tried again to scream, and waved her arms at the flight attendants, who stood expressionless near the cockpit door.

Now, she was falling into blackness. She could not see a thing, not even her hands flailing in front of her face. She heard voices, strange at first, resolving themselves into familiar sounds—Don's father, Charlie around the age of four or five, her father, and Gerrard. They were speaking to her, but try as she might, she could not discern the words. It was as though they were babbling in a foreign language.

Then she was on the plane again, screaming soundlessly in the aisle. Even though she was not near a window, she could somehow still see the approach of the mountain, right up until the plane struck and burst into pieces. There were shards of metal, smoke, and fire everywhere and she stood on the ground in the center of it all looking around. Figures inexplicably shambled by her, still going about their business, holding drinks and conversing. The flesh had been burnt from them and they looked like apocalyptic escapees from some science museum's body exhibit.

Oddly, despite their burned flesh, they still had shreds of garments on. A lady? passed her, wearing a new blue hat and a string of pearls around her neck, holding a martini with an olive. Julia surveyed herself, noticing that she was wearing Gerrard's T-shirt, still soaked in sweat, and holding a fancy cocktail of her own. She tried to drink from it but could not bring the glass to her lips. Then, she saw a family of ducks waddling through the chaos and she tracked them as they passed some toys, unaffected by the flames, heading toward a child of about three who lay dead. Julia didn't want to, tried her hardest not to look up, but did anyway taking in the entire scene again. Passengers from Flight 6242 continued to shamble around the wreckage and only the children lay dead.

She awoke in a state of complete disorientation. Her head hurt, and her face was sticky. Julia felt her heart racing as though she'd been running. She pulled the eye mask off and was immediately assaulted by bright lighting. The flight attendants were clearing the afternoon snack that had been advertised on the menu. As her mind reoriented itself, she attempted to bring her heartbeat back to normal by performing some yoga meditation she had tried once as part of her recovery, and eventually, she calmed herself and brought her seat upright. Glancing up at her monitor, Julia saw that it was only one hour until landing. She took a long sip of water from her bottle, sat back in her chair, and closed her eyes.

CHAPTER TEN

Julia and Don

OCTOBER 1998

JULIA WENT THROUGH THE days after their date in a haze. Nothing could drag her down—neither her father, nor the occasional looks from Ralph at the bar. These had really diminished of late, and she wondered if Kelly had said something to someone, maybe Robert.

It was Thursday, the first day of the new month, and the weather had returned to warm, sunny days which were expected to persist for at least another week. Julia decided to opt for a brisk walk today instead of a run and came into the house just as her father was pouring himself a large glass of whisky at the kitchen counter.

He often drank in the afternoons, usually starting around four o'clock and numbing himself by seven or eight. This behavior had seemed to lessen since Julia had begun working at Rick's, and she wondered if maybe her father had become conscious of his example as Julia reached drinking age, or perhaps he had simply time-shifted his drinking out of her sight. Either way was fine, as this spared her the risk of an unpleasant interaction with him in that state. It wasn't that he was a mean drunk, although he would become overly talkative and argumentative, it was more that, seeing her father yielding to the alcohol, slurring his words slightly, saying things he wouldn't normally say, disappointed Julia.

She cautioned him about drinking and driving, and he would usually let up about eight o'clock, switching to black coffee in anticipation of the drive to work at ten thirty. Julia's mother had long since given up the notion of telling David what he should do, opting for a well-honed indirect approach—a gentle nag here, an allusion there. This attribute of her mother's personality was Julia's least favorite.

Just then, Isabella came in from the living room with cleaning supplies for the kitchen. Her second client of the day, Mrs. Reddington, had canceled as her Mahjong club had decided to play that afternoon at her house, and she preferred not to have the intrusion of the cleaning lady. Isabella chose to take the opportunity to clean her own house.

Sometimes Julia found her mother exhausting; at times, she could be a large ponytailed hummingbird, flitting about the house, never stopping in one place too long. Julia occasionally wondered: *if her mother rested, might she be forced to think—about her life, her marriage, her future—and then not be able to get herself back in motion?*

Isabella glanced at the bottle of Jameson on the counter and then over at David, who had returned to the kitchen table with his glass and was lighting a cigarette.

"Do you need me to get more whisky from the liquor store, mi corazon? The bottle is getting low again."

Her mother was an expert at stealth attacks, subtle Trojan horses that superficially appeared helpful and kind, but which contained pre-packaged guilt awaiting detonation at some unforeseen time.

"No thanks, dear," David delivered in measured response, probably aware that they both knew another bottle awaited its turn in the liquor cabinet.

Julia wondered what had set him back to drinking earlier in the day again.

Maybe the cooler weather? She didn't know and couldn't be troubled to find out.

She had hardly broken a sweat on her walk but grabbed a bottle of Gatorade from the fridge out of habit and headed for the stairs with a quick nod to her father.

"Julia," her father called. She turned to face him from the bottom of the stairs.

"What's happening with this new boyfriend of yours?" Her father's voice was playful but firm.

"His name is Don, Dad, and not much. And he's not my boyfriend, just a friend who happens to be a boy. We're going to meet for drinks in Ann Arbor on Sunday night."

"Make sure you leave yourself something to talk about. I've heard you on the phone every day this week. Good thing we don't pay by the minute."

She burned.

Her father was right. She had talked to Don every day, getting up earlier to accommodate his class schedule and being unable to contain the volume of her voice as they talked about anything and everything on the phone. It had been as though they were trying to catch each other up on twenty years of missed history in a very old friendship.

Neither of them had siblings, so the storytelling had been about school, friends, parents and vacations—his, not hers, as she'd really had none. She didn't feel bitter, however, as she listened to Don's tales of his father's cabin. It sounded like something out of a fairy tale, tucked away in an enchanted forest, a place where everyone was happy all the time, and she found herself wanting, hoping, to see it someday. She had enjoyed these conversations so much that she had even allowed herself to skip Monday's run to spend the time on the phone with Don. She had spoken to him for nearly six hours the day after their date and it had felt like six minutes, neither wanting to hang up and sever the tentative connection they had made.

Isabella chose the right moment to rescue her daughter, reasserting her own position as head of the household—if not in totality, at least as it pertained to matters involving Julia.

"Go up and get your shower, mija. I'll get dinner going, and we can eat early tonight. I'm going to make some tamales."

Another subtle tactic to slow her father down, as he did not like to drink whisky with his supper. Julia seized the opportunity to turn and escape up the stairs to her room.

****

Sunday came, and Julia opted to hail a cab to go to Ann Arbor, though Don had offered, and even tried to insist that he would come and get her. She told herself this was her being a strong woman, taking control. Somewhere in the back of her brain lingered a thought—*You're just not ready for him to meet your parents yet. Coward.*

She brushed it off and got into the cab that was waiting at the curb. She felt her mood lighten as the cheap post First World War houses of Ypsi vanished in the rearview mirror.

It felt strange to be making the trip to Ann Arbor heading somewhere other than Rick's, driving with someone other than Kelly. She had almost forgotten her purpose as her mind dropped onto a pre-recorded track. She had set her coat beside herself in the rear of the cab, as she didn't want to sweat, and she felt her dress ride up slightly around her thighs against the cheap fabric of the taxi. She noticed a cigarette hole burned into the cloth and reflexively pulled her dress down, feeling exposed.

The taxi driver had a bushy mustache and full, dark curly hair, and Julia couldn't help but imagine an unkempt Saddam Hussein. He had grunted an approximation of English in a thick accent to confirm her destination and there was a vague, spicy odor about him. The rearview mirror was adorned with brown beads, and every time he glanced in it, she felt his eyes on her. Judging her. She almost felt like screaming: *This is America. I can wear whatever the fuck I want,* and she felt a twinge of guilt at the thought. She did not consider herself a prejudiced person but had no time for the judgmental ideologies of men.

Fortunately, traffic was light, and the route had been direct—I-94 to Main, where they took a left onto Liberty and pulled up to the Alley Bar. This was a hip area of town, new for Julia who worked on the southeast side of campus, and it was dotted with bars, restaurants, and shops.

Despite it being a cold Sunday night, it was a hive of outdoor activity. Julia noted the fare of thirty-two dollars, and she handed the driver two twenties and told him to keep the change, her generosity inspired by a desire for a speedy escape rather than altruism. He nodded in appreciation. The round trip tonight would cost her most of Saturday's tip money, but she could not care less at the moment. She stretched upright as she exited the cab, escaping into the fresh evening air.

Man, that was not comfortable, she thought as she wiggled her hips back and forth, pulling the hem of her form-fitting black dress down around her thighs and donning her coat.

Julia's dress had spaghetti straps that played to her strengths and had been a sore spot with her mother. At the start of that summer, a cousin of Julia's had invited her to a graduation party and Julia had bought the dress for the event. She thought it made her look good, but her mother had shamed her into wearing something more conservative, more *lady-like*, and she was angry at the memory of capitulating to Isabella's will on this point. Thankfully, she had negotiated further independence in the few short months since then.

She'd braved three-inch black heels today, confident she could navigate the short distance from the taxi to the table gracefully, and she wore the three-quarter-length black wool coat her parents had given her last Christmas. It was her big gift that year, unusually generous for their means, and from this month onward she would use it liberally. Tonight, it had served to shield her choice of attire from her parents as she had rushed down the stairs and out the side door, using the excuse of the waiting taxi's meter running to deflect their pleas for a kiss goodbye. Appealing to their practicality.

She felt a twinge of guilt at the shrewdness of this move but shook it off now as she approached the bar.

She saw Don at a table just to the right of the bar and made her way over. He hadn't seen her yet, as he was busy glancing at his watch. The date was for seven o'clock, and she had taken the liberty of arriving fifteen minutes late. Julia quickly removed her coat to ensure that she could make her best visual impression immediately, and as he turned his head toward the door to search for her she caught his eye. She could tell he tried to hide it, but she knew she had scored a direct hit.

They had covered so much ground by phone since the first date that this evening was remarkably comfortable. They picked up threads of unfinished conversations from their phone chats and talked over one another passionately. An observer might have easily mistaken them as married. The time flew past, and it was half past nine before they knew it.

"Well," she said tentatively, "I guess I should get going."

Don paid the bill and they moved to the door.

"Do you want to take a drive with me? There's a place I want to show you." he asked as they exited the bar into the cool night air.

"Sure," Julia replied after a brief pause.

They drove in Don's car for about ten minutes, and she didn't notice as they crossed the Huron River and passed into a largely green area. She was looking at Don - the lines of his handsome face, the dimple on his right cheek.

It was as though he could feel her staring and he turned his head to look at her.

"What?" he laughed.

"Nothing," she replied lightly. She turned her gaze to the right, staring out into the greenish blackness moving slowly by.

They came to a deserted parking lot near some children's play equipment. It was bound by trees on three sides, and about forty feet ahead, the river.

"Welcome to Gallup Park," Don said. "I come here sometimes with my bike when I want a break from campus...to read or just hang out."

They got out of the car and walked by the river hand in hand. It was cold and clear, and the stars shone brightly through the faint haze of Ann Arbor's lights.

After a time, Don finally spoke.

"Do you ever want to get married, have a family?" he asked, with a casualness that seemed to Julia a little forced.

"I dunno. I guess I hadn't thought much about it yet," she answered, looking carefully at the pavement as she negotiated it in her heels, feeling the blisters setting in.

She had only known this man for a little more than a month, but she could feel herself being drawn to Don, and was scared at how quickly it all seemed to be moving.

"Yeah. I guess I do. Someday."

"Yeah, me too," he said, smirking. "You know, when I finally meet the right woman."

She punched his arm and they both laughed.

They returned to walking and making small talk and Julia realized she was not focusing on what Don was saying, still stuck on the topic of marriage and children.

Feeling slightly annoyed, she stopped and turned to him, dropping her hand from his.

"Don, I want to go to school too. I want a life for myself." She looked at the river. "I don't want to be stuck somewhere like my mother, no life, no place to go. It's not for me."

"That's great," he said. "Good for you. You should go for it." His words echoing her conversations with Kelly. "What do you want to do?"

She hesitated briefly. "I want to be an architect."

"That's awesome," he said almost reflexively. "Why an architect?"

She took a moment and stared at her feet, struggling to find the words. Finally, she looked back at Don.

"When I was a girl, maybe fourteen or fifteen—it was a couple of years before we moved to Ypsi—my mother took me to a church for my cousin's first Communion. The church was called Sweetest Heart of Mary, I think. I remember laughing to myself at the name. When we got to the church, my mother had to tell me to close my mouth for fear of catching flies. It was...*magnificent*." Julia paused and grabbed Don's hand and she could see him listening patiently as they took up walking again.

"My mother had to pull my hand to get me to move inside. The church has these twin spires that reach up to the heavens, and the arch of the entrance is at least as tall as two grown men; it was overwhelming. I remember walking down the aisle looking around, trying to take it all in—the statues, the light from the stained-glass windows, the scale of it. It wasn't just the sights, I remember the sound, the way the footsteps and whispers of the people inside echoed, the smells of incense and old wood. It all felt so magical, and I felt so insignificant. I was Alice in Wonderland, shrunk down small, and wandering in a strange, mystical place.

Our little church in Mexicantown had been nothing like this and I tried to tell my mother how I felt. She told me that it didn't matter. God would hear you if you worshipped in a shed because he didn't care for showiness."

Julia paused and looked into Don's eyes.

"Up until then, I had always taken what she told me as truth. But sitting there, in that glorious building? I knew she was wrong. It *did* matter. *Men* had built this to make us feel small, humbled. It worked, and it felt like a great power to me."

Julia could see that she had Don's interest.

"After that, I found myself sketching," she continued, growing more confident. "Churches at first, and then houses. Places that I would want to live. I took out a book on architecture from the library at high school and taught myself a little. I guess it also showed me possibilities, how other people lived...that not everyone lived in a little box in a row of boxes in some shitty neighborhood. I loved the idea that a building made out of wood and stone could make you *feel* something. It was exhilarating."

She paused to take a deep breath. "Sorry, I got away from myself there."

"Wow," Don said, "You sound so passionate about it. But, you're twenty-one, why haven't you gone to college yet?"

Despite all the conversation by phone, and during their dates, this topic had not been explored fully, as Julia would simply redirect back to Don or another topic whenever the subject came up. She realized that she couldn't avoid it forever and decided to share a little with him.

"I lost a bit of interest when we moved to Ypsi because I was so self-absorbed," she replied. "Now that I've got some money, I want to do something with my life, and I guess I thought...*why not*? I can't work at Rick's forever."

Don began charting out to her the possibilities. Maybe, she could try to go to U of M, and he would work writing articles. His friend's father was going to get him an entry-level job at the *Detroit Free Press*, and though the distance would present some challenges, they could continue meeting on weekends. They would figure things out.

Julia felt as though he was tethering things, throwing anchors, and trying to solve problems that she wasn't asking him to solve. She was slightly sad, as though he had missed the point of it, but played along.

Inspired by the discussion of churches, she decided to shift topics before she grew impatient with him. They continued their walk, turning to work their way back toward the car.

"Do you think there's a God up there, directing traffic down here?" she asked, tilting her head upward.

He waited a while before answering.

"No, I don't," he said, the hesitancy in his voice out of sync with his words. "We just get what we make for ourselves. The rest is chance...random." Before she could respond he reversed the question. "What about you, Julia?"

She looked up again in deference to the subject.

"I don't know," she said. "I thought I did. When I was a kid. Now, I think..." She paused, realizing that this would be the first time she had voiced her doubts *out loud*. "I think that if there is something, someone out there, I don't think we can understand it; we've messed it up so far. Maybe you're right. Maybe there is nothing at all but us."

They continued this way for a time, discussing religion, the destruction of the planet, the state of politics, the plight of the underprivileged.

Like me, she thought, then quickly admonished herself. In the grand scheme of things, she knew she was a lucky woman. Sure, she had come from a humble neighborhood, but when she was feeling optimistic, she believed that she had always been surrounded by love, a web of support that extended across the cracked streets of the city and through its shops, her church, her school, her parents at the center of it. Julia continued to glance at Don's face as they walked, charmed by his voice and his good looks, but most of all, the combination of his intellect and humility, which was rare in her experience.

They returned to the car and Julia turned her entire body toward Don, face to face. It was as though someone had flipped a switch, charging them with electromagnetic force and she could no longer bear a sliver of space between them. She felt possessed as she pressed herself into him, seeking to connect with every part of him and she pushed so hard, powered by adrenaline, that she thought she might have hurt him. Yet, she longed to be closer still, to *fuse* with him. It felt like hours, although she knew it couldn't have been more than a few seconds, before he responded to her touch. She felt his warm breath, and then his mouth locked with hers and his tongue sought hers out. Her hand slid around the nape of his neck, her fingers intertwining with his dark, curly locks. They pressed their bodies tightly together, falling back against the side of the Corolla as Don fumbled for his keys, unlocking the car and then opening the rear door.

Julia pulled her coat off, letting it fall to the gravel of the parking lot and placed both palms against Don's chest. She lightly pushed him onto the rear seat of the car and hiked her black dress up over her hips, climbing onto him, opening his zipper and pulling his jeans around his hips. She sensed him take a deep breath and she held her own.

Was this really happening now, with him? She had never been here before, except in her mind, and though if felt right, here with Don, she worried. Worried that he would think less of her, worried that it would be painful, worried, that she would be punished somehow for her sin. But Don's charm had pierced something in her, a protective bubble that she had put around her desire after so many disappointments. And, once pierced, her raw human yearning had been exposed. She was tired of arguing with phantoms that told her - *No. You shouldn't.* Her mother. Her father. The priest at St. John. She sought to reclaim full sovereignty over her choices, starting now.

Her head was spinning in so many directions while her body felt alien to her, out of her control. She let herself go as she bent down to bring her face against Don's.

She had heard stories from her *experienced* friends about what it was like to *make love*, but as she turned her head to kiss Don and their eyes locked, she felt as though *no one* had ever experienced anything like this. It wasn't long before her body shivered and she felt an explosion of pure light course through her, from the tips of her fingers to her toes. They collapsed together and the moment receded.

As she lay with her cheek pressed to his, she felt embarrassed, wondering what Don would think of her now, but the worry moved to the back of her mind when he placed his hand gently against the side of her face and tucked a strand of stray hair back behind her ear.

"Well, that was unexpected," he said, grinning. They both laughed and embraced tightly in the back of the old car.

After a time she crept back off him, careful not to bang her head on the low roof of the car, and reassembled herself outside. She became keenly aware of her surroundings, hoping nobody had seen, and slightly irritated that she given herself over to such an animal instinct and relinquished self-control. She picked her coat up off the gravel, and as if to right things, she said,

"I think I should get home now, Don."

CHAPTER ELEVEN

Don and Julia

OCTOBER 1998

THEY CONTINUED THIS WAY for the weeks that stretched through October, talking daily on the phone and meeting on Sundays and Mondays when they could, making love in Don's room, walking through the park and occasionally going out for a nice dinner. Don found that he had to work hard to focus on his midterms. He was a solid A- student, but didn't want to blow it so near the finish line and his sleeping patterns took the brunt of the abuse, as he took to studying while Julia was working.

Twice, he'd shown up at the bar, just to tease her, *to see her*, but he backed off this tactic after the second attempt. He had gone in one Thursday night around eight and approached the bar. "What's good tonight, miss…" he asked, staring at her name badge pointedly, "…Julia?"

She had laughed, but it wasn't like her laugh on their first date. It was constrained, almost polite.

He realized she might view this mixing of worlds as an intrusion, and it had taken him a couple of days of inner coaching and reassurances from her that everything was fine, he had not offended her, for him to get his confidence back. He did not want to go down that rabbit hole again.

The last Sunday of October, Julia suggested they meet at the Alley Bar again. She still resisted Don's offer of rides, and he couldn't understand why she would want to waste so much money on cab fare; still, he knew better than to protest. He had arrived on time, as usual. They had agreed to meet early, at six o'clock, and she was late. He took his seat at the table and scanned the doorway until he saw her come in. The day had been warm, but it was cooling fast as the sun had nearly disappeared into the horizon beyond the city, and Julia didn't bother to take her coat off until she came to the table.

She smiled as she took her seat across from him.

"You're late. Don't you know what today is?" he asked in a playful tone, no longer fearful of challenging her a little.

"The best day of my life so far...?" she ventured, and he could see her digging deep for some charm.

He made an exaggerated gesture of being put out, his right arm lying flat across the table against his belly, left elbow atop it, chin on knuckles reminiscent of Rodin's *Thinker*. His face frowned in feigned disapproval.

"Today," he stated slowly, mimicking a teacher addressing a student, "is the anniversary of our first month together."

She rebuffed this quickly, protesting that since he had been an ass when she first met him, they should only mark the anniversary from their first *agreed upon* date. They bantered back and forth for a time until she extended her right palm outward, a crossing guard to prevent him from moving or speaking.

"Okay, if you insist," she said, sounding almost smug to Don, pulling a small, wrapped package out from under her coat with her left hand. She handed it over to him and he smiled, surprised, and unwrapped the gift.

It was a watch with a smooth, gold face flanked by two black leather straps.

"It's simple, the way you like. No numbers, just hands."

He made great effort to publicly cherish it, replacing the one on his wrist with the new one and dutifully admiring it. In truth, the thought of it—*that she had cared to mark the day*—was the gift he relished. He hoped he had uttered sufficient reassurances of its suitability and his love for it, and he allowed her a moment's pleasure in taking control of the situation. As their drinks arrived, he said simply, "I got you something too." He handed her a very small package.

****

For a moment, her throat seized, and Julia feared he may be intending a premature proposal—one she was decidedly *not* ready for. Oh, she liked Don very much, but they had not crossed that threshold, not yet uttered those words. Anyway, she had plans for her life, as did he. She was just enjoying the here and now, not trying to plot the course of their relationship. She approached it slowly, as if attempting to forestall the moment.

It was a ring box.

Shit.

She opened it gingerly, preparing her speech.

I care about you, Don. We're just not ready yet. We've only just gotten to know each other. You're still in school. I'm planning to go to school, and so on. She flipped the lid.

It was a ring, but not an engagement ring. It was a slim band of silver with two hands holding a heart underneath a crown embossed in the center.

"It's a Claddagh ring," he said, and she could hear a slight tone of disappointment in his voice at her momentary confusion. She pulled the ring from the box and gasped, a sigh of relief that he fortunately seemed to misinterpret as emotion for the gift.

"You like it?" he asked keenly.

"I know what it is," she said, continuing to admire the gift. Genuine emotion now filled the space left by her receding feeling of relief. She was touched by his nod to her paternal ancestry and she placed the ring, heart inward, on her right hand.

Things changed again after that evening. Julia started to spend time at Don's before work, when he didn't have class, having him pick her up in the late morning before her father awoke, and later dropping her at Rick's for her shift. She didn't know what her parents suspected, but she was twenty-one, and she didn't feel obliged to tell them everything. Her mother, true to form, did not waste time dropping hints.

"When will we meet this mystery man?" she'd ask, or she'd say, "Julia, let me look at you. I'm worried I'm going to forget your beautiful face." Or, "Julia, should I cut back on the groceries I'm buying? You aren't having dinner here often now and food is going to waste."

Then there was, "I hope you don't forget how I raised you."

Another clever depth charge.

Julia's favorite though, came from her father one afternoon. She was home, following her usual routine, as Don had an exam. She passed her father in the kitchen after a difficult run and he simply said, "I hope you know what you're doing girl. *Be careful.*"

She loved the straightforwardness of the man. Even when he irritated her.

Kelly, for her part, was clearly put out by the shift in their friendship and things grew cool between them, although she could still be counted on to adopt their routine when it suited Julia, which was down to about one or two nights a week. On those evenings, as often as not, she would simply want to sleep when they returned to her place. On the other nights, Don would pick Julia up at the bar and they'd return to his place. She wasn't going to be able to manage the rare nights at Kelly's much longer as it was early November, Julia was already walking home in blackness and when the snow came, it would not be enjoyable at all.

The first Sunday in November, Julia lay beside Don in his bed, staring at the ceiling.

"Everything alright?" he asked softly.

"I was just thinking," she said, "maybe it's time you meet my parents." She turned to look at him, to watch for any signal in the darkness that she had tripped a wire, gone into forbidden territory.

"I've been waiting for you to say that," he replied. "I want you to meet my dad too. You're gonna love him. He's a great guy, and he's dying to meet you. How about Thanksgiving?" he suggested.

She shook her head in the darkness.

"Too much stress. My mother goes bonkers trying to get everything ready because her aunt, and sister's family come for dinner," she explained. "It's chaos. I'm surprised my father doesn't flee for the weekend. No, I think the weekend before would be better."

In two weeks. She became anxious to clear this hurdle now that she had voiced the idea.

"I love you, you know," he said, and she could feel him searching her features in the dim light of the night.

"I know," she said softly. Wanting to give him more. She could sense his disappointment and felt angry with herself. "I can imagine spending a long time with you, Don."

"Well Jules, that's sweet of you to say," he replied.

"Please don't call me that," she said, "You know I hate that nickname."

"Okay," he replied, lifting himself up in the bed onto one elbow and looking down at her, "but I need a nickname for you. Julia sounds too formal sometimes."

She laughed. "You're thinking about this too hard. I can see smoke coming from your ears," she said, reaching up to tug one of his earlobes.

"I saw a 'C' on your ID the other day, when you left it on the table at the restaurant," Don continued.

Julia had forgotten it, and he'd picked it up for her on his way by after one of their dinners out.

"You looked at my ID?" she cried out in an exaggerated tone. "Hmm, boundaries. Cool." she teased, "And..?"

"What...does...it...stand...for?" he asked emphatically.

She made him wait.

"Oh my god," he said seeming genuinely exasperated, "Remember when I said on our first date that you might be a secret agent? Well, you really should forget about architecture and look into training at Quantico, or wherever they train the CIA. The enemy could torture you and never learn a thing. Seriously."

She laughed, wondering why she was hesitating to share this minor detail with him.

"It stands for Carmen, okay? Happy now?"

"Julia Carmen," he said. "Interesting. Who is this mystery woman?" he asked playfully. He kissed her cheek and lay back down, falling quickly to sleep. She lay awake for at least another hour, her mind racing.

The next morning, Julia decided to follow her normal routine. Don dropped her off at her house around noon, while he was in between classes. She crept quietly up the stairs and changed into long pants and sweater, with a light jacket for her run. She had been running for exercise, for meditation, for her mental well-being, since she had come to Ypsi three years ago. Initially, it had been a three-season diversion, but last year Kelly had shared her guest passes and brought Julia to her gym over the winter months. Now, if she went more than a couple of days without running, her body would let her know it.

After her run, she came in the house again feeling the sweat draining from her pores as she hit the wave of heat. She hadn't slept well, and she was feeling a little off. She quickly stripped down to her T-shirt in the kitchen in front of her father, who sat at the table reading and smoking a cigarette, a glass of Jameson at his side. Her mother, obviously having heard Julia's arrival, came hustling in from another room.

Julia had told Isabella she would be home for dinner, prompting her to cancel her cleaning job for the afternoon, and Julia felt a pang of guilt, sensing her mother's desire to capitalize on every moment with her daughter. Isabella had given up a hundred dollars just to be in the house while Julia was out running.

"I'm making beef enchiladas," Isabella stated, prompting Julia to smile at the thought of her favorite food.

"Do you need me to get anything from the store for you mama?"

"No, mija. I got everything I needed yesterday. I also have a surprise for dessert," Isabella added as though upping the ante to guard against a late change of heart by Julia. Julia made a point of extracting the secret from her mother and making the appropriate sounds of longing and hunger when she learned it was another of her favorites, arroz con leche. *At least it isn't too hard to make*, she thought.

"You didn't sleep in your bed last night, Julia." Her mother locked her gaze on Julia, awaiting a response to the unspoken question.

"I took a cab to Kelly's after my date with Don last night," Julia lied implausibly.

"Good."

It appeared to be enough for her mother's fragile mental construct, enough respect paid to her beliefs to not affront her with the truth. Julia's father just grunted, eyes remaining on his paper. Isabella ignored his cynical noisemaking, perhaps preferring to cling to the comfort of her fantasy.

After a brief shower, Julia helped her mother make dinner, both relishing the act of preparation more than eating.

Silently chopping tomatoes, grating the cheese, frying the beef. Speaking only in culinary terms to exchange tools or ingredients. Still, there was an intimacy to it and Julia felt the tension leaving her body.

She turned to her mother.

"I'd like you to meet Don. Maybe he could come for dinner?"

Isabella was clearly pleased by the prospect, and they plotted for a time. Finally, Isabella said, "I'll talk to your father about it." David had retreated to the living room, and they could hear some sports fans cheering.

Smells from their cooking began to drift around the room. This was always a trigger for Julia, and she felt a pleasant warmth melt the last of the butterflies that had been in her stomach. As they moved in a wordless dance around the food and dishes, she considered her mother for the first time as a woman - with desires and dreams of her own. Julia enjoyed being with Don so much, the closeness of him. It was hard when they were apart, and she found she needed distraction to move him to the back of her mind.

What about her parents? For once, she tried to just think of them as people, lovers, and considered life in their shoes. They had alternating work schedules, Isabella gone before David would wake, and David leaving just as Isabella would lie down to sleep, exhausted.

When do they make the time for each other? Or does that not matter anymore? Is this what it will be like for me before I'm fifty? Used up, just grinding through the motions? She shook her head at the thought. No, that would not be her fate, she resolved.

She moved to help her mother with the rice.

Dinner was quiet, but comfortable, and Julia did not have to rush off to work, so they lingered after the plates were cleared. Isabella had found a private moment to present the dinner plans to David and he was agreeable.

"You know, I'm glad your boyfriend is coming over," he finally said, rolling his tumbler back and forth between the fingers of his right hand as it rested on the table. David was savoring his first after dinner drink—and the moment. "It'll a give me a chance to show him my shotgun," he said, smiling at his own weak paternal humor.

She rolled her eyes.

"Be nice," she said, suspecting her father had never touched a gun in his life.

Plans were made. They would have dinner with Don's father on Thanksgiving weekend, and dinner with Julia's parents the Sunday before. Although it wasn't the holiday itself, Julia suspected her mother was secretly pleased at usurping the event, at capturing the celebration before they would share it with Don's father. In that vein, Isabella had insisted on a full turkey dinner with all of the traditional fixings and a few Mexican dishes thrown in. Julia had asked her mother to just make a traditional Mexican meal but was rebuffed and she wondered if her mother was just trying to ensure the broadest possible appeal to Don's palate, throwing the Mexican food in as a test. Scouting for information to be used to refine and improve subsequent meals she imagined would be coming.

After much anticipation, the day finally arrived, and at about three o'clock on Sunday, November twenty-second, Don showed up at the door dressed in his khaki pants and button-down blue polo. He had flowers for Julia's mother, which elicited the appropriate response from Isabella, though Julia rolled her eyes at the maudlin gesture.

Years afterwards, Julia often thought back to that dinner, wishing she would have known at the time that it would have been such a memorable day. She often relived it in her mind, but in her fantasy, she could do it right. She wouldn't worry what Don might say in answer to a question, or that her mother might say something embarrassing. She wasn't anxious about whether her father would, under the pressure of it all, have just a bit too much to drink. She wasn't stressing over every detail of their social interaction. Instead, she was just *being*, savoring these people, her family. She often thought back to it as their first, *and only*, pleasant dinner with all four of them laughing, drinking, and eating together.

It had gone wonderfully, and she had barely noticed at the time. Only later did she appreciate what a good prototype it had been.

A prototype for future family dinners that would never come.

CHAPTER TWELVE

Don

AUGUST 2019

DON WOKE TO THE buzzing of his phone at his bedside. Light was spilling in through the shears, but he fumbled toward the sound, not having the energy to turn his head to look. His fingers found cold metal. They traced their way over his father's pistol until they finally found the object of their search, and he pulled the phone up to his face and squinted at it. He had found, of late, that his vision took a bit of time in the morning to clarify, like sediment in a freshly poured beer. He had to patiently stare at something for a minute before he could read it and it was another reminder of his encroaching frailty.

It was a text from Diane.

Hey, Don. Didn't see you yesterday in town. Will you be coming in today? I'm sure you could use a drink. I took

Saturday off so that I could attend the memorial - if that's ok with you? Text me later.

He groaned at the reminder.

It really was thoughtful of Diane to offer, as it would be a four-hour drive for a one-hour occasion. *Occasion.* Sixty minutes to say goodbye and bury his son, a little less than four minutes for each year Charlie had been alive. It felt like such a small amount of time to mark nearly sixteen years together; fourteen of them wonderful, blessed years.

He wasn't sure how he felt about Diane attending. His reservations at the awkwardness of his own impending meeting with Julia were even more difficult to imagine with her there. In truth, he couldn't bear to imagine himself there, with or without Diane.

Finally, he rose from the bed, and after relieving himself he skipped the mirror altogether, failing to pause there even to wash his hands, and he shambled to the kitchen in his underwear.

He brewed a coffee and pulled open the fridge. Nearly barren shelves were dotted with condiments and a few other long-lasting items—cheese, eggs, some yogurt, a package of meat, all reinforced from below by a platoon of long-necked soldiers. They all stared back at him begging to be chosen and relieved from their neglect. In the end, he shut the door and opted for a granola bar from the cupboard as he wasn't very hungry anyway.

He dressed himself in blue jeans and an old sweater and took his coffee inside today. After guzzling it faster than usual, he picked up the Smith & Wesson, returning to the kitchen in search of the ammunition he had purchased the previous day. Finding it, he went to the back door of the cabin, first glancing to see that his trap had been unsuccessful.

Outside, it was cool but sunny.

Being at the rear of the house, he could feel the early rays of the sun directly on his face and he reflexively turned himself into them until, after a moment of basking, he returned to his intention. There was a small shed nestled at the rear left of the property, and he went to it, retrieving several items from far back on the top shelf inside. He returned to a small picnic table directly behind the house and set to oiling and cleaning his father's old gun.

He thought again of his father and how delighted he'd been to meet Julia. Their first dinner together that Thanksgiving, *two decades ago*. Then his train of consciousness took him back to the weekend when he first met Julia's parents, in Ypsi. How good he had felt taking *the next step* with Julia. They had enjoyed a wonderful dinner with her parents—a golden turkey with Mexican rice on the side. Sweet potatoes, corn, creamy black beans, and hot carrots. Julia had nearly shot wine through her nose when his face puckered as he put the carrots in his mouth. He had wondered if it was some kind of initiation rite until Julia's mother had said, *Ooh sorry, those are a little spicy,* and fetched him some milk, and the thought had vanished.

That dinner had been a first for Don, and today he felt he could almost smell that little kitchen again, taste the cilantro and lime in Isabella's rice; the heat of the Mexican carrots on his tongue. As Don remembered it, he had been comfortable instantly, warmly welcomed by Julia's mother and charmed by David's wit. Don had wanted to help with the dishes, but David insisted they retreat together with a drink to the living room, channeling some kind of machismo from the sixties. He remembered joking to Julia later, as they lay together performing post-game analysis of the dinner, that he had half expected the TV to be black and white.

When he and David had sat down in the living room, Don braced himself for some anticipated admonishments—*Be careful son, I love that girl dearly,* or, *If you hurt a hair on her head...*—but David had issued no such threats. Instead, he had taken genuine interest in Don, asking about his schooling, his father, and his goals in life. Don warmed as he remembered the conversation, and he wondered if David would be at the memorial. He had been close with Charlie, and although Don knew that

David had blamed himself, at least partly, for Charlie's disappearance, he suspected that he would make the trip.

Don hoped so, for Julia's sake.

CHAPTER THIRTEEN

Julia and Don

NOVEMBER 1998

JULIA SAT IN THE kitchen drinking coffee, a rare indulgence for her, and waiting for Don. In the short days since he had been there for dinner, she had become comfortable with him coming to the house, and so he had begun to act as a personal ferryman for her whenever his school schedule permitted. He would use school as an excuse to arrive just in time to get her for work, not ready to establish a dinner routine at the McCarthy household just yet, despite his enjoyment of the Thanksgiving meal they had shared together.

She heard the car enter the drive and rose quickly to make her exit. Her father was helping her mother with the dishes, an odd sight that struck her, felt slightly *uncomfortable* like a piece of ill-fitting clothing, and she brushed it off and said her goodbyes.

It was Saturday, and despite the holiday she still had to work. She expected it would be quieter today, with so many students migrating home with their empty bellies and full laundry bags. Kelly was gone to her parents' house in Troy and would likely return Monday.

As they drove to Rick's in relative silence, she couldn't shake the feeling that she was *missing something*, that something wasn't quite right. The thought wouldn't come to the front of her mind, and she decided to leave it for now. *A watched pot never boils.*

It was quiet at Rick's, occupied only by a small crowd of some regulars and locals—there wasn't even a band tonight in deference to the holiday—and she had time to chat with Robert.

"How are things going with Don?" he asked.

"Oh, great," she answered, always stingy with personal information. "We're going to his father's for dinner tomorrow."

As she said it, she realized that she didn't know much about Robert. *Is he married? Gay? Alone?* She chided herself for being so self-absorbed and asked, "How about you, Robert? Where are you going for dinner tomorrow?"

"Sheila and I are going to her parents'."

Mystery solved. At least partly. She chose not to press further, and they turned their attention back to their patrons, riding the shift out in relative silence.

She stayed at Don's that night. The next day, they fussed around the house, getting ready to make the one-hour trip to Lake Orion. Julia had bought a bottle of wine to take and was just packing a few last things when she cursed herself; she'd forgotten to grab some extra tampons from home before her shift last night.

Then it hit her—the elusive puzzle that had been gnawing at the back of her brain for the past couple of days.

She was a week late for her period.

Chapter Fourteen

Julia

August 2019

Julia nearly missed her connection in Newark. She'd cleared customs and gotten to the lounge quickly to wait out her ninety-minute layover. Her mind raced with thoughts of tomorrow, the day before the memorial, and she mentally ticked off all the practical details for the umpteenth time and thought about her father. She had e-mailed him, telling him not to come—that he wasn't welcome, or needed. He had pleaded with her via e-mail, *Could they talk on the phone? He was so sorry.*

Now, she was feeling sorry for her father for the first time in four years and wondering if she *should* call him when she arrived in Detroit. As she thought about it, she realized that it wasn't pity she was feeling for her father, although she did find her memory of him pitiable, maybe it was just a longing for connection. Since Charlie's death, it had dawned on her that, outside of her father she was the only other soul with McCarthy blood in this country. Her father was an only child, like her. Hers was a family tree that ran tall and straight, the one young branch she had contributed now broken, broken and gone forever. She felt the need to see her father, if for no other reason than for them to prove their existence to each other.

She was lost in her thoughts when she heard her own name through the public announcement system. "Last call for Detroit. Paging Ms. Rydell. Ms. Julia Rydell, please present yourself to the gate agent for immediate boarding."

Rydell.

She had grown accustomed to this as *her* name. She had taken it when they married—out of tradition, out of love for Don, out of the thought that they would be together forever. Out of love for their son. For some inexplicable reason, she didn't like the idea of him having a mother with a different last name, of not sharing that bond. She also hadn't liked the hesitancy of hyphenated names. Julia McCarthy-Rydell, w*hat a mouthful*. No, when Julia went for something, she was all in.

When she left Don two years ago, one thing she did feel entitled to keep was the name. Her name. She had now had it as long as she'd had McCarthy and that seemed like a lifetime ago. She wondered when, or if, she'd ever feel like changing it. She ran to the gate and pressed her phone to the scanner, bypassing the impatient looks of the airline agents.

Once on board, she accepted a water and settled herself in for the short flight. She watched, from her vantage point in a window seat, as they took off over the Hudson River and made the turn north, then west, into the setting sun. The sun's rays were dancing off the gray water, and the tall buildings of Manhattan were blazing gold as they receded from view, replaced by shimmering water that gave Julia immediate vertigo. She quickly pulled her gaze inside the aircraft.

The view of Manhattan sent her thoughts back to early in their marriage, when they had rented a place on West Breckenridge in Ferndale, a suburb of Detroit, about ten miles north of the city center. Ferndale was, in fact, the place where they had spent the majority of their married life, and certainly the happiest times.

Don's father had helped them find the place just after their wedding, and they joked that it was as far north as they could afford to go. Don used to like to say that they'd at least made it north of Eight Mile, if only by a mile.

Their rental was one of many similar clapboard houses on the street. They had chosen a one-and-a-half-story home with a triangular top, its peak running front to back, set on a square first floor, with dormers poking out of both sides of the roofline to make space for the two upstairs bedrooms. Baby blue siding with white trim was an odd choice, she had thought, but they weren't going to spend the money to repaint a rental.

When they had looked at the home with Don's father, Charlie laying asleep in his stroller, the first feature that had made it stand out for Julia was the front porch. It ran the full width of the home and was framed by multiple white pillars rising to the first-floor roofline, which extended forward from the house to cover the porch. Julia immediately imagined rocking chairs and a porch swing. Rocking Charlie on warm summer nights, listening to the crickets, and watching and waving as neighbors walked by on the little concrete sidewalk. The sidewalk, like the street, was cracked and heaved in places with sprouts of weeds peeking through, but it would be theirs and she knew she would like it. It would be a bitch, however, with the stroller.

Yes, the porch had warmed her to the idea of the place from the get-go, she thought. The second feature of the rental was unusual for the neighborhood – it had a small in-ground pool in the back, and Julia had hesitated on this point. She had liked to swim and relished the idea of teaching Charlie when he was older but feared for the safety of a toddler. True, she had not yet gone to work and could be around him all day, but the responsibility of it had worried her at the time and she winced inwardly at the memory now.

They had decided on the place in Ferndale at the turn of the new millennium, in June just after their wedding. They had been staying with her father in Ypsi, but Don had gotten a job at the *Detroit Free Press* after graduation and the drive proved to be unmanageable.

The house was cute, if dated, on the inside. The main floor was about twelve hundred square feet, with a small kitchen and dining area at the left side of the house, and a living room, bathroom, and laundry to the right. The upstairs held a bedroom for Julia and Don, and one for Charlie, as well as a small two-piece bathroom. Julia hated having to go downstairs to shower, but it was a small price to pay for their budding independence.

Sitting on the plane now, seeing the towers of Manhattan in the dying light of day had unlocked a memory in Julia's mind, and it came to her now as clear as if it had been yesterday. The year after they had moved to Ferndale, on September eleventh, Don left for work at about seven in the morning. It was early, but he had not earned the right to flexible hours at the paper yet, and he was working a deadline for an opinion piece about the state of democracy in America, using the contested Bush-Gore election from the year before as a centerpiece to build his thesis around.

That morning she had been ironing. Don wore jeans and dress shirts to work, and they could not afford dry cleaning. There was a white basket full of his shirts beside her in the dining room and Julia was using a mini ironing board that she had set up on the table. She was watching *The Today Show* while Charlie played with some toys beside her and had just fixed herself a coffee and returned to her chore, when the anchor broke into the program with news of an American Airlines flight that had crashed into the North Tower of the World Trade Center. Footage of smoke billowing from the building caught her eye.

Julia could still clearly remember her feelings from that morning. When the North Tower was struck, she had felt an obliged sense of empathy, her social responsibility. *How sad for those people and their families. What a terrible tragedy.*

But below that, somewhere deeper, was the self-serving gratitude that it wasn't them, didn't affect her, Don, or Charlie. A splash so far away in the water that its ripples wouldn't rock their little boat.

As events unfolded, she remembered feeling those ripples becoming a tsunami to shake their world, the fear that came with the uncertainty. She remembered trying to reach Don, but he had been busy as everything was chaos at the paper, trying like hell to keep up with the Internet.

For a moment she'd felt alone. Just her and Charlie in a big, nasty world.

Gradually she had rebuilt her connection to society, starting with Don at dinner that night, then calls with their fathers and shared conversations about the event from her porch with neighbors passing by. Finally, she had felt secure enough herself to feel for the plight of the millions of Muslims being wrongly judged in America at the time. She never forgot, though, the feeling of vulnerability that day brought. It was the first time she realized that she was dependent on others for her happiness. That she had everything to lose.

She slid the blinds shut on the aircraft window as though to ward off the irrational fear of her current flight that the memory had spawned, and realizing she was hungry, accepted a tray of cold chicken and salad. She also opted to take a glass of white wine, in spite of her pregnancy. She handed the tray back after a time, half eaten. Julia kept the wine but had only managed a few small sips.

Then she drifted, upright, into a fitful sleep. Again, dreams of Charlie came unbidden. After his disappearance, the dreams had been horrific—Charlie face down in the water, Charlie walking on the surface of the water, arms out, mutely pleading at her with his eyes. Charlie screaming at her soundlessly, with water pouring from his mouth, his nose, his ears.

Since the arrival of Don's e-mails, the dreams had changed. Charlie would be with her at their home in Birmingham. They would be sitting at the table in the outdoor garden at the rear of the house, flanked by her rose bushes.

Mom, I'm sorry for stealing your purse, he would say. *I'm sorry for the drugs. I'm sorry for not appreciating you and Dad more. I'm sorry for running away. I'm sorry.*

I forgive you, Charlie, she'd try to say, the words forming on her lips but not coming. *I forgive you for everything. I forgive.*

These dreams were worse, and she would wake up full of guilt that had to be assigned all over again.

This time, on the plane, she had a new dream, one drawn from a fantasy she'd secretly begun to harbor in the recesses of her mind. There had been a mix-up at the lab - it wasn't Charlie's DNA after all. He had been living under a phony name in a small town north of Saint Joseph. The police were terribly sorry for the mistake.

It's okay, I won't sue you, just give me his number. I need to talk to him. But they couldn't. *Just give me his number,* she'd plead. *Please, just let me call him and talk to him. Please. Please.* But he didn't want to speak with her. She dreamt of him there, running fishing charters for tourists. He still looked fifteen, of course, but he was grown up somehow and he had a beautiful girlfriend. She may have had green eyes like Julia. She cooked for Charlie, she cared for him when he was sick, she read to him. She loved him. The thought filled Julia's dream with warmth.

She awoke to the crash of the landing gear locking down, and for a moment, she panicked.

They were going to bury someone else's son. The memorial had to be stopped; there was another mother somewhere, searching, hoping, grieving. She had to know.

Ultimately, the merciless blade of Occam's razor returned to cut her fantasy to shreds.

She wiped the tears from her eyes, peering out of the window at the lights of Detroit shining in the blackness, and resolved to call her father first thing the next day.

CHAPTER FIFTEEN

Julia and Don

NOVEMBER 1998

JULIA HAD DISCUSSED WITH Don what she should wear to dinner at his father's house. He'd assured her that his father was a very easygoing man, and jeans and a sweater would be fine, but Julia, like her mother, would not dare go out to dinner without some attempt to dress up, even if only a little. Don had worn a comfortable, old pair of jeans and a University of Michigan sweater.

"I need room to put the turkey," he'd said, puffing his belly out and patting it.

In the end, she chose the black jeans she had worn to their first date, a green cashmere sweater—she knew it set her eyes off—and a pair of new black flats.

She had a natural beauty to her face and Don constantly told her that she didn't need to wear makeup. Today, however, she had bothered to put foundation, mascara, a little eyeshadow, and lipstick on. Don seemed to be growing impatient at her continual fussing, looking at his new watch frequently and pacing like a caged animal. Once, while she was putting her lipstick on, he even held his new watch toward her with an index finger gesturing toward its face, as though to remind her of the existence, and importance, of the concept of time. She turned and wordlessly extended a middle finger in return. Finishing with her makeup, she grabbed the bottle of wine and her purse, and just as they were ready to finally depart, she said, "I just have to pee first." After the false start they finally reached the promised land of the Corolla and Don appeared to relax, perhaps because the least-controllable variable of the day was now behind them.

During the car ride, she tossed scenarios around in her mind ad nauseam, none of them good, before her frustration boiled over.

"Why do you have to be so impatient, Don? You were an ass back there!" Losing control of her tone only magnified her anxiety.

He just turned to her and smiled, making it worse. She wanted to wipe that fucking grin off his face. He had no idea what they might have to deal with.

"Hey, I'm sorry, okay?" he'd finally pleaded. "I'm looking forward to this, and I guess I can't wait to introduce my father to my beautiful, charming girlfriend." With this, she found it hard to stay angry with him, and they managed a truce. By the time they reached his father's house in Lake Orion, the warmth had returned to their interaction, and they were chatting more comfortably.

Don Senior's house was on O'Connor Street, back off the main road through a winding series of subdivision twists and turns, nestled on the small street overlooking Lake Orion. The street looked beautiful to Julia, with its mature trees and older homes.

The neighborhood grew up in the sixties as the town had made its gradual transformation, from a vacation destination for auto executives and their families, to a small community in its own right. She didn't quite know what she had expected, but hearing that Don's father was the vice president of sales at a sizable company, she had thought of the mega mansions that she had only seen briefly when driving through Ann Arbor. This neighborhood was more modest, with older homes of varying sizes, but she could see the lake behind Don Sr.'s house and suspected the view itself was worth a pretty penny.

They exited the Corolla and approached the front of the home. Don Sr. had clearly been anticipating them, as he nearly sprung through the front door to greet them.

"Welcome, welcome. And you must be Julia, pleased to meet you!" he chortled, extending his right hand to grasp hers. Julia had to shift the bottle of wine over to her left hand and lift her left shoulder to keep her purse from slipping down in her eagerness to accept the gesture. Don's father placed his left hand over hers and did a gentle double-shake, making it feel a little more personal.

"Nice to meet you, Mr. Rydell," she said, Don's last name feeling strange on her tongue.

"Son!" Don's father turned his attention to his son after greeting Julia and gave him a brief hug. "Great to see you both. Come in, come in!" Before Don's father could usher them into the home, Julia thrust the bottle toward him, almost violently, in her enthusiasm to offer the gift.

"Oh, you didn't have to do that," Don Sr. said, clucking. "Ooh, that's one of my favorites!" He admired the bottle briefly before turning inward again. "Let's get inside and get a drink, shall we?"

They sat in the living room, on two opposing floral-print couches with a glass coffee table between. Don and Julia sat on one with Don's father opposite. Don Sr. was a tall, slender man, with a bushy white mustache and salt and pepper hair, and Julia knew from Don that his father was fifty-five, but looking at him now, it was hard to believe he was over fifty. He had such a youthful energy about him; he asked about Julia and her job, her family and hobbies, his voice a deep, soothing baritone, but she never felt as though it was an interrogation. It felt gentle, and she sensed him taking a genuine interest in her. She feared she might confess almost anything to this man and could see, after a short time, why he worked in sales.

Don and his father chatted about current events and Don's schooling, and Julia found herself wanting to initiate something in the conversation. She noticed a painting of an old aircraft on the wall behind Don Sr.

"Mr. Rydell?" she said to capture his attention.

"Please call me Reg. Most of my friends do. Mr. Rydell makes me feel old and it sure would be confusing with two Dons in the room." Don's father preempted the obvious question immediately, "My middle name is Reginald and I always liked Reg. Cynthia used to call me that when she was mad, but still, it reminds me of her."

"Okay, Reg," she complied. "That sure is a nice painting on the wall behind you."

"Oh that," he said, turning to acknowledge it. "That's a painting of the glider Amelia Earhart tested when she visited Lake Orion - in the late twenties, I think it was."

Julia was intrigued. She had learned about Earhart in high school and had always felt an affinity for her, a kindred spirit separated from her by a century.

"Oh yes," Reg continued, "she came here to meet William Scripps, a friend of hers and fellow aviator. He designed the glider and she tested it for him. The next time you visit, if the weather's good, I'll take you over to Scripps Mansion. It's near Lake Sixteen, not far from here, and you can see it, if you'd like." Reg continued on for a time, talking about the flight and his knowledge of the area, and Julia found herself swept up in his charm. Don and his father shared much more than names.

"Did you know, William's father founded the *Detroit Free Press*?" he asked, rhetorically. Of course she didn't know.

"Dad," Don interjected, breaking the spell for Julia, "shouldn't we be checking on the turkey?"

They worked together in the warmth of the kitchen, the steam drifting past the floral wallpaper like specters at a feast, the large meal for only three highlighting the fragility of Don's family tree. Julia was surprised at the amount of food Reg had prepared and she said as much to him while they worked.

"You didn't need to cook a whole turkey just for us!"

"It's okay, dear," he replied. "It's hard cooking well for one. This'll give me a chance to freeze some meals for myself for later."

Julia conjured an image of Reg's existence. Working and laughing amongst colleagues during the day, waving his goodbyes as they all left for their homes, their families, their lives in the suburbs. Don's father returning here to this big, beautiful, empty house. She felt a pang of sadness for him.

Julia and Reg laughed and drank and talked over dinner together. Julia cautiously stretched a glass of wine over the course of the day, with Don at times seeming the third wheel, sipping his water and trying to interject himself into the conversation. The time flew by, and Julia felt a bit disappointed when they finally took their leave around nine that night.

She found herself melancholy on the drive home, leaving the light and warmth of Don's childhood house, her mind worrying over her body. She thought, too, of Reg as she stared at the lights going by her window. Reg, framed by warm yellow light in the doorway of his house, smiling and waving as they backed out of the driveway. Catching just a hint of his smile fading as they pulled away, Reg slumping ever so slightly and turning back into the empty home.

Don was clearly pleased with the day's outcome, and they debriefed for a time in the car, but eventually their voices trailed off leaving only the hum of the tires rolling through the monotonous darkness of I-75. Julia's mind drifted to thoughts of Amelia Earhart, pioneer and boundary breaker, relentlessly pursuing some secret mission.

Forever lost in the vast blackness of the Pacific.

CHAPTER SIXTEEN

Julia and Don

DECEMBER 1998

THEY WALKED DOWN DON'S street, gloved hand in gloved hand. Julia could see her breath in front of her, and felt the cold air in her lungs, making her feel almost as though she was hyperventilating. Don was dressed in a thick, black sweater under his letterman jacket and looked comfortable, as always. Although it was already early December there had not yet been any snow, but they could both feel that it was coming soon. As they walked, Julia stared straight ahead, studying a fixed point in the distance, and she sensed Don looking at her face surreptitiously from the side.

She wore her hair down today, and it poured - a brown, silken waterfall, from beneath her white, woolen hat. She had worn a little makeup, perhaps to impress Don's roommates, and the cold December air had brought rouge to her cheeks, amplifying the effect in the pale light of the streetlamps. Her thick, wool coat hid her figure and thick fog plumed from her mouth as she huffed with the exertion of their walk.

"Jim and Jeff are actually nice guys," she finally said, rendering the much-anticipated verdict on their first joint dinner at the house. Up until that evening, she had seen them in passing going to and from Don's room, brief introductions had been made and social conventions followed. The evening's dinner had marked a new milestone in the relationship.

"It was funny watching the three of you try to cook. Like the three stooges." They turned left onto Hutchins to take their frequent walk, around Allmendinger Park.

"Well, I don't think we poisoned anybody. That's good, right?" he returned.

It was Sunday, around seven in the evening, and dark. As they approached the park, Julia could see splashes of color. The trees were wrapped in red and green lights.

"Let's go through the park," Don suggested.

Julia struggled to get into the festive mood. The lights felt more like traffic signals to her, a collection of conflicting demands to stop and go. Finally, as they got to the path into the park, she stopped abruptly, turning to Don. He mirrored her gesture and they stood facing each other, their breath mixing together in the cold December air.

True to form, Julia opted for directness. "Don, I think I might be pregnant," she finally expelled as a vaporous shock wave towards him.

It was as though the December air had frozen Don solid. His lips closed and she could not see his breath. She had rehearsed this throughout the dinner, attempting to smile and enjoy the company of the three men while planning for the moment. She trusted Don, but didn't know what to expect. *Would he deny the truth of it, or be angry with her?* She *had* been the one to initiate their only unprotected tryst.

"I know. At least, I'd guessed and I think it's wonderful," he finally said, his face breaking into a wide grin, after two seconds that had felt like an eternity to Julia. She fell into him, relieved and a little surprised, while struggling to get a grip on her own feelings.

Was this what she had hoped for? She suspected he still had not had the time to process what this all might mean. But that was okay, she loved him for his instinct. To reassure her. To protect her. She *loved* him.

That thought had hit her more than once in the two weeks since dinner at his father's. She had been so critical of other men, waiting for the other shoe to drop, not trusting what lay beneath the surface. She had no specific trauma in her past to justify the feeling, just her own determination to be self-reliant, to not place her emerging wants and needs in anyone else's hands. Meeting Don's father, a vision of Don's own future, had opened a pathway inside of her that she had never been down before. It scared and thrilled her at the same time.

She had taken a home pregnancy test the day after Thanksgiving. She took it at Don's, as though subconsciously by doing so she could keep this news from her parents. They would certainly be shocked, and hurt at the news. *If* she and Don chose to go forward with the pregnancy. She wondered, more than once in the past few days since she had learned the news, if she shouldn't just quietly go and get an abortion. The thought had tugged at her mind as a tempting solution to this messy complication that would preserve the status quo and keep their lives on track. She knew this wouldn't be fair to Don and wondered if she would be able to live with him, or herself. To love him fully afterwards. Bearing this secret alone; knowing the terrible deception she would be perpetuating. *No*, she had thought, *this would kill the relationship*. It would be a slow-acting poison that would spread through her until she could no longer even look at those eyes of his, feeling his honesty, his integrity, causing her to judge herself every waking hour. In the end, she knew she would have to tell him, but it had taken her days to come to this realization and she wondered why. She could love a child with Don, deal with her parents' wrath. They could work it out together and her own plans could wait. But only if he wanted to. She needed him to prop up her vague and fragile vision of this future together.

Now, she was relieved. At getting this off her chest, and at Don's reaction. But she *had* grieved the news at first, its impact crater centered on *her*—what this would mean for *her* relationship with her parents, for *her* plans for school and the future. Then she had projected the worst of her feelings onto Don and had expected a reaction coming from a place of fear about what others would do or say, about how this would change things for them.

The relief passed, and now, in the darkness of the park, surrounded by a barren, wooden audience and kitschy lights, it was replaced by a feeling that had been gnawing at her since she first learned of the life inside her.

Shame.

Shame, that the impact on Don—her lover, her child's father—had not been the first thought on her list. Shame,

that she had not had the strength she thought she had. Shame, that he had shown the reaction she wished she could have felt herself.

Joy.

CHAPTER SEVENTEEN

Don

AUGUST 2019

DON SPENT THE EARLY afternoon engaged in target practice in the bushes at the rear of his yard. He did not remember exactly when his father had bought the pistol, but knew it was not long after his mother's death. His father had told him about it when he was eight - *not to go in his nightstand drawer, not to touch it. It was dangerous.* A year later, perhaps deciding that prohibition was not reliable, Reg had taken him to the range to instruct Don in the safe handling of a firearm. Don liked to think it was a macho thing with his dad. Something guys did—own a gun—rather than fear, or worse.

Don sometimes wondered, though, while lying in the darkness at the cabin, if his father *had* felt fear after his mother's death. Fear of the darkness, fear of being alone. The kind of fear that kept Don company on the nights when he was sober, and sometimes even on the nights when he wasn't.

He returned inside, and his stomach reminded him that he'd only had a granola bar and coffee that day. Food was a joyless affair for him at the cabin; he enjoyed eating in town, and the social implications of it, but cooking for himself was a chore. Dinners anymore were odd combinations of long shelf-life items from tins and boxes, like some kind of distorted food pyramid.

He boiled water for some pasta and grabbed a jar of sauce from the pantry. His father had retrofitted the old wood stove for gas after purchasing the cabin, and its blue flames licked the bottom of the pot fiercely. Don put the sauce in a bowl in the microwave, setting it to heat, and the aroma assaulted his senses bringing back a memory of Julia. Of them, cooking together in Ferndale.

The two of them had been in the kitchen together making pasta and Charlie was sitting in a little chair near the doorway to the dining room. It was a furry little orange faux-armchair made to look like Tigger, stuffed with sturdy foam to hold its shape. Charlie was maybe three and he'd sat in that chair, his eyes fixed on a picture book, his dark hair plastered thinly to his little forehead.

A chip off the old block, Julia had said, gently teasing Don's love of reading. *But I bet his has fewer pictures.* He'd flicked sauce at her with the spoon and she'd chased him around the kitchen, Charlie watching intently from his foamy throne, finally squealing in delight at his parents' laughter.

They'd continued that way, bantering and teasing, all the while making dinner together and drinking wine. Forgetting whose glass was whose. After clearing the dishes and putting Charlie to bed they'd collapsed together on the porch swing with the last of the bottle, where they rocked together for a time, Julia's head resting on Don's shoulder. Suddenly, Julia had sprung up full of energy. *Let's go for a swim,* she'd suggested, grabbing Don's hand, and not waiting for an answer.

They'd stripped naked in the darkness behind the house, giggling quietly like kids, and slipped into the water silently not wanting to take any chance to wake Charlie. Julia had clung to his neck and wrapped her legs fiercely around his waist.

Are you strong enough to hold me up? she'd teased, and Don had suspected that she knew the water was doing half the work.

They'd made love in the pool that night, under a moonless sky. In that cheap pool behind that little clapboard house, nestled in cracked concrete and asphalt, Don had felt as though he'd found heaven.

The sizzling of water boiling over startled him. He cooked his pasta and ate in silence until a buzz on the table stirred him. It was Diane.

Hey, haven't heard from you. I'm a little concerned. Text me.

He thought a moment and texted, *Thanks, Diane. I'm fine. I appreciate your offer to come to the memorial, but you really don't need to make the trip. I'll be fine. Thanks.*

He felt a pang of guilt as he pressed send.

A moment later, the phone rang; it was her. He silenced it, taking note of the day on its display, and took his dishes to the sink. He didn't know where Julia was, but suspected she was on this side of the Atlantic by now. Tomorrow would be Friday—a day for her to prepare, organize, set things in order.

Don grabbed a beer from the fridge and went to the front porch, where he could see light from the setting sun still filtering through the tops of the trees and began his nightly vigil.

Chapter Eighteen

Julia

August 2019

Julia's taxi pulled up to the Best Western. Gerrard had located a few rare five-star options in the city for her, but she had dismissed the offer. She did not feel she deserved luxurious grief and opted for practicality, staying just off I-94 near River Rouge about ten minutes from the church.

She had not slept well on the plane, her dreams having left her exhausted, and it was close to midnight by the time she had checked in and reached her room. She dumped her bags, used the toilet, and brushed her teeth. Julia then opened her carry-on bag and pulled out the long, black dress that she had carefully folded inside. She held it aloft like a delicate thing, examining it as it unfurled toward the floor. After hanging it carefully in the closet and grabbing one of Gerrard's T-shirts from the bag, she took off her bra and threw the T-shirt on. She collapsed into the bed—at least the mattress was comfortable—and reached for the lamp. A Gideons Bible, left out on the nightstand, caught her eye and she thought of her mother for the first time in a while. She laid back on the pillow and fell into a deep sleep, mercifully free from dreams.

She woke up disoriented. Light bled in around the shade on the window.

Where was she? When was she? The red lights of the old clock radio on the nightstand blinked twelve o'clock and were of no help in answering the latter but did serve to remind her of where she was, and why. She realized she had forgotten to set her alarm and fumbled for her phone. It had automatically adjusted to the local time, and she saw that it was ten.

Good. She wasn't due to meet the priest with Lisa until noon, so she would have time for a shower and some breakfast. She didn't feel hungry, rather, she felt a queasy reminder of the child in her belly. She got up and made a pseudo-coffee from the one-cup machine in her room, clearly for the true addicts, but she didn't care for coffee enough to drink it and left the cup on the dresser, nearly full.

Her mind felt foggy, and her body felt limp as she forced herself to the little chair and table near the window and opened the blinds. Sun poured into the room, and its rays served to offer up the gray concrete of the city and its river in the best possible light. She sat to bask in their warmth and attempted to reconnect her body clock to her place on the planet.

Julia's pregnancy served as some kind of strange umbilical cord to the past, bringing memories of her first pregnancy with Charlie. And of her mother. That day she and Don had stood in the kitchen to share the news that Julia was pregnant. Her father clutching his glass tightly, so tightly she thought it might shatter in his hand, and the look on his face—had it been fear? Anger? She hadn't been able to tell in the moment. Later, she had settled on disappointment. Disappointment that his little girl had grown, that he could no longer indulge himself in the fantasy of her innocence. She was an adult, choosing—being forced onto—her own path. He was mostly silent as if waiting, waiting for Isabella to speak first, to find the words for their feelings on it.

Isabella had looked horror stricken.

"How could you do this, Julia?!" she had scolded. "To your father...to me? To yourself? What were you two thinking?!" The words were washing over Julia in waves. She detached and fixated on a point on the stove to the right of her mother. There was a chip in the enamel she hadn't noticed before. *When had that happened?* she wondered. She stared at it as her mother's voice continued to smother her.

"Look at me, Julia!" her mother shouted. "I don't want to be a mother again at my age. How are the two of you going to manage?"

Julia and Don had anticipated this question.

"I'm going to quit my job at Rick's," she began hesitantly. "I don't want to be around all the smoke anymore. I have almost five thousand dollars saved up already. We'll live at Don's place until he finishes school. Then we'll find a place together. Don's friend, Jeff, his dad works as an editor at the *Detroit Free Press* and he's going to get Don a job there when he graduates. We'll move closer to the city and rent until we can afford something. We'll get married."

Julia spilled the pre-recorded message out quickly, as though fearing interruption. Fearing that her parents would find a hole in the plot that she and Don had carefully constructed together. A moment of silence passed, marked by the ticking of the kitchen clock. Isabella was still in shock, processing the wealth of information packed into Julia's prescription for the future.

"Haven't you two got the order of things all backwards?" her father had finally asked, reflexively putting out his half-smoked cigarette in apparent deference to Julia and drawing Don's responsibility into things.

"Mr. McCarthy, we know we don't have much. I love Julia. We want to get married. I'm going to support her and the baby," Don had fumbled.

David's face had frozen briefly.

"Don, I told you to call me David," her father had finally said softly, looking up at the couple. It had felt like an absolution, a subtle statement of support in the face of her mother's fierce disapproval, and she had loved her father so much in that moment. Her mother left the room in tears to isolate herself from the news she couldn't digest.

Isabella had come around eventually, out of love for her daughter, the prospect of a grandchild ultimately outweighing the forces of her own upbringing. She had insisted on an engagement and knowing their firm plans for the wedding.

The engagement was straightforward; Don had stopped Julia on one of their winter walks through Allmendinger Park and dropped to one knee.

"I don't have much to give you, Julia. I can't afford a diamond ring. But I love you and want to be with you forever. Will you marry me?" Even though the gesture was much anticipated, and uninventive to say the least, Julia had found herself overcome with happiness to hear it.

"I love you too, and yes," she'd replied, smiling and feeling stinging at the corner of her eyes. She pulled him upright and they had embraced. He had taken her gloves off, puzzling her at first, and took the Claddagh ring from her right hand moving it to the ring finger on her left hand, flipping it around so the point of the heart faced outwards, to show the world that her heart was now claimed by another but they were not, as yet, married. She'd dramatized holding her left hand out, palm down, as though examining the ring for the first time.

"I love it," she'd said as they both laughed. Don had insisted that he didn't want to marry until he was finished school and had secured a job, so they set the date for June, a year and a half from then. It would be the turn of the century and a new life for them both.

They had separated briefly over the few days of Christmas, Don spending the time with his father, and Julia working to mend her relationship with her parents. By New Year's Day, Don had felt comfortable enough to come in for a drink and celebrate quietly with the McCarthy family, but the conversation was stilted and awkward. He busied himself in January and February under the pretext of focusing on his final term. He needed to do well now more than ever, and so he continued to minimize his interactions with her parents.

Part of Julia's penance had been to attend church with her mother once a week throughout Lent, which had come early that year in the middle of February. Julia had quit her job at Rick's at the end of the Christmas term, and no longer had her late Saturday shifts as an excuse. She and Isabella had connected again on those cold walks to and from St. John's, both members of some secret maternal club. Isabella had insisted on Julia confessing her sins to the priest, and Julia remembered feeling ashamed at having to share such personal things with this man in the shadowy booth, but she did it to please her mother.

Julia's immortal soul thus preserved, Isabella had clearly begun to look forward to the arrival of her grandchild. She even accompanied Julia to one of her doctor's visits to listen for the heartbeat of the baby. Julia vividly pictured Isabella grinning proudly while looking up from Julia's belly, the stethoscope dangling from her ears.

That had been a Tuesday – the day before St Patrick's Day. In her hotel chair, now, she could almost feel how hard her mother had hugged her goodbye, when Don and Julia had dropped her at the house on North River Street. They had planned to celebrate there with a dinner together the next night—a happy occasion to mark the end of the cold winter between them. She now, too, could almost hear her father's shaking voice coming through Don's cell in the early hours of that St. Patrick's Day morning. The tremble in his voice that had alarmed her more than the fact of the call itself. She remembered sitting up in Don's bed, him quickly shaking off the dregs of sleep as he realized something was wrong. She recalled the shock and the fear that she would miscarry on account of it.

Her mother had died in her sleep at the age of forty-two. The same age she was now.

As Julia sat in the sunlight in her cheap hotel chair, she tried to shake the unwanted feelings the memory had stirred. Finally, she forced herself up and into the shower.

She wanted to have time to call her father.

Chapter Nineteen

Julia and Don

April 1999

Julia walked around Prospect Park in the warmth of the spring sunshine, her hands involuntarily cradling the fullness of her belly. She felt good on her walk and realized that she was smiling, and this brought with it fresh feelings of guilt and loss at her mother's sudden and untimely death the month before. Julia found herself thinking back to the funeral, how sad and alone her father had looked standing there in the church, eyes cast downwards, wearing his one good suit, almost lost amongst the vast columns and arches. He had worn a rumpled brown two-piece with thin stripes and a red rose in his lapel to mark Isabella's love of gardens. David had lost weight, and the suit had clung to him reluctantly.

Father Peter had delivered the eulogy as David was far too uncomfortable with the idea of speaking in public, and as the priest delivered his boilerplate commentary on Isabella and her short life, Julia had perceived the further diminishment of her father. Seeing him at a loss for words, looking so fragile, had pained her almost as much as her own grief.

She did have to grapple with her own sorrow eventually, and this had been difficult for Don, as grief was new for him. His mother had died before he could recall, and up until now, things had gone smoothly for him. Perhaps Don had felt that, with the premature death of his mother, his cosmic share of misfortune had already been dealt, that it should be smooth sailing from here on out. Or perhaps it was just his positive nature. Julia didn't know. She did feel, however, that Don's good fortune since the age of five had created the fiction for him that life was *supposed* to go that way for everyone. According to the plan. At times, she loved that about him. His innocence and optimism; his faith—rather, *his expectation*—that the world would bend itself to suit his dreams, their dreams.

At times this past month, she had also found this trying. While she was grieving the loss of her mother, his antidote was to remind her of the exciting future that lay before them. Prompting her back onto the track of plans for baby and wedding, plans she didn't feel she could savor in her moments of sadness and loss. All of this changed for her the first time she felt *movement* at the start of April. She marveled at the thought that she was creating new life, and it was almost like finding out she was pregnant all over again. From that moment on, she was able to quarantine her grief somewhere behind thoughts of her child. Something to be felt and dealt with, but not at the expense of the here and now.

After the funeral, she had decided to spend more time at home with her father, and Don had agreed to join her there after graduation. It was a fluid arrangement, with Don staying progressively more often as March turned into April, until he was practically living at the house by the middle of April when his regular classes had ended. David had harbored fewer moral reservations than Julia's mother *would have,* once summing it up as, "No point closing the barn door after the horse has gone."

Julia had always found that expression funny, and when her father had used it in this context, she almost wanted to ask the question that always came to her mind—*What if there are other horses in the barn?* But she was happy to have her father's support and decided not to deal some of his own wit back at him. When Don did finally "move" into Julia's bedroom, Julia had redundantly instructed him on the importance of stealth in the mornings, adopting a protective stance toward her father, and Don took great pains to comply.

It had felt strange. Having Don in *her* room, making love on *her* bed, surrounded by *her* things; this was her inner sanctum. It wasn't as though the room itself was intrinsically sacred as she'd only occupied it for four years, but the idea of it was very personal for her. She didn't know why it bothered her—she was going to marry this man and they were having a child together. The puzzle of it gnawed at her and it did put a brief chill between her and Don, which was only amplified by her sorrow and irritable moods. Her only remaining solitary refuge came from her brief walks alone around the neighborhood.

She had been so lost in her thoughts while walking that her body had navigated her usual running route on autopilot, and she was surprised by the sight of her own house before her. Even more surprising was the sight of Don and her father, hunched down in the cool sunshine trimming back the rosebushes.

"Well, if it isn't two of my favorite men," she said with a lighthearted tone that had been rare that year. "But this can't be," she continued, teasing them. "You're both working—and in the garden no less."

Don looked up and smiled, deferring to Julia's father for the riposte.

"I've done more work in my life so far then you ever will, girl," David said, looking up at her sideways from where he was kneeling in the dirt. It wasn't his best, but it was so good to see him making the effort. "Your mother would have done this last month, before it started to get warmer," he added, turning back to the task at hand.

"How was your walk?" Don asked. "You feeling okay today?" He hadn't been awake when she had risen to start her Sunday morning routine.

"Good, and good," she answered. "You hard workers want a coffee or something?"

"Not for me. More than two cups upsets my stomach," said her father, intent on his pruning.

"Yes, please. You know how I like it," from Don, perhaps savoring her role as wife-to-be a bit too much.

"Okay. I'll get changed and bring it out."

She changed into grubby pregnancy jeans and a sweater, fixed Don's coffee which was easy as he liked it black, and returned to the garden, kneeling to help the men.

"Don't strain yourself," David had said, ignorant of the modern tenets regarding activity during pregnancy.

"I'm fine, Dad, the baby's fine. The doctor says I can stay fairly active almost until the baby's born."

The three of them pruned silently until all the heads had been trimmed off the bushes.

"Oh," Don said, looking up at Julia. "I just remembered. My dad asked us to come up to the cabin after my graduation, to celebrate. He has a week of vacation and thought we might like to join him."

She had heard Don talk about the cabin so often before, how peaceful it was being out in nature, but she had yet to experience it for herself. She knew she could use a little vacation but was nervous about the idea of being away from her doctor, her father, and their newly established routine.

"Okay, sounds good," Julia said after a slight hesitation. She would go, for Don. "Will you be okay?" she asked, turning to her father.

"Don't worry about me, my love. I'll be fine. The break will do you good, just don't exert yourself too much."

As they began to bag the decapitated flowers for the trash, Julia grew excited about the prospect of a vacation with her fiancé.

This will be good for us, she thought as she tied the last bag tightly, sealing the dead flower heads inside.

Chapter Twenty

Julia and Don

June 1999

Julia inhaled deeply through the open car window. The air smelled so much better up here, she thought. She gazed at the trees speeding by on her right and rested her hands protectively over her extended belly, which was framed by the shoulder strap and belt across her lap. In addition to switching from running to brisk walks she had redirected her diet to healthier foods, and her father, for his part, had taken to smoking only when she was out or going outside to dose himself with nicotine.

"Wake up, Julia," Don said softly from the back seat as he touched her shoulder, "We're almost there."

Although she hadn't been sleeping, the gesture startled her and she inhaled and sat straighter, as though to prepare for an aircraft landing.

The three of them were in Reg's new Cadillac and it had been a comfortable ride with several pee stops along the way for Julia. She felt as though her bladder had shrunk to half-size.

"It's about twenty minutes farther and this is the last gas station before we get there," Don's father had cautioned. "Do you need another stop?"

"No, thanks, Reg, I'm fine."

They pulled into the driveway at last, and Julia, Don, and Reg took their things into the cabin.

Julia loved it immediately, the serenity of it. She felt her anxiety, her melancholy, and even some of her grief slip away into the fresh air of early summer. They spent a glorious week together, during which Julia spent a lot of time just rocking on the front porch with a lemonade, taking walks in the woods, or sitting reading a book. They took a couple of trips into town for ice cream and Don and Reg seemed proud to introduce her to the regulars there.

Reg kept a boat at the marina in town, a twenty-seven foot bowrider with a big inboard engine under the rear deck. It held ten passengers comfortably, and when the weather was good, he would take it out along the coastline and fish. He'd named it *Fire Horse*, explaining to Julia that had been a nickname used by Amelia Earhart for her transatlantic plane and he'd liked it; he didn't care that he was mixing air and sea references.

Over breakfast at the cabin one morning, he told Julia that he would sometimes stay out in that boat right until the last moment of daylight when it was becoming less safe to navigate back to shore. He would take the small risk just to take in the sunset over Lake Michigan and catch the appearance of the evening's first stars.

There was nothing like it.

Reg clearly wanted to share the experience with her and his son, but the wind had been high for most of the week, and Julia worried she would be seasick. They would have to save it for next time.

On the last night of their holiday together, the weather was clear and cool at dusk, and the wind had finally settled prompting Don to suggest a campfire. There was a pit off to the right of the rear patio where Reg set to building a fire, and in no time they were seated in old wooden Cape Cod chairs around its glow. Julia had a gray wool blanket draped across her knees and she looked at the two men with her at the fire. Their faces were bathed in cascades of red and orange.

Reg was a handsome man, she thought, and if they had a boy maybe it would be nice to carry the name "Don" down another generation. It would be something to talk about with Don later, she decided, although having their child called "the Third" was not an idea she liked. She just hoped that whatever the child's sex, he or she would inherit the best qualities of these two men. And herself.

Shattered sparks of burnt wood and sap exploded in front of them like little fireworks, and the smoke hung in the still air. Don stood up and excused himself to go inside as the last logs were burning down. "I'm going to hit the hay," he said.

"I'll be in shortly," she countered, not quite yet ready to leave the spell of the fire.

"I'll stay here and see to putting it out when we're done," Reg added, as though still gently instructing his son in the protocols of life at the cabin.

It fell quiet as the future in-laws gave witness to the slow death of the fire. As Julia stared at the coals, watching them slowly fade from hues of red and orange to hot, white ash, she marveled at the idea of fire walkers. She tried to imagine the courage it would take to set your bare foot onto something that hot, something that your conscious mind told you was to be avoided at all costs. She just couldn't wrap her head around it. Eventually, she turned her mind back to the man across from her.

"Reg, how come you never remarried? After Cynthia."

Reg peered into the pit, his brow wrinkling slightly in the fire's dying glow. It seemed a long pause and she thought to apologize for such a forward question, but Julia just felt as though she had known him for so long already.

"When Cynthia died," he eventually began, still staring down, "we'd fought so hard together. Put all our energy into beating the cancer. It was the biggest rollercoaster of my life those last five years. First, Don was born, and we had everything in front of us. Cynthia and I used to argue because I only wanted to have two kids and she wanted three. She'd joke that we should compromise on two and a half—which rounded up to three." He chuckled at that memory and fell silent, until Julia began to feel uncomfortable. Now, only the occasional cricket chirp and the subtle hiss from the fire served to cut the heavy stillness of the evening.

Reg's voice cut through the evening air. "Cynthia was staying home to raise him, and she was such a good mother. Singing to him at night, playing with him all day, reading to him, holding him. I knew then that we could have as many kids as she wanted and we'd be alright." Reg paused again, more briefly this time, as if he had needed to warm himself up to his story.

"Then, when Don was only a year old—" Reg looked up intensely at Julia, his voice cracking on the word "year", and she scolded herself for asking the question in the first place. But Reg continued, returning his gaze downward as though his story was burned into the pit somewhere.

"After Don turned one," Reg tried again, "she felt the pain in her gut and she shrugged it off as cramps. Her body adjusting after having Don. I accepted that," Reg nodded his head firmly. "I accepted that because I wanted it to be true. I was self-absorbed at work and distracted with my own stuff. Then one night, I looked at her at dinner. She'd hardly touched her food and I wondered if she was eating enough but didn't say anything. She looked...off, almost *yellow,* like she'd put some kind of makeup on, or the light was playing a trick. I asked her about the pain. She told me it was fine, and I went back to eating. I wished I'd have pushed harder then."

"Reg, I'm so sorry," Julia interjected, feeling unsure of what to say or do. He just nodded again without meeting her eyes.

"A week later, she collapsed when I was at work," he continued. "She called me in a panic because Don was walking around the house, and she couldn't get to him. I rushed home and called for an ambulance," he paused. "Sorry," he said, "this wasn't what you asked me."

"Please, Reg, go on," Julia said softly.

"Well, long story short—I won't trouble you with all the gory details—we tried everything. For nearly three long years, we fought the thing. Surgery, chemo, radiation. It was terrible. In the end, she just asked me to let her go." Reg finally looked up from the few remaining flames into Julia's eyes. "Like I could just give her permission."

Julia thought she saw little red drops rolling down Reg's cheek, blood in the firelight. His gaze was strong, daring her to touch his grief, to approach some measure of his pain. She wanted to reach out, to rise and hug the man, but the intensity of the moment filled her with fear. She was immobilized until Reg spoke again.

"I told her to go. I would take care of Don, raise him right. Tell him all about his beautiful mother. Ahh." He sniffed, clapping his big hands down on the thighs of his jeans and slapping himself back into the present. "I think I just needed time. Time to heal. Time to raise Don. Time to forgive myself. I always wondered how things would have been if I'd pushed harder, sooner. I don't know. I think I've come to terms with it. As to your question, I dated a few times, even had a steady girlfriend a couple years back, but nothing seemed to stick."

"I'll tell you one thing," Reg said as he looked directly into Julia's eyes for only the second time in the conversation. "I still love Cynthia as much today as I did twenty years ago." Reg got up and went for the hose.

As Julia left the remnants of the fire to go inside, she felt as though she carried the hot embers with her, deep in her belly.

Chapter Twenty-One

Don and Diane

August 2019

Don had followed his normal routine that morning but remained at the cabin. He hadn't been into town for two days now, preferring solitude, and he thawed some bacon in the microwave to make his favorite breakfast. He even took some bread out of the freezer and toasted it. As he sat to eat his breakfast at the kitchen table, his phone vibrated beside him. He ignored it and after finishing his breakfast in silence, took his dishes to the dishwasher.

Don went into his father's old bedroom to the desk, dusty from lack of use, and grabbed some paper from a drawer. He fumbled around in the other drawers until he found an envelope and a pen.

He returned to the kitchen table and sat down, scattering the paper on the table in front of him beside the black Smith and Wesson he had left there the night before. It pointed at him, a steely black finger of accusation, and he could hear his father's voice warning him about never letting the barrel point at anyone. He leaned back in the wooden chair, causing it to creak in protest. Don closed his eyes and took a deep breath.

For a second, he thought he could hear the gun speaking to him, but the noise resolved into something more tangible. Julia's voice. Screams were now echoing in his head—Julia's screams that *she couldn't take him anymore, they needed time apart,* followed by a memory of his reflexive assurances that *they would be alright, that they just needed to work through this together,* that *maybe he's somewhere hiding.* A runaway who would tire of his adventure and return. The prodigal son, their last shared fantasy.

"You're a fucking robot!" she'd finally said, throwing her fists at him. Pummeling his chest like some hyper paramedic trying to revive a stopped heart.

"I'm grieving just like you!" he'd shouted back. "Just because I don't cry myself to sleep every night doesn't mean I don't feel anything!" He'd wanted to release his rage back at her in kind but knew he could never be capable of such an act. Don taking the abuse just made her seem angrier until she had collapsed, exhausted and sobbing at his feet, a puppet whose strings had been cut.

They had replayed variations of this drama in the weeks and months after Charlie's disappearance, a skipping record of blame and apology.

"I can't be with you anymore," she'd sighed finally. No more shouting, just resignation. She stared at his feet, as though willing them to move away from her.

He'd pleaded with her—*He loved her. He needed her. They needed each other.*

Through all the arguing, the shouting and screaming, she had never once accused Don of being to blame for their son's disappearance. She had never said so in words, but he had felt her judgment just the same, the unspoken accusations of his neglect, neglect when Charlie had needed the reassurance of a strong man in his life, of his father.

Don's train of consciousness had a full head of steam now and it force-fed him a memory of Charlie at twelve, working on a science project he'd had to do for school. Charlie had asked Don to help him make a working volcano, after he had learned how from a science magazine. He was so excited about the project.

"Sounds great, Charlie," Don had said. "Can you see if your mother can help you? I've got work I've got to do here." Some trivial piece on comparing American democracy today with its Greek origins.

Sitting now, at his kitchen table with a sprawling of white before him, Don was freshly assaulted by memories of Charlie and Julia shaping the clay together, getting the baking soda and vinegar and testing it out in the driveway.

"Can't you pull yourself away from your laptop for five minutes?" Julia had asked him.

Couldn't he? He had, reluctantly, and then he had provided the expected expressions of amazement and congratulations. But Charlie wasn't little anymore; he was a smart, sensitive kid and could tell when he was being patronized.

He just said, "Thanks, Dad," and turned his attention back to Julia as they worked to clean up the mess and get the project ready for school.

Don had gone back in his mind and replayed that and countless other scenes a thousand times, re-writing and re-directing them with a better script. He'd drop his papers and laptop immediately - "That sounds great, Charlie! Let's do it together!" Hopelessly attempting to channel Ward Cleaver in his black and white, idealized, revisionist history.

It had been his companion these past four years, this constant mental torture. He thought that if there was indeed a hell, it couldn't be worse than this: *to know your sin and be unable to make atonement.* He opened his eyes and looked around at the table as though just realizing his purpose for the first time.

Julia, he wrote simply on the exterior of an envelope. He grabbed a piece of paper and held the pen over it, not knowing how to begin.

He didn't know how long he sat, the blank paper staring back at him, mirroring the emptiness he felt. He had come to the point where there was nothing he could think of anymore. His mind felt like it was shutting down.

There was a loud rapping at the door.

"Don? It's me, Diane. I know you're home. I see the truck. I've got some rolls for you, Don."

He grabbed his phone and saw the text: *I'm going to drop by with some cinnamon rolls from the bakery. Hope you're home.*

He sighed and shuffled some papers over his father's gun, heading reluctantly to the door to open it.

"Hey, Diane, how are you?" Don said, attempting to put a smile on his face. Diane looked slightly horrified, and he imagined seeing himself through her eyes - baggy eyes under tussled, unwashed hair, two days stubble on his face. Breath reeking, body smelling of sweat and desperation. His white T-shirt stained with fat drippings from this morning's bacon, and gray, ill-fitting track pants stained with paint from some household chore. Bare feet poking out reluctantly from underneath.

"Can I come in?" she asked, and Don could detect a slight tremor in her voice.

"Sure," he said, turning his back to her to lead her into the kitchen.

Diane set the box of rolls on the counter and made her way over to the coffee maker.

"You want a coffee?"

"I've had my fill, thanks," he replied, eyes on her.

"How do you work this damn thing?"

"Just put your cup under the spout and press the button that looks like a coffee cup."

She brewed herself a coffee.

"Sugar?" she asked.

"It's in the cupboard above, in the yellow container."

"Thanks. I missed you in town yesterday."

"Yeah, I just had some things to do around here. Sorry I didn't answer your texts."

"Do you want me to drive you to the memorial tomorrow? I really don't mind," she said.

"Look, Diane, I really appreciate your thoughtfulness. I'll be fine. Thanks for the rolls."

"Are you trying to get rid of me, Don Rydell?" she asked, in a playful tone that Don suspected was a little forced. "Can I at least have my coffee first?" She moved toward the table to take a seat, setting her shoulder bag on the chair beside her.

"Of course. I'm sorry."

Don eyed her warily as she sat across from him at the kitchen table, the papers between them.

"What have you been busying yourself with, these last couple days?" she asked, holding her cup in her hands, her eyes never leaving his.

"Not much. Just some chores. Set a trap out for the damn bears."

"Any luck?"

"Nope."

She looked for a place to put her mug down. She started to move some papers and Don jumped in his chair.

"I'll get those," he said abruptly.

It was too late. She had disturbed the papers enough to expose the tip of the gun's barrel. It was unmistakable. Don swept everything over to the side of the table, and the papers again fully covered the weapon.

****

Diane felt that she was a strong woman; she'd grown up in Oklahoma and knew her way around guns and men. She thought she knew Don pretty well, *but did she really?* She thought she had known Darryl and she had never been so wrong. Was Don capable of hurting her? Normally, she would swear *no, never, not Don*. She watched him watching her and she could almost smell the fear and sorrow on him. The silence was becoming uncomfortable, and she knew she needed to make a decision. Maybe she should just make her exit and leave him to his business, whatever that was, but she knew she might never forgive herself if she did.

In the end, she put her coffee down and surprised Don by grabbing the gun from under the papers. "I'll just take this for now," she said simply, ejecting the magazine and making sure the chamber was clear. She put the gun in her shoulder bag. "Let's go outside and talk."

The thought of arguing with this woman apparently didn't occur to Don in his stupor as he followed her timidly out to the rear patio. She pulled two chairs together, on a slight angle like the setup for an intimate talk show, and indicated for Don to sit. Then she sat and faced him.

"Don, I know this is unbelievably difficult for you," she said softly. "I can't imagine what you must be feeling right now. I just want you to know that I'm here for you. Please let me be here for you." She put her hand gently around his shoulder. He looked into her eyes and was silent.

At last, he succumbed and fell into her, a tree cut to the breaking point, slowly at first then collapsing suddenly, sobbing.

Chapter Twenty-Two

Julia

August 2019

Julia got into the cab the hotel had arranged and tried her father's number, but to no avail. The driver pulled away from the curb, navigating the late morning Detroit traffic, and Julia decided to write an e-mail to her father: *Dad. I want you to be there tomorrow. I'm sorry for what I said before. Please come if you can. Julia.* She had not given her new cell number to her father, but she now included it in her email. The taxi continued to weave in and out of traffic on the way to the church, and as they passed a hospital the sight of it triggered a good memory for Julia.

She thought back to how David had helped her and Don out after Isabella's death, welcoming them into the home in Ypsi, and cooking for them. He couldn't cook like Isabella, but she remembered that it was good. He had continued to work nights, but he was a changed man, doing the shopping, fixing things around the house, trying to make sure that Don and Julia were settled and happy there. It was almost as though David had clung to them as he bobbed adrift on his own turbulent and lonely sea.

Then, Charlie came. Julia recalled the contractions. It was a Thursday in the last week of July, hotter than hell, and her father was at work. Don was with her, not having yet started his job at the *DFP*, and he had helped her out to the Corolla where she had sat in the front seat huffing. She remembered worrying over the seatbelt, not wanting to put pressure in the wrong place, and Don coaching her with words of encouragement. She also remembered wanting to kill him when he joked on the way to the hospital, "Hey, this baby was conceived in this car, maybe it wants to be born here too." She had laughed and winced from the contractions at the same time.

She knew that the delivery had been painful, but she couldn't remember that now. She just remembered the feeling of pure joy when they handed Charlie to her. Pure joy, and *relief*. He had a little bit of silky black hair plastered over his round head, and he cried a toothless cry as she pressed him to her chest. Maybe her memory had been retroactively edited by Charlie's death, but she thought that she clearly knew the moment she learned what real vulnerability was, and with it the inevitable fact that she would gladly lay down her life for another human being—her own flesh and blood.

They had decided to call him Charlie, after David's father. If it had been a girl, she would have been Cynthia, for Don's mother. Julia had never met her own grandfather, but they wanted to pay respect to their roots, and Don was adamant that he didn't want another Don. They had briefly considered Reg, but in the end, Charlie seemed to fit the best.

Her father had come up to meet them at eight the next morning, right after work and a quick shower. She smiled now in the taxi, as she pictured Don and David proudly passing Charlie back and forth like a trophy, wanting to be photographed with him, to be near him. She had also wept, there in that sterile hospital room full of men, for her mother, and for herself.

Julia was shaken from her daydream as the taxi came to a halt outside the church. "Eighteen dollars, please," the driver said. She gave him a twenty, and as she left the cab she looked up at the red-brick church, its one red tower capped in a round green belfry, rising from among the collection of two-story shops and old houses. She imagined it as a red arm and green fist raised up to God, and she looked to her right, past the suspended traffic lights bowing back and forth in the breeze, at Vernon Street and to her old neighborhood beyond. She'd passed under those lights countless times, walking with her mother to come here through sun, rain, and snow - trudging past the houses, the credit union, the hair salon.

A walk of hope and faith amongst those who needed something to have faith in.

The house she had lived in until the age of seventeen was on McMillan, three blocks east of the church, and it was smaller and humbler than the place in Ypsi. When they lived there, Isabella had not yet found her calling in housekeeping as there were few houses with demand for such services in Mexicantown. Isabella had to plead, using friends, family, people she knew at the church to help her find work, however temporary. She had tried and failed as a beautician, then bounced from server jobs at local taquerias to a job at the religious artifact shop across the street from the church. Housekeeping in Ypsi had been a promotion from life in the city, her struggle culminating in a broken heart at the age of forty-two.

Julia winced at the thought, making the natural comparison to herself at forty-two.

But what had she accomplished, really?

Failed to pursue her dreams, failed as a mother, a wife. Working for graphic design shops doing the clerical work, living paycheck to paycheck, *living off of Gerrard*. Pregnant and alone. If not for her share of the money from the house, she would be destitute. She imagined working in some nail salon in the city, in a crowded room full of hollow eyes and toothy smiles, the place reeking of cheap perfume.

Julia entered the church, which like most churches, was an assault on the senses, and she found herself not fully prepared. The temporary truce she'd had with religion had ended long ago with her mother's death, and she felt ill at ease going in. Holding the service for Charlie and burying his ashes at Holy Cross was her last act of contrition to her mother.

For two decades, Julia had struggled with a crushing sense of guilt that her pregnancy with Charlie had been the trigger for her mother's untimely death. She had never shared this thought with Don, out of shame and a desire not to spread the disease to him. Over the years, she had repeated a cycle of self-recrimination and healing, even forgiveness. Then something would trigger her to pick at the wound again—a missed birthday, a milestone with Charlie. It had taken years for her to come to terms with it, but today she added the guilt of her mother's death again to her load and started down the aisle.

The smell of incense drifted amongst the worn, dark, wooden pews. There was a hushed atmosphere, and she could see Lisa and a priest talking quietly in the transept to the right of the altar, bathed in the glow of the stained glass. Dispassionately watching her approach, the risen Christ loomed large, painted in peaceful pastels amid a sky of blue in the half-dome over the altar. Ivory pillars with rounded arches supported his blue sky, and intricate engravings filled the space in the spandrels, so that there would be nothing bare to bore the eyes on their upward journey from the floor.

She took note of the words, wrapped like a banner between the top of the arches and the dome. Like some medieval stock ticker, they wrapped around the curve of the dome's base, forever frozen on the words of St John: *These things I command you, that you love one another, as I have loved you.*

You have not loved me, Julia thought bitterly, as she closed the distance to Lisa and the priest.

CHAPTER TWENTY-THREE

Diane

AUGUST 2019

DIANE LOCKED DON'S GUN in the glove box of her car and returned to the back patio with two beers from his fridge. The sun had passed over the house and she suggested they go to the chairs on the front porch to avoid the chill of the shade. They sat, quietly rocking for a time, until Diane finally broke the silence.

"Don, I've never really asked you before," she began, softly. "What was Charlie like?"

They had discussed Charlie before, on their occasional evenings in the park, with Don slurring out an abridged version of Charlie's disappearance, the difficulties when he was fourteen, fifteen. She had usually veered carefully away from probing more deeply, preferring that both of them focus on the present rather than the past with all its ugly demons. It was not a comfortable subject, but she knew it was, and would always be a part of the man, and that maybe he'd needed to talk more about it.

Don exhaled, clearly taken aback by the question.

"What was Charlie like?" he repeated the question, pausing as though struggling to piece together memories that had been shattered into a thousand pieces.

"He was a wonderful kid," Don finally answered. "When he was in sixth grade, they told us he was 'gifted.' We'd suspected; he always loved puzzles, games...books, but they had done some testing at school."

Don's voice trailed off, and Diane could see that his eyes were transfixed, no longer translating images from the outside world into his brain. He was lost – lost in some alternate universe where Charlie went to school, hung out with friends, had dinners with Julia and Don. Diane was beginning to regret asking the question until Don's voice rang out, more firmly.

"Julia was all for it," he said, "I think she was determined to make sure that he didn't squander his talents so she got him in some after school programs: math club, computer club, whatever she could find. We couldn't afford any private schooling, so she tried to find whatever public resources she could for him. Charlie seemed to really take to the after-school stuff, especially anything to do with art or music."

Don paused and furrowed his brow.

"My father passed away the summer Charlie finished sixth grade and that was tough for all of us. But then, for Charlie, seventh and eighth grade were great; he was doing well in school, had friends. Julia had found work as an assistant at a graphic design company, and I was becoming known outside the paper. I was finally being published."

Listening to the energy in Don's voice, Diane felt as though she had pierced something, and she thought of her own father. She could remember the strength of his embrace and his calloused hands, rough from working construction jobs, touching her cheek to wipe away a childhood tear. Once, when she was maybe seven or so, she had seen him at the stove heating a sewing needle against the electric element. She had asked what he was doing, and he had turned his head and stuck his left hand towards her, exposing his thumb. She was surprised to see his thumbnail, black from a misplaced hammer stroke and asked him what that had to do with the needle.

I'm going to prick my nail, to let the blood out, he had said.

But won't that hurt, daddy?

Not as much as it does now. I hit my thumb and made it swell up, but the blood can't get out. This needle will hurt for a second, but I'll feel much better when the pressure's gone, don't worry Dix.

Dix. This had been her father's pet name for her, his gentle teasing of the southern drawl she had inherited from her mother, the accent she'd worked so hard to tone down when she had moved north. She found herself lost in the memory of her father. He was a rugged man who worked construction jobs ten months of the year in Tulsa. He would then find work welding or doing odd jobs for little car repair shops during the short off-season. He was a rough man, but he had always been a loving father. She felt her eyes misting and tried to focus in again on Don's words.

"We were doing okay," Don continued, "My father's estate had finally settled, bringing enough money to provide us a safety net and we thought it was time to make the step up. We felt that we deserved a better life and wanted to own our own place. So we found a little place in Birmingham."

"I didn't know you lived in Alabama," Diane questioned, interjecting for the first time.

"What?" he said looking up at her from his beer. "Oh, no, Michigan. I guess I always just told you I was from Detroit. That's easier when people ask. Birmingham is a little suburb of Detroit about fifteen miles northwest of the city. We thought it would be a good place to raise a family - a lot of people do." He turned his head away as Diane grabbed at the thought.

"Did you want to have other children?" she asked.

"Oh yes," he said as he looked back at the half-empty beer warming in his hand, "At first, Julia wanted to focus on Charlie, and we felt strapped financially. Then, when Charlie went to school, we talked about it. We tried...but Julia miscarried, twice. It was hard for us, getting our hopes up, starting to plan for a brother or sister for Charlie. Then we'd lose the baby."

"Sometimes, I think she felt cursed. She wasn't—" He paused, catching himself, "—*isn't* superstitious. It was just bad luck. After the second miscarriage, she threw herself into working and started talking about maybe trying to go to college after all. Then, well, it just seemed too late. Like we'd missed the window. We tried a couple of times, but I honestly believe her heart wasn't in it and I think I wanted another child more than she did."

Diane hadn't expected all this, but it was good. Good to see Don talking, his energy growing with the effort.

"Then, the troubles started with Charlie, and we never talked about having more kids again." Don stood and poured the last of his warm beer out on the gravel. "I think I need a shower," he stated plainly.

"I'll be right here when you're done, Don."

About half an hour later, Don returned to the front porch, freshly showered and dressed in clean jeans and a black turtleneck, carrying two fresh beers. Diane thought, that in that turtleneck, he looked a little bit like Jon Hamm.

"Hey, who's this?" she teased, accepting one of the longnecks from Don. It was about four thirty in the afternoon, and the sun was starting to touch the tops of the pine trees lining the driveway. It was silent but for the constant undertones of nature—birds, a tree toad, leaves rustling in the cool evening breeze.

"Don," Diane finally said, starting the speech she'd carefully rehearsed while Don was showering, "I know you beat yourself up over Charlie's accident but you really shouldn't. It was a terrible, terrible thing that happened but beating yourself up forever won't bring him back."

There, she'd said it. The firm message she thought he needed to hear.

"Accident," Don muttered, staring at the gravel in silence for a moment. "*Fire Horse* was my dad's boat. We used to drive to the marina in town here and go out cruising in it together. Catch the sunsets. One day, Dad, Julia, Charlie, and I—I think he was about ten at the time—even took it up over the point and down into Traverse City. We had a picnic lunch there and came back the same day. We'd had to leave at seven in the morning to have time to make the round trip. Dad probably blew three hundred bucks on gas, but we did it... because we could, and because Charlie loved the boat. By that time, Dad was letting him run it for long stretches at a time so he knew how to dock it, how to operate it. He knew every inch of that boat. Hell, he knew that boat better than my father." Don was becoming slightly agitated, pressing his right index finger down on the arm of the chair to emphasize each point he was making, all while holding his beer steady in his other hand.

"I thought it was Julia's dad that owned the boat?" she questioned, wanting to slow the pace a little.

"Yes," Don said, shifting down a gear and pausing to catch his breath. He continued more calmly. "After Dad died, David was living in Saint Joseph, working at the marina. He loved boats, like Charlie, but couldn't afford anything. Julia and I were doing better financially, and we had talked about buying a newer boat to keep up at the marina near the cabin, so for Christmas the next year we gave *Fire Horse* to David. Then, we never got around to buying our own boat. We had just moved to Birmingham and everything changed. It became the furthest thing from our minds."

Diane felt as though she was twenty-three again, working at the Lucky Seven casino in Oklahoma City, dealing poker and blackjack and watching tired, old men lose money they couldn't spare. Working the casinos had been her way out of Tulsa since her family didn't have money for college. In Oklahoma City, as a young woman from Tulsa, she was just 'Diane'; she had left Dix far behind, resting somewhere with her father in his early grave and living on only in her mother's gin soaked memories. Now, as Diane listened intently to Don's story, she watched *him*; studying his eyes, his face. Looking for the tells and trying to figure out how this day was going to end.

"After ninth grade, Charlie was not happy. About the move, about school, about being landlocked with us at the cabin. Things were becoming different with him. The summer he turned fifteen..." Don paused, "...he wasn't angry, there was no shouting or screaming. He was just, withdrawn. We would get one-word answers to anything we asked; it was like pulling teeth. I can't believe it now, but I even joked that Julia's genes were coming back to give her a dose of payback." Don paused on that point, and Diane could sense he was chiding himself.

"Julia did some research on the Internet, saying this was normal with a teenager, we should love him, be patient. Ride it out."

Diane chose to wait in silence rather than interrupt.

"We took him down to Saint Joseph that year," he continued, "the last weekend of vacation. To visit his grandfather. Julia hadn't been at her new job long and only had two weeks' vacation. So, we celebrated Charlie's birthday at the cabin and stopped to see David on the way back."

Don looked up at Diane. "You should have seen the look on Charlie's face. David took him out on the boat, just the two of them that weekend, so Julia and I could spend a few hours alone together. It was a great weekend." Don turned back to his beer, drawing a long sip. "Charlie loved it so much, he begged to go back the next weekend. We said no, but he was persistent."

"We thought that Charlie had made some good friends in ninth grade, that he had made a good start. He kept complaining about leaving Ferndale, missing his old friends, but his marks were great, mostly As, A plusses. For some reason, when he was in ninth grade, he made a friend who was a grade up, Geoff. Some kid he met at an art camp or something, I think. Geoff's parents were split up and his father lived out in Kalamazoo. Geoff had alternating weekends with his father and was driving himself back and forth, and on one of those weekends, in August, he offered to take Charlie to Saint Joseph to visit his grandfather. Julia didn't want to let Charlie go. She thought that they were too young, and it wouldn't be safe."

Don paused, as though considering what he was about to share with Diane. "But I talked her into it. We had given Charlie a basic cell phone for his birthday that year. It was another way to try to stay connected to him, and I told Julia she could call him any time. He promised he would text updates along the way. Geoff assured us he would drive slowly. They were only allowed to drive in daylight, zero tolerance for alcohol, etcetera. So, I talked Julia into it."

Don paused and looked again at Diane, shrugging his shoulders as if to say, *Kids. What are you going to do?* He was silent for a long moment, lost in thought.

"I had suspected, it turned out rightly, that Geoff and Charlie might be doing drugs together, getting up to no good. I thought, we all went through that, give him a little space. Deep down, though," Don took a deep breath and looked to the sky for a moment, "Deep down, I think I wanted a break from him, wanted Julia to myself." He continued, "She had been putting so much energy into him, and her new job, that I was…jealous. Maybe I resented it a little. So, yeah, when the chance came up for a weekend alone with her, I told her it would be good for Charlie, but really, it was good for me."

Diane considered the universal guilt of parenting trade-offs and hindsight second guessing that she could recall having herself with Chelsea during the teen years, when she and Darryl were growing distant. She ached for Don.

"Everything went fine," Don continued before Diane could say anything. "No problems. After that, we let them make that trip a couple more times that year before school started. Every other weekend."

Don shook his head. "He could be so focused on things. A book, a song, the boat. They were fixations for him that he had to experience. Over and over."

He looked at Diane. "He got Geoff to take him without asking us, just after he started school that fall. Maybe he thought we'd say no because of school. I don't know. We punished him, of course, but we thought that a kid could do worse things than sneak off to spend time with his grandfather. Other than that, things were good. It seemed like tenth grade was going to be good for him too, like he'd settled into his new surroundings."

The sun was visible now only between the trees and Diane could feel pangs of hunger. She didn't want to interrupt, but she risked a glance at her watch while Don was draining the last of his beer. Almost five thirty. The days were starting to shorten.

"So, what happened, Don?" she prompted.

"I guess I never told you all the details, huh?" he answered, simply.

"No, you just said that he drowned in the lake, and I never wanted to push you about it. I'm sorry I didn't ask more before," she replied, her voice trailing off and her cheeks blushing.

He turned to look at her again.

"The next year, the summer he died, he made the trip again a couple times without telling us." Don frowned, puzzled. "I had grounded him several times that year, but still, I don't know why he wouldn't tell us." Don paused.

"Another beer?" he held up his empty bottle, wiggling it gently, as though trying to entice her.

"I think we should maybe eat something first," Diane suggested, making motions to get up from the chair. It was getting cold.

"I think he killed himself," Don said flatly, staring back down at something in front of him on the driveway.

The abruptness of it shocked Diane back down into her chair.

"He knew how to operate that boat," Don continued, still staring at a random piece of gravel beside the truck. "When the police told us two weeks after he went missing that they'd found *Fire Horse*, there were no signs of damage. The lake had been calm. The boat had half a tank of gas, the engine started fine and there was no water on board."

He turned to look at her. "Diane, they never recovered a lifejacket. I think Charlie committed suicide."

Diane tried to read Don's face in the dusk, but she could discern no expression on it. She didn't know what to say.

Diane followed Don's hard gaze through the trees, due west to the setting sun. To the setting sun, and, somewhere miles in the distance, the lake that he believed Charlie had chosen to die in.

Chapter Twenty-Four

Julia

August 2019

"Hey," Lisa said, elongating the word, as though to add an appropriate note of sympathy and warmth, when she spotted Julia coming to the front of the church.

"Hey," Julia said with a forced smile as she turned right into the transept without pausing to make the sign of the cross. They embraced.

"How are you? Not too jet lagged, I hope?" Lisa asked.

"No, I slept okay."

The priest watched the friend's reunion patiently, his hands clasped together in front of his black cassock. Lisa and Dave Wight had become good friends after helping Don and Julia purchase their home in Birmingham. Before Charlie's disappearance, the foursome would get together on weekends for dinners out, cards and backyard barbecues.

Lisa and Dave had two girls, both younger than Charlie, so the kids had not truly been able to form deep friendships like their parents. Julia wondered if Don still talked to Dave and found that she hoped so, for Don's sake. She wasn't going to ask Lisa about that, didn't want to pry open doors that were closed.

"Everything's ready for tomorrow," Lisa reassured her. "How are *you*, though?" She adopted a small downward frown and slightly tilted her head to the right, placing her hand on Julia's right arm and giving it two quick strokes up and down.

"I'll be okay," Julia responded matter-of-factly, not permitting herself the grief at the moment.

Lisa picked up on the cue and appeared eager to move into task mode. "This is Father Willis," she said, gesturing with her right arm toward the man in black, inviting him into the conversation.

He quickly closed the three steps to the two women and extended his right hand. He was tall and slim and probably in his sixties, with a fringe of white hair around a bald dome.

"Hi, I'm Father Willis, nice to meet you. I'm so sorry for your loss."

You know nothing about my loss, Julia thought bitterly, while smiling and placing her hand in the priest's. She braced herself for a cold, clammy handshake and was surprised to feel the man's hand was dry and warm.

"Lisa and I were just going through some of the details for tomorrow," he said. "The service will be here at eleven. You have requested that the service be conducted without Mass." As though a question, giving her a final chance to right the wrong.

She nodded affirmatively.

"I understand you wish me to deliver the eulogy," Father Willis continued, eliciting another nod from Julia. "I think I got what I needed from you when we spoke on the phone, but if there's anything else you'd like to share, like me to incorporate into it, please don't hesitate."

No, she thought as she nodded. "Thanks," she said a little more dryly than she intended. She sighed inwardly as he began a description of how the service would proceed.

"...then, when the service is ended, the altar servers and I will process out through the doors of the church with the casket," he continued. "The church ushers will serve as pallbearers and will place Charlie's casket into the hearse."

She perceived a silent judgment. *Who is this woman with no loved ones to carry her son?*

"The congregation will remain," he continued, "as the luncheon will be served immediately following the service in the great hall adjacent to the church. Charlie will then be taken to rest at the crematorium where we will perform the cremation Monday morning, bringing the ashes to Holy Cross for burial that afternoon at four o'clock."

"Is that all okay for you?" he asked.

Four was later than she'd thought it would be, she must have mixed something up. She had booked her flight back to the UK that Monday evening and it would now be tight. She would take care of that later.

Yes, Julia nodded, wondering how many more nods would be needed to get this over with. Just then, her phone buzzed in her purse.

"Excuse me a moment." She grabbed it, turning away and leaving Lisa to make small talk with Father Willis. It was her father.

"Dad?" she said, answering.

"Julia?" David sounded uncertain, even though it was obvious it was his daughter on the line.

"Dad, I'm sorry for my e-mails. Can you make it?" She felt like she was twelve again.

"Of course, dear. I'll be there. Sorry I missed your call before; I was out getting my hair cut and I forgot to take my phone with me."

Julia wondered how much there was left to cut these days. "That's okay, dad," was all she could manage.

"I'll be leaving shortly. I don't like driving at night now," David said.

"I thought you didn't have a car." She hadn't thought of that until now.

"I rented one. A little foreign thing. It wasn't expensive."

"Where are you staying?" she asked.

"The Marriott in Dearborn. I should be there by six."

Julia looked it up on her phone and saw that it was about fifteen minutes from her hotel. She didn't know what she expected, speaking to her father for the first time in over two years. A few months ago, she would have sworn this moment would never come, but strangely it felt natural. As though the past few years had been a dream that could just be put to the side.

"Do you want to meet for dinner tonight?" She'd made plans with Lisa, but suddenly felt the need to be with her father.

"That'd be lovely, Julia."

"Okay, call me when you're settled and I'll Uber over to get you."

"I can drive."

"No, I want to get you. Don't worry about it."

She figured he'd be drinking and did not want him to take chances.

"See you then."

"Bye, Dad."

She hung up and approached Lisa.

"Lisa, is it okay if we have a late lunch now and skip dinner? My dad is coming into town."

"Sure, no problem. Whatever you want."

They finished making plans and left Christ's benevolent gaze to get lunch.

Chapter Twenty-Five

Don and Diane

August 2019

"Thanks, that hit the spot. I didn't know I was hungry." Don pushed the plate to the middle of the kitchen table and wiped his face with a paper napkin.

"Oh, I just threw that together. You don't have much to work with here. Do you want me to get you some groceries?" Diane asked, while taking his plate to the dishwasher.

She had found three potatoes, an onion, and a few other staples, and together with the last of the eggs, had made some kind of southern-fried hash. *It had been good*, Don thought, if a little spicy.

"No, thanks, I'll get some when I get back," Don replied.

"I can still go with you, if you want," Diane countered, eyes looking down at the kitchen counter where she was cleaning up the last of the dishes.

"It's okay, Diane. Really. I think I can do this. I really appreciate it though."

She changed the subject, "Does that fireplace back there really work?"

"That?" Don said, turning and looking behind him to the rear of the cottage. "Oh, yeah. It works." He turned back to look at her face. "Wait, would you like me to light a fire?" he asked.

"That'd be nice. The air is so chilly now."

Don found some kindling and a lighter, and soon a little fire was crackling in the stone fireplace. The two couches opposed each other, but were perpendicular to the fire, leaving the single easy chair to offer the only direct view. This had not been a problem for Don for four years, in fact, he couldn't remember the last time he'd lit a fire here; he had almost forgotten to open the damper, remembering only at the last minute.

He pulled the coffee table back, and moved the easy chair over to the side, then pivoted one of the couches ninety degrees to face the fire. He put the coffee table back in front of it and they both sat there on the couch, basking in the warmth of the flames.

Don had never been a fan of gas inserts. Sure, they were easier - flick a switch and voila, fire. But Don enjoyed the process of splitting the wood, drying it, splitting it further into kindling. Preparing it and coaxing it to life. Like most things around the cabin, he felt that the work he put into something earned him the right to its enjoyment. This notion crossing his mind tickled a memory; something he'd studied in one of his literature classes. Don loved literature, rather he used to anyway; he had been an avid reader and his books were still scattered all over the cabin.

"Have you ever heard of *The Little Prince*?" he asked Diane.

"Where is he from?" she asked, clearly puzzled.

"It's a book," Don said, becoming animated, "by Antoine de Saint-Exupéry. He wrote it back near the end of the second world war. It's about a little prince traveling the stars and visiting planets. I guess it's really a kind of philosophy book."

"Never heard of it." Diane said, "Do you have it here? Maybe I could read it sometime."

"I think I do."

Don got up from the couch and searched the cottage with growing enthusiasm. "It might be in the cellar," he exclaimed, grabbing a flashlight in the laundry room and opening the trap door. He paused momentarily before switching the light on and disappearing into the cellar, leaving Diane watching from the top of the stairs. His descent was mostly free from cobwebs, having been freshly tread two days ago, and he turned toward the darkness on the far side of the basement with his flashlight. The beam of light danced over his ghosts until he found the object of his search: a large storage bin. He went to it, and setting the flashlight on the top, hefted the bin and carried it back to the landing; it must have weighed nearly fifty pounds. In the light, he could see dozens of paperback books inside, and after a time searching he found what he was looking for.

Finally, he emerged triumphant from the basement with a book in his right hand and his flashlight in the left. *Don Rydell - modern-day tomb raider,* he thought, chuckling to himself.

"He was a pilot, you know," Don said as they settled down on the couch, Diane to the far left and Don stretched out to her right, leaning into her side. "Saint-Exupéry."

"The author?" she asked, looking at the book cover.

"Yeah. He flew for the allies in the war. He disappeared on a reconnaissance mission out of Corsica near the end of the war." Don thought briefly about the connection to Amelia Earhart. One that had never struck him before.

"Will you read it to me?" he asked, looking up at her face.

"Uh, okay, sure," she replied, smiling as she opened the book.

"'Once when I was six years old,'" Diane began to read.

Don could see her scanning the childish illustrations and he realized that she might mistake this for a child's book. She glanced at Don briefly.

"No, I haven't lost my mind, Diane," Don replied to the unspoken question, "please, just read."

"'I saw a magnificent picture in a book called *True Stories from Nature*,'" she continued.

"Wait," Don said suddenly. He got up and went to the door at the rear of the cabin, switching the outside light on. "Sorry," he said. "'Nature' made me think of my trap. Nothing there. Maybe the bear has moved on." Smiling sheepishly, he returned to the couch and his position of comfort.

Diane continued to read, and Don could sense her becoming wrapped up in the little story. Don, too, found himself falling under its spell again, hearing it through Diane's ears. The book was one of many wormholes to his past and it now conjured bittersweet memories for him. He remembered the last time he'd ever read the book. *How old had Charlie been? Seven? Eight?* Don had read a chapter each night when he put Charlie to bed, and he smiled at the memory now, soothed by Diane's steady voice.

The fire was dying down but neither of them wanted to disturb the warm cocoon that they had made. Diane eventually came to the end of the book and Don thought he could see diamonds in the corners of her eyes.

"Did he die? Did the snake bite kill him?" she asked, turning to Don.

"It's a mystery," Don replied. "They never found the Little Prince's body. Perhaps he just left the earth to roam back amongst the stars. That's part of the point, if you don't know for sure, then you can look to the stars in their beauty and imagine he is on any one of them. Hope can go on as long as the mystery is there." Don's smile faded.

"My favorite was the rose," she said.

"Yes, you remind me of her a little."

Diane frowned and Don could see that she wasn't sure how to take his words.

"What was that line about the rose again?" she asked, testing him.

"'It's the time you spend on your rose that makes it so important,'" he said over his shoulder, eager to accept the challenge. "There are millions of roses out there, but the one you spend time on is what matters *to you*. The time you put into something creates its value, bonds it to your heart. That's what it means, at least to me."

She smiled. "I like that."

They sat pressed together in the dying glow of the fire. Darkness and cold were filling the room and Diane pulled a blanket over them, pushing herself down and putting her head on the arm of the couch.

"Don?" She hesitated. "When I came over this morning," she turned her head to look right at him, their faces nearly touching in the tiny glow from the remaining coals, "what was your gun doing on the kitchen table?"

Don was silent. He wasn't sure he knew the true answer himself, but he knew what Diane was expecting to hear.

"I was planning to write a note to Julia, apologizing for the things I've done wrong, for what happened with Charlie. Saying goodbye."

He watched Diane for any reaction. Her eyebrows were raised slightly, and her expression was soft.

They each waited for the other to speak.

"It's hard for me to believe now, but I think that maybe I was going to use the gun on myself, I guess," Don finally said, feeling shame at his cowardice.

Diane put her right arm around Don pulling him into her, and Don felt himself crying, for the third time this week.

"The world needs you, Don. I need you too," was all she would say.

Don lay there in the darkness, warm against Diane's body, and thought about the Little Prince.

Nothing ever goes away until it teaches us what we need to know, the Little Prince had said.

Don drifted off to sleep, wondering what it was that Charlie had taught him.

CHAPTER TWENTY-SIX

Julia

AUGUST 2019

I'M COMING DOWN. FIVE minutes. Julia stared at the text from her father. She was in the back seat of a Corolla and her driver, Trayvon, was waiting patiently in the front seat. He was a young black man driving for Uber to make a few bucks to fund his classes at Wayne State and he was wearing a white dress shirt and jeans. They had chatted a little on the brief drive over here, and his Uber profile stated that he was known for *Great Conversation.* Julia would probably give him five stars, as he had been courteous and efficient, and she knew four stars had become the new sacrilege. *What did you have to do to earn one star anymore?* she wondered silently.

When she had climbed into the back seat of the Corolla and felt the cloth under her rear she smiled, briefly transported back to a happier time. The pleasant memory was short-lived, however, for as she awaited her father in front of his hotel, her thoughts were drawn to him and to one of their last face-to-face encounters. Her mind replayed the accusations she'd screamed at her dad in his little rental a block from the marina, in Saint Joseph.

Why didn't you keep the key locked up? Why do you have to drink so much? We could have been looking for Charlie last night!

David's unit was a small two-bedroom that offered him no nooks to hide from her wrath, and so he had just taken it all, mute. He had found refuge by throwing himself into the search, borrowing a boat from his boss at the marina and scouring up and down the coastline over the first two days following Charlie's disappearance. When they'd found *Fire Horse* empty, Julia had stopped speaking to him almost entirely. In the beginning she would send short e-mails, little fact bombs, in response to his outreaches, then she offered only silence.

She now knew it had not been her father's fault; Charlie would have found a way to do what he wanted. He was clever, resourceful, and stubborn but she hadn't been able to see that clearly back then.

Trayvon snapped her from her reverie, twisting in his seat to look back at her as if to say: *Is this guy coming, or what?* and she felt compelled to reassure him.

"He'll be right out, he just texted me."

Just then, David emerged from the lobby doors and Julia got out of the car to hug her father. She didn't know what she expected—*gaunt? Unshaven? Drunk? Looking eighty instead of seventy?* He was none of these. He looked...good. He had a golf shirt on under a windbreaker and blue jeans that fit him well, though he had put on a few pounds since she saw him last. Overall, Julia thought he looked *healthy*, and she said so as she hugged him; he smelled good too.

"Thanks, love. I wish I felt good. It's so good to see you. I'm so sorry." Unlike Lisa's consolations, this hit home.

"Let's go eat," she finally said, a little irritated that a part of her brain was worrying over keeping an Uber driver waiting.

The lady at the front desk at her hotel had recommended a restaurant called Ford's Garage. She had asked if Julia was here for business, or pleasure, a straightforward question that had momentarily stopped Julia cold.

Arriving with her father, Julia could see that the restaurant looked like an old garage from the outside and it had a green Model T parked out front. She had noticed numerous Ford buildings as they approached and wondered if they were near the Ford compound now. She thanked Trayvon, clicked on five stars, and they went up to the restaurant.

"Do you need a smoke before we go in?" she asked her father.

"No, love," he said smiling. "I quit those damn things last year. Couldn't afford the habit anymore."

She realized then that she had missed the smell of tobacco on him. He pulled the door open for her and they entered the building.

"Thanks," her father said to the hostess, who led them to a booth in the back. They had no sooner taken their seats when a young server approached. She was sporting a brown ponytail and a smile that revealed a small gap between her two front teeth.

"I'll just give you a minute," she said cheerily as she tossed them menus and rushed off to another task.

Everyone's in such a hurry these days, Julia thought, already accustomed to the courtesy of time that Gerrard's money had afforded her - servers who let you have a table for the night, drivers who would wait all morning for you if that's what you wanted. She had almost forgotten what it was like to be on the clock.

"What's good here?" her father started, looking at the menu.

"Maybe the burgers?" she answered, recalling the hotel clerk's comments.

"I hear the weather will be nice tomorrow." David continued.

"Yeah. Me too. I met the priest today and everything seems to be in order."

They continued like this for a while, filling time and space.

Where was that server? Julia wondered.

"Julia," her father finally said in a tone that indicated they were moving to *real* conversation. "Thank you for letting me come. I wanted to be able to pay my respects. I wanted..." He paused, looking down briefly and then back up at her. "I wanted to see you."

"It's okay," she replied. "Dad, I wanted to see you too." Her eyes grew misty.

Goddamn it.

She blinked slowly, hoping that tears would not break free from her eyelids and there was silence while each waited, considering the risk of saying what had to come next.

She had rehearsed this moment, but had worried that when the time came, her hurt and anger would rise up and consume her yet again. Still, she desperately wanted to explain things properly to her father - why she had lashed out, why she hadn't wanted to see him these past few years. She had to rid herself of the sickness, the anger...and the fear. She thought back to something a therapist had told her in the early months after she and Don separated, a quote from Nelson Mandela. *Forgiveness liberates the soul and removes fear.* She wasn't sure she could do this for her father yet, but maybe she could do it for herself.

"I want you to know—" she paused and took a big breath, her green eyes glistening with tears, "—I forgive you; it wasn't your fault. I was just so hurt and angry and afraid. Most of all, I was afraid. I wanted to blame anyone but myself. You, Don, the police. Anyone but me. Or Charlie."

David held her gaze.

"I know," he said softly. *I know.*

Their server, Mindy, chose that moment to interrupt them for drink orders.

"Sparkling water, please," Julia said.

"I'll have a coffee," David answered, surprising Julia.

"Doesn't that keep you up at night?" she asked, as Mindy left to see to their drinks.

"Doesn't matter," David replied. "Everything keeps me up at night. I don't think I've been able to retrain myself after being a creature of the night for so many years. I don't need much sleep anyway," he said. Then, after a pause, "I haven't had a drink in fourteen months."

No wonder he looks so good, she thought.

"Good for you, Dad."

"Yeah, it feels good now. I can taste food again. Maybe a little too much," he said, patting his belly.

He was a different man than she remembered. Different, and yet, unchanged where it mattered. It *was* good to see him.

"I felt that way too, you know, after your mother died." David said quietly, drawing Julia's attention. "I wanted to blame the world. Isabella wasn't supposed to go before me, so young. It wasn't fair, we were supposed to grow old together. Die, together. I was angry at you, at Don, at the world. Then, mostly at myself. When I went out to Saint Joseph..." He paused, as though considering his words carefully, "...I wanted isolation, to find a way to cauterize myself, and I guess I started drinking more to help with that. Your visits were the only thing I had to look forward to in my life."

Julia could see her father struggling to hold it together and she fought to keep herself from sobbing. She told herself that she wanted him to be honest and not hold back because his daughter was weeping, but maybe she still feared to show weakness in front of her father; a man she could never remember seeing cry, not even at Isabella's funeral.

"Then your visits became fewer and farther between, and Charlie started to come on his own," David continued, bringing Julia back to the moment.

Mindy returned to set the drinks on the table.

"Are you ready to order?" she asked, holding her stylus at the ready over the digital pad.

"I'm sorry, I think we need another minute or two," Julia apologized.

"No problem, I'll be back in a few," Mindy replied before leaving to tend to her other customers.

"Go on, Dad," Julia encouraged.

David cleared his throat.

"Well, then. As to Charlie's visits, I knew you didn't want him to, that he was running from you, but I was selfish. I found myself looking forward to seeing him, going out on the boat with him. To not being alone for a night or two." David grabbed a handkerchief from his pocket and blew his nose.

"Did I ever tell you…"? He paused, pocketing the handkerchief, and looking to the side as though scanning the restaurant for an accomplice. "Did I ever tell you that I read poetry to him on the boat?" His voice was nearly a whisper.

Julia had to edit this into her imaginary memories. She didn't really know what they had done on the boat, but all of her imagined scenarios involved her father drinking, and he and Charlie boating recklessly through the waves. *But this?* - this was not an image that had ever come to her mind.

He read the look on her face.

"I know, I can't believe it myself. Charlie was such a keen reader. So clever, that boy. So I introduced him—and myself really—to the Irish greats: Yeats, Thomas, Kavanagh.

She watched her father, this man who she'd thought could barely finish a crossword puzzle, don a look of concentration, and with a little red coming to his cheeks he began to recite from memory:

"On Raglan Road on an autumn day I met her first and knew,

That her dark hair would weave a snare that I might one day rue;

I saw the danger, yet I walked, along the enchanted way,

And I said, let grief be a fallen leaf, at the dawning of the day."

"That's beautiful, Dad," Julia said, almost at a loss for words and wondering who this man across the table from her really was.

"You should hear it set to traditional Irish music," he said. "My favorite is the version with Sinéad O'Connor and The Dubliners."

"Who wrote it?" she asked, truly curious.

He made a show of feigned pain, drawing his fingertips in towards his chest.

"Patrick Kavanagh, of course. The greatest modern-day poet to come from Ireland. Making him the greatest modern-day poet in the world...by definition of course," he added, in a playful tone.

Mindy broke the spell, her patience for her slow, teetotaling patrons wearing thin. "What can I get you both?"

They ordered their burgers, and after a few more hesitant exchanges, David said, "I'd like to speak tomorrow, if you'll let me."

She did not think long.

"Of course, Dad. I'd love that. I'll let Father Willis know first thing tomorrow."

This man—father, grandfather, widower, worker, poetry lover—had far more to say for Charlie than a strange man in black ever could.

They finished their meals amidst volleys of small talk and Julia felt a gaping wound in her heart begin to heal.

CHAPTER TWENTY-SEVEN

Don

AUGUST 2019

DON AWOKE WITH A start and his first sensation was of Diane's warm body under his face. Her warmth felt good, and he was reluctant to leave, but he lifted himself slowly in the blackness careful not to disturb her. Rising from the couch he fumbled in the darkness for his phone, left somewhere on the coffee table in front of them. Finding it, he tiptoed to the kitchen, pointing the phone's face away from Diane before tapping it lightly to reveal that it was four fifty a.m.

Good timing, he thought, and he felt good, like he'd had a full night's sleep. He had set his alarm for five, wanting to be sure he would get to the memorial on time, and it was nice to wake up just beforehand so that it wouldn't disturb Diane. He hadn't set an alarm for over a year and now almost forgot to switch it off. Using the light of the phone, he crept to his bedroom and closed the door.

After a brief shower, he dressed in his suit—a simple navy, off-the-rack purchase that Julia had helped him pick out for some meeting with an important publisher in the *before time.* He threw some clothing and toiletries into an overnight bag, though he hadn't decided whether he would stay through until Monday. Less than twenty-four hours ago, he had thought he would never go anywhere again, ever, so he had simply been unable to contemplate being at the church, seeing Julia, *needing a room.* He tried not to dwell on it.

Just keep moving, one task at a time. Don't think too far ahead.

He tiptoed to the front door with his things and paused, looking back at Diane still asleep on the couch. He set his bag down and made his way across the foyer to his father's old room, where he closed the door and turned on the light. He decided to leave a note for her, so he grabbed some paper and a pen and wrote:

Diane,

Thank you for being there for me. You are literally a lifesaver. I'll text you when I get there. I'm not sure how long I will stay, but I'll let you know.   Don

He paused. He didn't have the time or capacity to think about how he felt for Diane at the moment, nonetheless he added *Love* before his name. She deserved that.

He placed the note on the kitchen counter, folded conspicuously into a tent, and went out to his truck for the long drive east into the sunrise.

CHAPTER TWENTY-EIGHT

Charlie

APRIL 2015

"CHARLIE? CHARLIE, WAKE UP. Class is over," Mr. Gander said from the front of the room to the snickers and snorts of twenty-five students in the tenth grade. Geoffrey Gander had been teaching math to teenagers for twenty-two years and for the last ten years the students had been calling him Ned Flanders because of his mustache and nasally voice.

"I'm sorry that my class can't hold your limited attention span," he continued. "Maybe you should try getting some sleep tonight."

Charlie startled from his trance as his classmates rose eagerly to make their way out.

"He's tired from working nights cutting peoples' lawns," Brick said to Jazz two desks up, looking back at him to make sure Charlie could hear them. "Isn't that right, Chico?"

"Fuck you," Charlie said halfheartedly.

Brick and Jazz had been two of his faithful tormentors since he had arrived at Ernest W. Seaholm High in Birmingham one-and-a-half years ago, but they were mostly harmless, and he had learned to just dish it back when they gave it. Steven Davis was a linebacker for the Seaholm football team and was a big guy. Everyone just called him 'Brick.' Greg Djaza didn't do much of anything, but the name lent itself to 'Jazz,' and that had stuck. Charlie doubted he'd ever heard jazz in his life, if he even knew what it was.

"I'm gonna tell your momma you said that when she's over cleaning our house on Saturday," Jazz said, eager for Brick's approval.

Charlie didn't have the energy to respond.

"Go get some sleep weirdo," Brick said, cutting the harassment mercifully short.

Charlie grabbed his things and joined the procession out the door. Everyone else was already comparing videos on their smartphones; twenty second bites of nothingness that didn't do anything for Charlie, and anyway his phone was an older knock-off that didn't have all the apps of the latest "i" wonder, leaving him to old fashioned texting and talking.

Charlie broke away from the crowd and headed into the restroom where he glanced in the mirror. Superficially, he looked like the other kids, but sometimes he felt like he was of another species. They cared about who liked whom and who had posted the coolest video online. Drinking and parties. Cars.

He liked books, classical music, poetry, even philosophy. He knew that he spoke the same language as his classmates, but they didn't *communicate*, not really. Physically, he could see that he had his father's brown eyes and smile while his skin and hair came from his mother. Shiny, dark brown hair that was fine, almost silken, falling straight over his tan skin.

Charlie Rydell thought that he had the least Mexican name you could imagine, but the kids had caught wind of his ancestry in ninth grade when he asked a question while filling out a school form.

He had to answer what his ethnicity was and he put his hand up bringing Mr. Holmes to his desk.

"My mother is Mexican, but my father is white. What should I put?" This was new information for Charlie's seatmates and it didn't take long for it to make the rounds.

"Pick whichever one you feel suits you best then, Charlie, or cross out the Hispanic origin answers and write in *Both*," Mr. Holmes had said impatiently, clearly not giving a shit about whatever this stuff was used for, if anything.

Charlie had struggled. He liked to get things right. He chose *Not of Hispanic origin,* feeling like he'd insulted his mother even though she would never see the form. He knew Grandpa was Irish, but his grandmother was Mexican and his mother *looked* Mexican, so Charlie had seen her that way ever since he could remember.

Some boys burst noisily into the bathroom, stirring him. He dried his hands and made his way to his locker.

Charlie had managed to avoid after-school activities that year, despite the heavy push from his mother. He wasn't athletic and that was all that counted around there. Science club, literature club, photography club—all the things that could potentially interest him, would just feed the fire for the likes of Brick and Jazz at Seaholm, and Charlie couldn't be bothered. He could do those things on his own time and he wouldn't make it easy for them. It wasn't like all the kids at Seaholm were mean, there were really only a few bullies, and the vast majority of his classmates were just indifferent. Somehow that was worse. If it wasn't for his friendship with Geoff and the bullying from Brick and Jazz, he might even begin to doubt that he was real.

Dropping his books off he grabbed his backpack and made his way out into the April sunshine. It was cool, but Charlie just wore a blue T-shirt and jeans with ASICS sneakers. He took his time as he walked down the front steps of the school; he didn't have to rush to catch the bus as he lived less than a mile away, and he set out onto Lincoln Street, turning left for the twenty-minute walk home.

Lincoln was a busy street divided by intermittent center boulevards of grass and trees. There might as well have been billboards advertising *Upscale Suburban Living* or *Safe, White Lifestyles,* Charlie thought. Straight, freshly laid concrete provided sidewalk paths on either side of Lincoln, but Charlie stayed on the same side as the school and continued east, finally coming to Pleasant Street, where he took a left to head north to his house. He had laughed when his parents told him they were moving to Pleasant Street in Birmingham. They had said it with so much enthusiasm like it was the solution to life's problems, problems Charlie didn't know they had.

Charlie had liked the house in Ferndale. He liked having a pool and he had friends there. But when his parents told him they were moving, that things would be better for them, he would be going to a great school, he wondered aloud, *why*? He'd argued that he wanted to go to high school in Ferndale with his friends, and his mother and father had to patiently tell Charlie *how lucky he was*. His mother had explained that *when she was his age, they lived in poverty. In the city. Charlie would have opportunities they didn't have. He should be grateful.* So, he had taken their cue and stopped complaining about the move.

They lived in a nice two-story brick house on the left side of the street, just past Pleasant Court. Charlie got tired of being not-so-subliminally assaulted about his feelings and ignored the street signs deliberately. When kids at Seaholm had asked him where he lived, he sometimes told them Sesame Street.

One advantage of the move though, was the house. There was more space - more space for Charlie to find peace and quiet. It was a four-bedroom two story with red brick and a little dated, but nice. Except for his mother's rose garden in the backyard, his parents could never find the time for gardening, so they had kept it simple out front. Grass and a few bushes lined the curved walkway off the driveway to the front door.

They had delegated the cutting of the grass and pulling of weeds to Charlie. It was one of his *chores to pull his weight around there*, part of a lesson they'd needed to teach him after some of his behavior last year. The fact that he was responsible for their gardens made the earlier stings from Brick and Jazz cut a little deeper. Self-conscious, Charlie would do his lawn chores as quickly as he could, always glancing to the sidewalk, hoping no one he knew from school would walk past.

Charlie had a lot of chores around the house now. Last fall, he'd gotten caught stealing his mother's purse; he hadn't even really known why he did it. He *had* needed the money—he owed a friend of Geoff's for some weed he'd bought—but he could have stretched that out. Geoff would have covered him.

His father had been furious.

"What the hell were you thinking, Charlie?! How are we ever going to trust you again?" he'd said, while handing down a two-month grounding.

Charlie had taken the purse from Julia's bedroom the prior October, while she was making dinner downstairs on a rare night when she'd gotten home early. He had taken it to his room and searched through it - gone through his mother's *personal* things. Charlie knew that the violation of trust was far worse than the two hundred and ten dollars he had taken, and he burned with shame now at the memory. He had heard his father coming up the stairs and stuffed the money in his jeans and put the purse under his bed, intending to return it later.

That night at dinner, they had gotten into an argument about something, maybe Geoff and the illicit trip to Saint

Joseph a month earlier, and he had stormed off to his room and gone to sleep.

The next morning, his mother was searching everywhere for her purse. "Has anyone seen my purse? Charlie? Have you seen my purse?" She knocked on his bedroom door.

"No," he'd said stupidly, feeling the inevitability of discovery descending upon him. His father told his mother that he would look and call her when he found it. She was pacing the halls.

"Charlie, don't you have to get to school?" Julia called out. He'd felt trapped. He couldn't move the purse and had left it under the bed to go to school.

He remembered coming home that night, last October - the crunch of dry, dead leaves under his feet, the sight of the grand Halloween decorations that lined the street, and the smell of the smoke from fireplaces in the crisp air. He had almost forgotten what he had done; maybe he had just imagined it—he wouldn't *actually* have done something that stupid, and he had prayed that this would just be an evening like any other. Then, the knot in his stomach grew as he had walked up the drive. The feeling that he was caught. *Knowing it.*

His first clue had been that it was four in the afternoon and his mother's 328i was in the driveway.

He had wanted to turn and run, but he had already given most of the money to Geoff and it couldn't be returned, so in the end he had just braced himself and gone in for his punishment. They couldn't hurt him, really. His father had ranted and raved, his face beet red. Charlie couldn't remember ever seeing him like this, not even last month when they had snuck off to his grandfather's.

Why was he so angry? Eventually, his words turned into static. It was his mother that stung the most, sitting there at the kitchen table, looking frail and disappointed. His proud, fierce mother who was never at a loss for words—silenced. She had not been able to look Charlie in the eye.

He shook the memory off as he passed the walk to the front door—*that* was for guests, whoever they were. Even Dave and Lisa used the back door when they came to visit. The driveway was empty tonight as usual, and Charlie made his way through the wooden gate and around the back of the house. About a third of the way in from the rear corner of the house, off of the stone patio, Charlie found the door and entered.

The back door opened into a sizable mudroom, maybe eight by twelve with a landing and stairs continuing down to the basement at its innermost end. To the left was a small area for hanging coats and a bench where Charlie dropped his backpack. On his right, the mudroom opened to the kitchen and dining area, and past the table was the kitchen itself, its pantry, fridge, and white cupboards lining the wall to the left and a U-shaped counter with a sink centered under a window facing the backyard on the right.

Behind the left-most kitchen wall, was a living room at the front of the house. A separate office was at the front corner of the house on the opposite side of the front door from the living room. The stairs to the second floor of the home ran over top the basement stairs and greeted front-door visitors slightly to their right, off the hallway between the two front rooms.

Charlie expected his father to be in the office at this time of day, around four, as usual. He worked, often from home, for the newspaper writing political stuff. Charlie thought it was boring, but they would talk about it sometimes when his dad was in the mood. Charlie was surprised to see his dad at the kitchen table.

"Hey, Charlie," his dad said, looking up from his tablet.

"Hey. Aren't you working today?"

"Nah, I'm in between projects for a week or two," his dad answered. "How was school?"

Charlie hoped his dad hadn't noticed his involuntary eye roll. He was counting on grabbing a snack, quietly mumbling hello, and escaping up to his room to watch some Netflix.

"Charlie? How was school today?" his dad repeated.

Boring. Monotonous. Brick and Jazz picked on me again. I fell asleep, he thought. "Fine," was all that escaped his lips.

"Did you learn anything new today?"

"We did an experiment in science class. Made a tornado in a jar."

"Oh, that sounds neat."

Neat. It was funny to hear his dad try to talk like a teen. Connect on his level. *Did he think Charlie was still ten?*

"I saw your mid-term grades online," his father said, dropping the mood into low gear.

"So?"

"You know we were thinking of putting you into Advanced Placement next year in math and science. Now your grades are slipping. What's going on, Charlie?"

"I dunno. My math teacher sucks, and Mr. Sorensson missed a mark for an assignment I handed in for science."

"Are you going to talk to him about it?"

"No."

"Charlie, you are almost sixteen. You've got to start taking responsibility for yourself. Your mother and I can't do everything for you."

Charlie waited.

"Your mother and I expect those grades to come up by year end, Charlie; you can do it. If you need some help, let us know. Talk to your teachers, they're paid to help you."

With that, his father finalized the topic, returning to the news on his tablet, and Charlie made his way to the kitchen to heat up some leftover spaghetti.

They had been eating later in the evenings since his mom got the job over at Design Studio in Birmingham a couple of years back. She used to be in the kitchen when he came home in Ferndale, greeting him with a small snack to tide him over until dinner, while already working at some home cooked dish she'd learned from her mother, the grandmother he'd never met. Charlie felt like he knew his grandmother though, since his mother talked about her often. Now, except for holidays and that one fall night last year, his mother wouldn't be home until five-thirty or later and it was his dad who would often start something on the stove, leading them to eat around six-thirty or seven o'clock. This suited Charlie well as he could eat what he wanted when he got home, and usually slip away for his own private time before dinner.

"See you," he said to his dad as he passed with his plate of pasta to head up to his room. He didn't think his dad even noticed that Charlie had left his backpack on the bench.

Charlie got to the top of the staircase, which opened into a narrow hallway either side of the landing. The house being designed for maximum square footage rather than architectural appeal, there were four bedrooms over the four corners of the house. His parents' room had its own bathroom and was to his left, over the kitchen at the rear of the house. His room was past the shared bathroom at the right and front of the house, over his dad's office. Charlie came to it and entered.

The room was sparsely decorated but the first thing that would likely draw one's eye was a large poster, over the bed and on the far wall, of the heavy rock band, Disturbed. *The Guy*, as he was called, had flaming orange eyes that burned beneath a gray cloak, seemingly staring at Charlie as he entered. Charlie was not really a fan of heavy rock bands, but he tried to like the music because Geoff did, and he wasn't going to put posters up of his favorite books and classical composers like a nerd. So, the walls had a couple of shelves with a few books, The Guy, and a poster of Kate Upton in a bikini that his mother hated. He hadn't been on any dates—he didn't know how he could work up the nerve. He liked girls, though, he felt *pretty* sure of that, but he also really felt close with Geoff and it could be confusing at times.

Under the poster was a small, single bed in the rear corner of the room. The headboard lay against the wall, and to its right at the level of Charlie's shoulders, was a small window overlooking the square postage stamp of green that his parents called a yard. His parents had planned to build a deck, but hadn't gotten around to it yet, so there were just stone pavers by the back door with a couple of loungers and an outdoor table and chair set on them. The only part of the yard that looked truly cared for were his mother's rose bushes. They framed an L-shape around the edge of the pavers by the table and Charlie was often drawn to their bright red color when they were in bloom.

He pulled himself back from the window. He had a wooden desk next to the door, and overtop of it were a couple of shelves with some books and a microscope set his parents had gotten him for Christmas the year they had moved here. He had looked at it on Christmas Day, but it had remained in the box ever since. He sat on the chair and pulled Netflix up on his phone.

A text bubble from Geoff interrupted the program.

Wanna come over Saturday? Xbox?

Xbox was their code for *smoke some weed*. Geoff lived a few blocks away and they had met during a summer writing camp that their mothers had enrolled them in last year to encourage their interests. It was fun, and Geoff and

Charlie had bonded over their love of good books and films.

Sure. Let's talk at lunch, Charlie replied.

Charlie would be sixteen in July, but Geoff had already turned seventeen last month. Geoff was in the eleventh grade and he spent every other weekend in Kalamazoo at his dad's place. It had been a pain the previous spring, with Geoff's mother and father, being recently divorced, having to meet at a gas station somewhere near Ann Arbor, in some kind of one-sided prisoner exchange. But last summer, Geoff got his license and his father had promptly bought him a used VW Golf so that he could now drive himself back and forth.

Charlie liked hanging out with Geoff for lots of reasons. He was more mature than Charlie's classmates and he understood and liked the things Charlie was into. Charlie still kept in touch with Gabriel and Michael, his best friends from Ferndale, but with his parents only having one vehicle visiting each other was difficult. They would send snaps to each other like little lifelines and they sometimes teased him about thinking he was better than them now because he was in Birmingham. *Soon,* they said, *you'll be off to Country Day or Cranbrook.* Even though Charlie knew that would never happen, it still stung and Charlie could feel them slipping away.

He couldn't get into his Netflix show and abandoned it ten minutes in as he was tired. He fell into his bed and slept until a text from his mother woke him.

Dinnertime.

As he made his way groggily down the stairs, he could hear his parents.

"...so, Shelley got the assistant manager's job. I've been there over two years and she's only been there a couple months," his mother's voice said.

"Did you talk to Marty about it?"

"I couldn't get a straight answer out of him. You know, I sometimes wonder if she's sleeping with him."

"Whoa?! How do you know that? Wait, are you worried about your job?"

"What?! No," his mother said, as though his father had no clue what he was talking about.

Charlie paused near the bottom of the stairs, eavesdropping.

"Maybe I should try to get my college degree after all. Everybody else who works there has one. Marty hinted that he could help with that, put me on part time. We'd have to pay the tuition though."

It was silent for a moment.

"Julia, we've got a mortgage payment now, much bigger than our rent was, the car payment, your clothing bills, and I'm not working much myself right now. We need your income more than ever."

"What the fuck does *my clothing* have to do with this?! You weren't worried about money when you decided we should get the BMW. What about the money that just came from your father's estate?"

"That's for retirement. Or emergencies."

"I guess we really were in deep shit before, then," she said, sounding pissed. "And maybe this *is* an emergency. I don't want to be a glorified secretary forever."

Charlie blushed.

"Don, I want to go. I *need* to go," Julia finally pleaded.

"Charlie's grades are slipping," his father said abruptly. Charlie wondered why he'd brought that up now.

"What?"

"Math and science have gone from A to B minuses. Both," his father said.

"Did you talk to him about it?"

"Yes, he's going to study harder."

Charlie frowned.

"Does he need tutoring?" Julia asked.

"I don't know. If his grades don't come back up, he won't be able to handle AP next year."

"Let's not push too hard," his mother declared, bringing her prescription for what she clearly thought Charlie needed. "He's a sensitive kid. He's just going through what every teenager does."

"I know. But he needs boundaries, and he needs a push now and then. He just doesn't seem motivated to do anything but play video games and sleep."

Charlie cringed at his father's image of him. He didn't understand anything. Class was boring because it was so remedial for Charlie, and his daydreams were much more interesting. His parents thought he wasn't motivated, but his problem was he cared too much—about his grades, what other people thought, what his parents thought, about his future and the future of the planet. He worried about so many things, there were times he thought his mind would explode.

"I'd better check on him," his mother said. "Charlie?" She said it like a singsong bird call, pitching up on the "Char" and down on the "lie," extending both syllables.

He started walking as though he'd just reached the bottom of the steps.

"Oh," his mother said. "There you are. It's dinner time."

They sat mostly in silence at dinner, his mother and father having exhausted substantive conversation and having just enough energy left for small talk.

"I might go over to Geoff's tomorrow night, play some Xbox," Charlie said matter-of-factly.

"Only if your homework is done. You need to get those grades back up." There was his father, setting the ground rules.

"I know."

They finished in silence.

****

"Wait till you try this stuff out. My cousin got it from somebody out in Colorado. It's called Red Dragon."

Geoff lived with his mother and sister in a small house on Wallace Street. It was just past Linden Park on the other side of Southfield, and only a twenty-minute walk from Charlie's place. They sat in Geoff's backyard at a cheap box-store table and chair set, the weeds poking up between the pavers at their feet. The yard was private, with eight-foot arborvitaes lining the three sides at the back, making it feel like they'd escaped into some secret garden. The sun had just set to Charlie's left over the bushes, and it was growing dark.

Charlie sat back in the chair, the hard metal of the chair back pressing against him. A pizza box lay empty between them, and Geoff leaned back on the matching chair opposite. They both lit up and smoked and as the familiar sour smell drifted between them, Geoff tucked his frizzy, shoulder-length brown hair behind his ears and smiled, his crooked teeth gleaming in the pure white of the LED porch light at the back of the house. He watched Charlie, as though to gauge his reaction to the Dragon.

Charlie felt his muscles release and his nerves go numb. It was as though he'd entered a zero-g world - everything seemed so light, and the hard chair melted into velour. He couldn't understand how he ever could have worried about anything.

"It's almost May. Soon, my grandpa will be taking the boat out again," he said slowly and deliberately, as though just realizing these things for the first time.

"I could take you there. I'm going to my dad's next weekend."

"My parents would never let me. They took a shit when we went there without telling them last fall, remember?"

"They let me take you last summer, before that," Geoff said ambivalent.

"That was then," Charlie said. "They are on my ass about grades now. My dad's gotten strict."

"Darth Vader?"

This was their nickname for Charlie's dad and Geoff loved to use it whenever he could. "He's harmless."

"I'll ask this week," Charlie said.

"Do, or do not. There is no ask," Geoff said, putting on his best Yoda impersonation. Charlie snorted; it was hilarious.

"Yeah, yeah. I just don't need the hassle."

"So? You'll get grounded for a bit. It'll totally be worth it."

Geoff's sister, Maureen, poked her head out of the patio door. "You guys aren't supposed to be smoking!"

She was eleven and clearly loved to take the opportunity to raise hell with her older brother.

"Mom smokes all the time. Get back inside and watch TV," Geoff said over his shoulder.

"Where is your mom tonight?" Charlie asked.

"Out on a date with *some guy*," Geoff replied, taking a long drag and sitting back.

Tina could always be counted on to be out on Saturday nights, clearly relishing the freedom that Geoff and Maureen's ages afforded her. Liberated, to hear her tell it, from the *overbearing bonds of her ex-husband*. She didn't seem to worry too much about Geoff and Maureen, and they reciprocated. Nobody in the household wanted to ask too many questions, or dig too deep, as they all had what they wanted. Geoff had once told Charlie that his greatest fear was that one of his mother's random encounters would turn serious, upsetting the status quo.

"You're almost sixteen, dude. In two more years, they won't be able to tell you shit."

Two years. That felt like forever.

"I'll drop you right at his door. Easy, peasy," Geoff emphasized, spreading his arms wide.

"Yeah, that might be awesome." The idea began to grow in stature in Charlie's brain.

"I love you, man," was all he could think to say.

CHAPTER TWENTY-NINE

Don

AUGUST 2019

DON PULLED INTO THE parking lot across from the church beside the Ave Maria Religious Shop advertising *Libros y Artículos Católicos* and looking around he realized he had forgotten just how run-down this area was. He thought of when Julia had first brought him here, and how she had been so determined to show him everything. At the time he had sensed that it meant something to her—walking together through her old neighborhood, and that it was *important* sharing this with him, revealing a deeply held part of herself. He decided now that it wasn't pride on her part, touring him through the streets to her old church and the old house, rather, it was something like defiance. She had been daring him to judge her.

He always sensed that she hated the fact that she grew up here and that she almost took it as personal *flaw* of hers, like the birthmark on her hip. It didn't matter to Don; Julia could have come from the gutter for all he cared. He wondered if he ever told her, and if he did, had she believed him?

He decided to text Diane.

I made it safe and sound. Did you see my note?

Don watched the bubbles dance on his phone.

Yes. Thanks. I'll be thinking of you today.

He typed clumsily. *Thanks. I think I'll be ok. Take your time. Help yourself to the little I have in the fridge.*

I'm going to get some groceries for you and clean the place up a bit.

Don inhaled sharply. This was intimate and he suddenly regretted signing his note as he did.

He typed again: *You don't have to do that.*

I want to. And you can't stop me :-)

Don paused, before typing: *Thanks. Got to go. I'll text you after.*

He took a deep breath, got out of the truck and quickly surveyed its gray exterior. He had taken the time to run it through the car wash during a gas stop on the way down, exposing the truck's weaknesses for all to see. He took note of the rust that was beginning to eat away at the bottom of the doors and checked his watch—ten fifty a.m. His wrist felt weird, and he realized that he hadn't worn a watch in nearly three years.

Mourners passed him by, all dressed for the occasion, and he wondered who the hell they were. Like extras in some horror movie, they shambled past him to cross the street, making him wish he could just blend in.

Put one foot in front of the other and you'll get through this, he told himself.

Just then, he heard a voice to his right.

"Don! Don, we're so sorry."

It was Dave Wight, walking up to the truck, alone.

"Dave. Thanks."

They briefly hugged before Don inquired, "Where's Lisa?"

"Oh, she's in with Julia. I just had to come back out to get her reading glasses. She left them in the car."

"Thanks for coming."

"Of course," Dave coughed uncomfortably before continuing, "Sorry it's been so long, we should catch up...at the lunch."

"Yeah. See you then."

Dave seemed happy to postpone the awkwardness. "Hey, let me know if there's anything we can do," he added, already stepping backwards from the side of the truck.

Sure. Just bring Charlie back for me and erase these last four years please, Don thought.

"Thanks. Will do," he muttered.

Dave jogged away eagerly, as though Lisa's glasses were needed for some lifesaving procedure, and Don continued his slow walk across the street to the church.

As he passed through the doorway, his eyes immediately fixed on the coffin straight ahead before the altar. There was a picture of Charlie on an easel to the left, but it was too far away to see clearly. Don closed his eyes and tried to picture his son. He was afraid he would faint; he fumbled for a pew and held on.

Steadying himself, he scanned the church and could see that there were fewer than fifty people scattered around in the pews. He saw Lisa and Dave with Julia – and was it David beside them at the front, on the right-hand side?

For two years after Julia had left, Don had rehearsed a fantasy meeting with her. Sometimes, it would be at a coffee shop, or Rick's. He had also imagined a romantic gesture, like dinner at The Sidetrack, maybe on their anniversary. He'd bring roses, her favorite flowers, and apologize for everything. He could never quite frame the speech in his mind, he just vaguely imagined his words conveying the right sentiments to melt her resistance.

In his fantasy she wouldn't argue, she would just listen patiently and accept his explanations. Then, the guilt and anger would evaporate and he would imagine her face softening, her hand reaching out for his.

I've missed you too, she would say. *Of course, we belong together, Don. You're the only one who ever understood me.*

Of course, he was. There could be no one else for her.

Organ music brought Don back from his daydream. Yes, he'd imagined this meeting a thousand times, but never at Charlie's funeral. He quickly took a seat to his left at the back of the church and bowed his head.

CHAPTER THIRTY

Charlie

MAY 2015

CHARLIE CAUGHT HELL FOR not letting his parents know he was sleeping over at Geoff's.

"You know our rules," his dad said, sternly. "If you aren't going to be home, you call."

"Were you guys drinking last night?" Julia asked. It was harder to lie to her. Luckily, he didn't have to on this point.

"No. We just had some pizza and played Xbox."

"Was his mother home?"

"She was out for a bit and came in later." *At two a.m., plastered,* he thought to himself.

This had been a fluid point for his parents. They didn't seem to know or agree on whether it was okay for him to be at a friend's house without adult supervision and they had even argued about it openly in front of him. He knew his mother felt some guilt for uprooting him two years ago and wanted to encourage his friendships. His father, ever logical, seemed to have an invisible manual that covered just this circumstance and he returned to it over and over again.

"Okay. I'll ask first next time."

He'd made sure to check his eyes for redness before going home to face the interrogation that Sunday. Geoff had given him a bag of weed to bring back, and Charlie had hidden it in a pocket in his laptop bag. He would have to re-hide it somewhere in his room for safekeeping.

He tried to do some homework that Sunday afternoon but couldn't concentrate. His mind kept drifting to thoughts of his grandfather and the boat, bringing memories of Grandpa Rydell and sunset cruises. Everybody laughing and shining in the sun and swimming off the back of the boat, a mile out from shore. Eating sandwiches and drinking ice-cold Cokes around the little aft table. Learning to water ski.

Sometimes the memories were so good, so perfect, Charlie wondered if they were just a vivid dream he'd had. Going to Grandpa McCarthy's was a touchstone for him, a pinch to prove it was all real, and these days he felt the need to pinch himself more often than ever.

He had been upset, at first, when his parents had given the boat to Grandpa McCarthy. It was *theirs* and he didn't want to part with it. He didn't understand what the gift had meant to his grandfather at the time, so he complained at every opportunity to his parents. He finally guilted them into the promise of a new boat *next year*. A promise that, like others, had been broken.

Grandpa McCarthy was not a waterskiing kind of guy like Grandpa Rydell. He liked slow cruising or anchoring a mile out and reading. Still, the first of the precious few weekends they'd spent together last year had been wonderful. His reunion with his grandfather and *his boat,* without a cloud in the sky. Charlie, with his shirt off, laying at the front of the boat, burning in the sun then jumping in to cool off.

Grandpa, always sitting at the the little table at the back. Smoking and reading.

"You should learn your heritage," his grandfather had said one Saturday afternoon while they bobbed lazily on the water.

"My heritage?" Charlie had asked, puzzled.

"Your mother carries more of your grandmother's genes in her, I think. But you're at least one quarter Irish. We'll start with Yeats and work our way from there."

Charlie hadn't had the foggiest idea what his grandfather was talking about, but he had soon fallen under his spell.

He didn't know if it had been the sun, or the sound of his grandfather's smooth Irish voice, or the rolling of the waves, or all of them together, but he'd felt hypnotized that day. He couldn't remember all of what his grandfather had read to him, but he knew the first poem by heart. He'd reread the copy David had given him over and over:

Where dips the rocky highland

Of Sleuth Wood in the lake,

There lies a sleepy island

Where flapping herons wake

The drowsy water rats;

There we've hid our faery vats,

Full of berries

And of reddest stolen cherries.

Charlie found himself dozing at his desk. He tried to go back to his studying but he could smell garlic and onion coming up from the kitchen below and knew it would be dinnertime soon.

That week at school turned out to be uneventful, but he found himself fighting knots in his stomach as the weekend approached. He was a model citizen at home, helping with dishes, doing his homework, subconsciously accruing goodwill ahead of his premeditated sin. Friday morning, he stuffed some underwear, socks, and a T-shirt into his backpack and left for school. His mom had already left for work and his dad was in his office working.

"Have a good day at school. See you tonight," his father said casually, looking up briefly from his tablet.

"Bye," Charlie said, not wanting to acknowledge the lie.

He met Geoff in the school parking lot at three thirty in the afternoon, feeling sick. Guilty at deceiving his parents, he thought about calling it off.

"Hey bud, ready to go?" Geoff smiled, waving from the window of the Golf.

"Yeah," Charlie said, throwing his backpack in the rear seat, and jumping into the front. As he felt the click of his seatbelt, his fingers tingled against the cold steel of the buckle and he realized that he was now a passenger, an amusement park patron who had just been harnessed into a rollercoaster with no turning back. "Let's go," he nearly shouted.

The drive was uneventful, but about halfway, around five, he'd gotten a text from his father.

Charlie, where r u?

Then, a minute later: *U know the rules.*

Charlie turned the phone off.

They pulled up to his grandfather's place just as the sun had disappeared, bringing cold dusk. It had taken three hours to make the drive, Geoff being cautious with his speed and the traffic being thick at times.

David's house was a simple one-story building with green siding and black trim. Two front windows, bleeding yellow light and flanking a black entry door, stared back at them. *That looks like a green Halloween pumpkin, how weird,* Charlie thought as they sat in the gravel driveway, the Golf's engine idling quietly.

"You want me to wait while you see if he's home?" Geoff offered.

"Nah, you need to get to your dad's before it's totally dark. I know where the spare key is hidden." Charlie grabbed his stuff and closed the door.

Geoff waved, a single salute. "Text me Sunday. I usually go around two, but we can decide then."

Charlie waved back and turned toward the house.

He knocked on the door and his grandfather answered. He was a little disheveled, with unkempt hair and a floral button-up shirt untucked over dirty jeans.

"Charlie!" he said and reached both arms out to embrace his grandson. Then, puzzled he asked, "Where's your mom and dad?" He looked around Charlie to the driveway.

"I came without them, Grandpa. I wanted to see you."

"How'd you get here?"

"Geoff dropped me off."

"That was nice of him. I didn't know you were coming. Come in."

Charlie and his parents called David a few times a month, checking in on what was new and sharing their news of the week. It was rare that they had the time to make the trip as a family all the way out to Saint Joseph. David couldn't visit them either as he no longer had a car, which Charlie's mother had said was probably for the best.

They went back into the small home to the kitchen at the rear. Two bedrooms were mirrored around the entrance at the front of the house, the living room and kitchen were at the back of the home. It was an open concept and Charlie could see a glass of amber liquid on a little table by an easy chair in the living room. The television was blaring some news program.

"Can I get you a Coke?" David said, turning down the volume on the TV with a remote.

"Sure, that'd be great, Grandpa."

Charlie sat on a chair at the kitchen table.

"Do your parents know you're here?" David asked, obscured by the door of the fridge. A hopeful shield from the truth.

Charlie paused. He didn't want to lie to his grandfather.

"No," he confessed, feeling slightly relieved at the effort.

"They'll be worried sick. I'm going to call them right away."

Charlie could only hear his grandfather's side of the conversation, but there was a loud female voice on the other end, he could discern that much.

"Charlie's here at my place." David paused, listening

"About half hour ago. Geoff dropped him." Another pause.

"No, wait." His grandfather pulled his cell phone from his ear and looked at the side of it before putting it back against his head. "Shit, it was on mute. That's why I didn't hear the phone ring earlier. Sorry, I forgot to turn it back on this morning.

"No, he's gone now.

"Yes, he's fine.

"He can stay with me until tomorrow.

"Sure. Whatever works.

"It's okay. He's okay."

Then his grandfather turned to him.

"They want to talk to you."

Charlie grabbed the phone. "Mom?"

He sounded more like a lost ten-year-old than a teenager of almost sixteen.

"Charlie," his mother exhaled. "You had us worried sick! What were you thinking?! We were about to call the police." Her relief was winding up into anger.

"I just wanted to see grandpa. Help him get the boat in."

"You need to ask permission. You can't run off like that, Charlie. We've been through this before."

"I know, Mom. I'm sorry. I won't do it again."

"No, you won't," she said. "Your father wants to talk to you."

Charlie's shoulders stiffened.

"Charlie. Don't you ever pull a stunt like this again. You hear me?" His father's voice was shaking with rage.

"Yes."

"First thing tomorrow, I'm heading up there to get you."

He must really be pissed if he's willing to make a six-hour round-trip drive to get me, Charlie thought.

"Can I talk to Mom, please?" he said.

"Well talk about your punishment when I see you."

Then, his mother's voice came on the phone. "Yes, Charlie?" Her voice was flat, emotionless.

"Dad doesn't need to make that long drive. I don't want to make more trouble with this. It was stupid and I know that. Geoff can bring me home first thing Sunday. This way, I can help grandpa out a bit and visit with him."

"I'll talk it over with your father. But don't think you won't be punished for this."

In the end, the elixir of mercy, convenience, and guilt proved effective, and they'd agreed to let him stay with David until Sunday. But he was to leave his phone on and respond to all texts immediately. David set Charlie up in the spare bedroom, moving clothing and other clutter off of the bed to do so.

"That was stupid," he said as they retired for the night.

"I know."

"We'll see to putting the boat in in the morning," David said smiling as he closed Charlie's door.

It was cold but sunny that weekend, and Charlie and David spent a good part of Saturday on the water. His parents only ended up texting once. Geoff arrived at noon on Sunday to take Charlie home.

Charlie waved bye to his grandfather, threw his bag in the back seat of the Golf, and got in the front. They backed out of the driveway, waving.

"Good weekend?" Geoff asked somewhat rhetorically, as they had been texting back and forth.

"Yeah," Charlie said. "It *was* totally worth it."

They passed Benton Harbor and pulled onto I-94.

Geoff hit the accelerator and they punched east, toward Don and Julia's wrath.

CHAPTER THIRTY-ONE

Julia

AUGUST 2019

JULIA WATCHED AS LISA breezed through the hotel lobby—a bundle of pent-up energy packed into her five-foot-three frame. She was a petite woman with short blonde hair in a bob and a smile of perfect teeth under ice-blue eyes. Today Lisa was sporting a gray pantsuit, with a brown Louis Vuitton bag tucked firmly under her arm as she hustled over to where Julia stood by the Starbucks kiosk.

"I'm not going to ask how you are dear, but did you manage to sleep last night?" Lisa asked sweetly.

Julia considered the question. Sometimes it was just easier to lie. "Yeah. I slept okay."

"Well, I've been over to the church and things are ready. You don't need to worry about a thing."

"I want to pick my father up to get him to the church, so he doesn't have to drive," Julia said.

David now lived walking distance to the marina and a store, and until yesterday hadn't driven in years, and Julia thought, for the first time, about how much her father's world had gradually shrunk in the twenty years since Isabella's death. *Maybe that's how it is*, she pondered, *We grow up and our world expands, then we get old and it shrinks. You don't even know it when you're there – the point where your life is as big as it's going to be. You only know it*, she thought, *after the fact.* When you look back and realize it's been years since you went anywhere, or tried anything new, and your world has been closing in on you without you even noticing. Shrinking until it's just a home, a bedroom, a bed. Rare and lucky was the person who passed from a big world to the great beyond. *Charlie was one*, Julia thought, as she wondered where she stood on that morbid continuum. She had woken up feeling good about her dinner with her father, but she was a little nervous about him speaking today and her somber thoughts didn't help.

Julia considered the coffee board while Lisa tapped away on her phone.

"Can I help you?" the barista asked, smiling.

"Uh, a tall cappuccino for me, and..." Julia glanced back at Lisa, who sensed the pause. Lisa looked up from her phone, thumbs frozen over the virtual keyboard. "Tall black for me, thanks." Her thumbs immediately returning to their tap dancing the moment she finished speaking.

"Name?"

"Julia."

"That'll be eight forty-six."

What had happened to manners? Julia wondered as she handed the girl a ten. She put the change into the tip jar, her brief time at Rick's so long ago having ingrained in her a sense of kinship with hospitality staff.

They moved to the end of the counter to wait.

"Okay." Lisa returned her phone to her purse. "Dave will pick us up out front at ten. We can go get your dad and then we should be at the church by ten thirty. Plenty of time."

Julia texted her father to inform him of the plans, and he responded affirmatively.

"Did you talk to Father Willis about the eulogy?" Julia asked.

"Taken care of. He'll invite your dad up to the lectern. He just has to move the microphone to where it's comfortable and talk."

"Thanks."

They grabbed their coffees, found a table, and Julia noticed as they sat down that it said *Julie* on her cup.

She then watched as Lisa put three sugars in her coffee; the woman was a hummingbird and Julia briefly envied her metabolism.

"Have you talked to Don?" Lisa asked after a few silent sips of coffee, without looking up from her cup.

"No. He doesn't have my phone number or e-mail."

"I know, remember?" Lisa replied, looking up. "I just thought you might have reached out. You have his."

"I don't even know for sure if he's going to be there."

"He's going to be there, Julia. Trust me."

"I'm afraid it will just be awkward. I don't want it to be, but it will be. And I don't want Don to go through that," Julia added. "Four years ago, when we split up, I said a lot of things. Things I shouldn't have."

"You were grieving," Lisa said, shrugging her shoulders as though Don was sitting with them at the table, and she could make the case to him directly. "You don't need to apologize for things you *might* have said at a time like that. It's totally understandable."

Was it? Julia wondered. Four years ago, she'd channeled everything bitter she'd felt at that man. That man she'd once loved. *Maybe did still love on some level,* she thought. She had projected all her regret, self-loathing, and grief onto him, and, as with her father, she now knew that hadn't been fair. She wondered what life had been like for Don these last couple of years, after they'd sold the house. Tucked away at the cabin. Isolated.

Or maybe he'd found love again and was happy with another woman. When she thought of him, and she wasn't feeling sorry for herself, she often chose that scenario. Don and a mystery woman taking long walks in the woods, snuggling under a blanket by the fire, sitting with coffee on the front porch, listening to the birds. She pictured them shopping in town for antiques and could almost hear the sweet voice of her nebulous replacement. *That copper pitcher will go great by the fire Don, don't you think?*

She blinked and twisted her head to the left. *Shit. Gerrard.* "Lisa, can you excuse me for a minute please?"

"Sure, sweetie, I'll be right here."

Julia got up and found an alcove near the washrooms and called Gerrard.

"Hey."

"Hey. I saw your text when I got up. I'm glad the Blackburn meeting went well," Julia said.

"Thanks. How are you, love? I was starting to worry but didn't want to disturb you. I know this day can't be easy. Is the hotel okay? Are you eating?"

Julia thought that women were supposed to gravitate to men that reminded them of their fathers, but Gerrard was more like her mother, needing to focus on the little details to point out how much he cared. She wondered what a psychologist would make of that, but it was probably the least of her pathologies.

"I'll be okay. It's fine. I changed my return flight though. I leave late Tuesday and get into Heathrow around eight Wednesday morning now because the burial isn't until four in the afternoon on Monday. I thought it was going to be earlier. There was a hundred pound change fee."

"Oh, That's unfortunate. I have to survive without you for another day," he said, pausing briefly before continuing, "I'm swamped on Wednesday, but no worries, I'll get someone to pick you up in any event. I'll be thinking of you today, love."

"Thanks, Ger. I'll talk to you later," Julia said softly as she disconnected the call.

Speaking with Gerrard had turned Julia's mind inward towards her womb, and the complication she'd have to deal with when she got back to England. *One mess at a time,* she thought.

The call had been a convenient way to interrupt Lisa's line of questioning, and when Julia returned to the table, they moved back to small talk of lunch plans and travel and *wouldn't it be nice to get together under better circumstances,* before exiting the hotel to the car and the next steps in what Julia knew would be a very difficult day.

They stopped outside David's hotel to see that he was already outside waiting. He was in the same suit he had worn to Isabella's funeral, but it looked better on him now. Julia got out and embraced him, and after getting back into Dave and Lisa's Escalade they made their way to the church. It was ten forty when they parked and crossed into Holy Redeemer where they quickly took their seats near the front. Julia looked back, scanning the congregation and finding no sign of Don. She went alone up to the closed coffin, again feeling angry that she'd been denied a proper goodbye with her only child.

There's nothing to be done for it now, she thought, *this is not him. He is gone, and these are only remains.*

Lisa had arranged for Charlie's ninth grade class picture to be placed beside the coffin on an easel, and despite

Julia's admonition to herself, the sight of the picture made everything real.

She felt waves of emotion rolling through her, unstoppable now in their ferocity, a storm that had to be endured for however long it lasted. She internally recited her well-worn rites, attempting to telepathically commune with Charlie's photo. - *What happened to you, Charlie? Why? Why wasn't I there for you? I shouldn't have gone to work. We shouldn't have pushed you so hard in school. We shouldn't have let you fall in love with that boat. Should have drilled you more about safety. Cut you off more firmly from Geoff. Called the police sooner,* and on, and on. She had to press these pointless replays down, for the Charlie that stared back at her was innocent of these things. They had not happened in his world, and he couldn't answer her even if he were flesh and blood standing before her.

She rested her hand lightly on the coffin and whispered, "I love you, Charlie. I hope you are at peace." Weeping, she turned back, crossed to their pew, and embraced her father.

The organ began to play, and Father Willis followed a brief procession into the church. The smell of incense drifted from a silver ball he was waving, and Julia felt her stomach lurch. She turned back briefly under the guise of observing the procession and saw him. Don was alone at the back of the church in his navy suit, the one she had helped him pick out once upon a time. He saw her and lifted his hand, palm outward in a timid motionless greeting. She mirrored the gesture and offered him a grim smile, then turned her head forward again.

"The grace of our Lord Jesus Christ and the love of God and the fellowship of the Holy Spirit be with you all," Father Willis intoned.

"And also with you," the congregation replied in unison.

Father Willis flicked a silver ball at the coffin, sprinkling holy water on it.

"In the waters of baptism, Charlie died with Christ and rose with him to new life. May he now share with him in eternal glory," the priest continued.

There was music and a nice reading from Lisa and words from Father Willis. But to Julia, it all became like a droning in her ears and she thought maybe she was getting a migraine.

"David McCarthy, Charlie's grandfather, will now say a few words." Father Willis gestured toward Julia's father, and Julia was drawn out of her trance upon hearing his name spoken aloud.

David stretched himself up and walked deliberately up to the lectern. "Thank you," he said, as he pulled a folded piece of paper from his pocket and put it on the shelf in front of him, his hands trembling.

"I had the good fortune of being Charlie's grandfather." David's face was twisting, his voice uneven. "It was not easy to get to know Charlie. For many of you, he may have seemed quiet, maybe shy, introverted even. Like many teenagers his age." David looked down at his page of notes, picking them back up to bring them into better focus.

"But I had the pleasure of getting to know the *real* Charlie. He was intelligent and passionate, like his mother." David said, as he looked fondly at Julia. "He was well read on so many topics, so interested in the pursuits of his elders, and in this way, Charlie was *nothing* like most teenagers his age. He was older than his years and he cared *deeply* about so many things.

"He was kind and thoughtful, like his father. He visited me, a precious few weekends, over the last couple years of his all-too-brief life and he was always asking to help out, to help me with things around the house, with my boat." David's voice cracked at the mention of the source of their collective grief and the page began to shake more violently in his trembling hand.

"Charlie loved the water so much," he continued, pausing for a deep breath. "I spent a lot of nights after Charlie's death wishing I'd never let him near the boat. Forbid him from it. But it has been said many times, that if you love someone, you have to set them free. He was the happiest on that boat, and I couldn't deny him," David paused to look across the congregation. "So, now, I try to think back on the times we *did* share together, cruising on a sunny day, or just reading poetry and watching the sunset. Talking about his dreams for the future."

David stopped to wipe his eyes with a handkerchief. "He wanted to be a writer and I think he would have been a great one. He was so observant and smart. I wish," David sniffled, "I wish I could just read one thing by him, for I know it would have been wonderful. For a young man his age he knew *so much* about God's world, and the miserable creatures in it. He knew of sorrow and longing…he knew of lust and weakness. But most of all, he knew of love.

"He loved his mother and father. I knew that just from the way he'd talk about them while we were together and the stories we'd share. And I know he loved me, and I him. I'll miss him dearly."

Tears were flowing freely and silently down David's cheeks, pooling at the sides of his chin and threatening to fall. He continued, "I'd like to finish with a short poem by Yeats that Charlie and I liked:

'I will arise and go now, for always night and day

I hear lake water lapping with low sounds by the shore;

While I stand on the roadway, or on the pavements grey,

I hear it in the deep heart's core.'"

Julia found herself weeping too, and she silently embraced her father as he returned to their pew. He had forgotten to grab his paper.

The service ended and Father Willis and the ushers processed out with the coffin, sending Charlie onward in his journey. Julia stayed behind at the front of the church. She couldn't bear to watch them put Charlie in the hearse, so she watched as the coffin slowly shrank out the front doors and then turned her gaze back to the altar. Soon, the coffin would all be burned to ash and she fought an irrational urge to chase after it, to stop them from immolating her child. Finally, she forced herself to get moving again. She wanted to talk to Don when the congregation dispersed, but first she had a thought to take her father's notes, as a keepsake. She went to the lectern and grabbed the page, gently refolding it and tucking it in her purse.

Chapter Thirty-Two

Charlie

May 2015

THE TOILET FLUSHED AS Charlie and Don looked on.

"Now it's time to go start on your homework," his father said, his face strained red from the effort of holding back emotion, as a tangle of green spun down to oblivion.

Pain relief for the sewer rats, Charlie thought.

Charlie wondered if his father knew how predictable his rants were. They would come on strong, filled with anger, threats and punishment, and could last a few days. Then, as his father was distracted by other things, he would calm down and the new rules would be relaxed, sometimes even with an apology for overreacting. Charlie thought that his mother's influence was responsible for slowly chipping away at whatever rules his dad tried to apply, as she hated to see her son upset. But Charlie feared that this time might be different.

He'd gone home today, like any other day, expecting to just roll with his usual routine. He had noticed his mom's car in the driveway and he didn't even guess at the reason this time; he was so self-absorbed, so sure it had nothing to do with him. But when he'd come into the house, his parents had both been at the kitchen table, waiting.

He had tried to read the room, still oblivious to what was going on. His father's face was set hard, like someone engaged in a staring contest and he now couldn't remember if he even saw him blink. His mother, still dressed for work in a simple green dress, her dark hair down and heels still on her feet, had her head slightly turned, a look of pity on her face. For the first time, he noticed wrinkles around her eyes. His first thought was that they were going to tell him that his grandfather had died.

"Hey," he'd said, trying to force the news away. "You look nice, Mom. Why are you home so early?"

"We want to talk to you about something, Charlie. Come sit down." His father's even tone stood in stark contrast to the look on his face.

"Okaaaayyy. This looks serious," Charlie had replied, trying to lighten the mood while dropping his backpack and moving slowly to the table. All he had wanted at that moment was the power to be invisible, to just be left alone to go to his room in peace.

The three of them sat in silence, Charlie flanked by his mother and father. His father had given his mother a wall clock years ago, it was round with a backdrop of flowers—a disposable Christmas gift that she had, for some reason, treasured. It now hung on the wall to the left of the fridge and Charlie could hear it ticking. It seemed so loud and he'd never noticed that before. *Was it really only four-oh-five?*

"Charlie," his mother spoke. Her hands were folded in front of her, as though she feared they might do something unpredictable if not restrained, perhaps hit him. "We've been worried about you. Going off to your grandfather's again without asking."

Why were they going to rehash this?

"Your grades are slipping. You've missed four classes in the last two weeks."

She produced a piece of paper from the unoccupied chair beside her.

Evidence.

His stomach sank as he stared at the page.

Ernest W. Seaholm. The white "S" logo on a circle of red. It said *Academic Attendance Record* at the top.

What a strange piece of paper, he'd thought. *Why did she bother to print that?* Everything was online now.

His parents sat, stone statues glaring at him.

Was he supposed to say something?

"Uh, I wasn't feeling well. I went to the cafeteria to study by myself."

That was the best he could come up with, and he felt his cheeks beginning to burn. He was supposed to come home, head to his room, play some games, take a nap. No interaction until dinner at the earliest.

He saw motion to his left where his father had flicked something onto the table. Charlie stared at a bag of what looked like…weed.

Huh. Where did that come from? he wondered briefly, before the neurons in his brain could connect the correct pathways.

That's mine. They searched my room. This is some kind of—intervention? His stomach did a slow-motion somersault.

"You know what this is?" his father had asked. Like he wanted to draw things out, maybe savor the torture.

Okay, you've made your point, Charlie wanted to say. *What's my punishment? Now can I go to my room?*

Instead, determined to go down swinging, he replied, "It's not mine."

"Charlie," his mother said in a tone which implied, *Give me a break.* "We weren't born yesterday."

"How long have you been smoking marijuana?" his father asked.

Marijuana.

That word sounded funny and Charlie couldn't remember the last time he'd used it.

"It's Geoff's. I'm keeping it for him." He looked back and forth between the two of them, his thoughts so intense he feared he'd say them out loud. *Please, it will be easier for all of us if you accept this little white lie.*

"I have Tina's number right here," his father said, producing his cell phone. "Shall we call her so you can tell her what you just told us?"

Charlie's brain scrambled. This was a nightmare. His heart hammered in his chest, and he felt sick.

"Geoff gave it to me. To try. I haven't used it yet. I didn't know what to do with it."

"Charlie, we are considering calling the police," his father stated bluntly.

They wouldn't.

"How long have you been using marijuana, Charlie?" This, coming out more like a statement than a question.

Was his father deaf?

"I haven't been. Geoff just gave that to me," Charlie protested.

"When?" Another trap. Charlie quickly tried to guess when they'd found it before answering,

"Last Friday."

"Charlie, we just want what's best for you, you know. We love you." his mother said, softly now.

They continued to exchange platitudes and questions for lies and half answers and Charlie wondered what was the point of it all?

Did they enjoy this?

Finally, his father was ready with his sentence.

"Charlie, there's a program called Harmony Hills. They do boys youth boot camps in the summer. Full time, in residence. Starting the end of June, after school's done."

What. The. Fuck.

"I'll get my grades up. I promise."

"You are not allowed to see Geoff anymore," his father continued.

"Until when?" he'd asked.

"Until ever."

"Come on," Charlie pleaded. "He's the only friend I have at Seaholm!"

"Well, you need to choose some new friends. Better friends. He obviously hasn't been a good influence on you," his father said firmly.

Julia looked down at her hands.

"Mom!" he pleaded to her. "Don't take away my best friend. You moved me here and I hate that I don't have friends like I did in Ferndale. I've tried hard to make new friends. They're all stuck up at this school. I hate this!"

His mother would not meet his eyes, but Charlie thought he had gotten through to her. Maybe she could talk his father down on the punishment, when he'd had a day to calm down. But Charlie wasn't sure.

This felt different.

Charlie's father looked over at his mother before continuing,

"You are to text me when you leave school. I will be waiting here for you. You will do your homework at this table, in the kitchen," his father continued. "While you are doing your homework, I will hold your phone. You are not to have any contact with Geoff. Is that clear?"

"Yes." Charlie felt his stomach sink. Geoff understood him like no one else in this world. Of course, Charlie called Geoff his best friend, but the term somehow didn't seem *big enough* for what they had. When they were apart, he couldn't wait for the next time they would be together, listening to music, talking about the world, playing games. He had been looking forward to the end of the school year, when he and Geoff could spend the summer together, doing things they both loved.

"We expect you to do well on your exams next week. We know you can do better, Charlie," his father said, in a measured tone.

"Charlie," his mother spoke softly. "We put a roof over your head, feed you, *love* you. You have it better than most kids out there and our rules are simple and reasonable. When you break them, you are disrespecting us."

"I know, Mom," he'd said. "I'm really sorry."

Penitence was all he had left.

In the end, he'd talked them out of Harmony Hills and negotiated a lighter sentence, but still home felt like prison – cells tossed every week, no freedoms left. He had told Geoff the truth, mostly. About getting in trouble, about the lockdown. He'd shaded his confession regarding Geoff's part in it though, casting himself as a brave man defiant in the face of his parents' questioning, refusing to give Geoff up and claiming that he gotten the weed elsewhere, implying that the communication ban applied to all his friends. Not that he really had any others. Charlie hoped that he could turn his parents around on this point by the end of the school year. So many problems would vanish with the end of the school term. Three weeks.

He had to hang on for three long weeks.

CHAPTER THIRTY-THREE

Don and Julia

AUGUST 2019

THE SERVICE HAD BEEN beautiful, Don thought. David's eulogy had been touching, especially the recognition he'd afforded Don. Acknowledging that he existed, and that he was grieving along with Julia and David. Don was glad David had been there, for all their sakes.

Just before the service she'd waved to him. He couldn't read the look on her face—it looked like a mixture of pain and relief at the same time. He had wanted to go up and embrace her, comfort her, and it had felt cold for him to stay politely at the back of the church, obeying social convention.

As he looked around at the backs of peoples' heads during the service, not knowing most of them, he resolved to leave for the cabin before the lunch. He would drive back to

Detroit on Monday for the burial but right now, he needed to be in the environment that held his few comforts in life.

And what about Diane? he asked himself.

That was a complication he still couldn't deal with, he could only think of Julia right now. Seeing her had opened a floodgate of memories for him. Memories that came rushing back in unwanted, tearing at callouses and creating fresh wounds as they replayed in his mind.

Julia at Rick's, behind the bar, those green eyes lifting to meet his gaze as she wiped a glass with a rag. Making love in his old rental in Ann Arbor, feeling her warmth beneath him, her hot, sweet breath in his ear. Walking together in the park. Cuddling on the swing, swimming in the pool.

How he'd loved her.

Somehow, his mind only previewed for him the happy memories of Julia, editing out the most painful scenes of the three of them together, and he now felt a burning longing for the past. Oddly, this was almost as painful as the bad memories, the yearning in his soul for something his intellect knew would be forever out of reach.

Most of the parishioners had filed past on their way to lunch but some stopped to shake his hand, nodding thoughtfully - bobbleheads in their suits and dresses. Don attempted to be courteous and appreciative.

Yes, it was a beautiful service. Yes, Charlie was gone way too soon, thank you. Oh, I'm doing okay considering, and so on.

He continued to glance up to monitor Julia's movements. She had gone to the lectern to retrieve something and was now coming his way. Lisa, Dave, and David continued to talk together at the front of the church.

As Julia approached, she offered him a brief smile and said simply, "Don."

So much in that one syllable. Her tone was soft, and it carried no weight. No recriminations or hatred that he could discern.

He wanted to tell her everything in that moment. *How he loved her. How he was so sorry. How he wished everything had been different.* That he would give his life to change it all.

****

Julia took Don in. He was still handsome, perhaps a little lighter than the last time she'd seen him, hair a little thinner. She thought back to that day, the moment she left, backing the BMW out of the driveway to follow the U-Haul, with Don staring at her silently from the end of the driveway, a lost look on his face. As she had driven away on Pleasant Street, she had resolved not to look in the mirror, hadn't wanted to see his pained expression shrinking behind her as she left him for good. But she'd been unable to resist, glancing once to see him, reflected pitifully in miniature above the words – 'Objects in mirror are closer than they appear'. It was an unsettling image that would never leave her.

He had the same pained expression now; he looked like a lost little boy in a grown-up man's suit. She knew what she had to tell him, but she couldn't find the way. It didn't feel right, here, now in this building. She could only utter his name. Acknowledge him. Should she embrace him? Offer her hand? She felt paralyzed.

In the end, he took the initiative and hugged her. It was warm, but brief. She moved on to the ever-comfortable practicalities of life. "Are you staying for the lunch?"

"No, I've got to be going."

"Will you be there on Monday?"

"Yes. Julia, I wouldn't miss it."

"Okay. I'll see you then." She felt relief that she could postpone the conversation.

"It was beautiful. Please thank your father for me."

"I will."

She wanted to call out to him, but instead stood, frozen, as she watched him turn to go.

CHAPTER THIRTY-FOUR

Charlie

JUNE 2015

THE LAST TWO WEEKS had been difficult for Charlie. It had been a cycle of mind-numbing classes followed by cold, wordless dinners, study, then bed. He would wake up to the blaring of his annoying alarm, rise, rinse and repeat. Keeping his distance from Geoff was difficult; though they would acknowledge each other in the halls, they hadn't texted for over a week now. This was making Charlie feel sick inside, and today that queasiness was compounded. *Today*, they would get their final math exams back.

Mr. Gander made his way up and down the aisles between the desks. All the grades would be posted on the school's virtual "blackboard," and his parents would know the results soon, whether Charlie liked it or not. Mr. Gander was old-fashioned and preferred to hand out the papers first. Perhaps he enjoyed torturing the students and savoring their reactions, exacting his petty revenge for their ridicule.

His mustache twitched up and down as he provided inaudible commentary while handing the papers out. He slowly made his way over to Charlie.

"I expected better from you, Charlie," was all he said. A red *C+* screamed at Charlie from the front page and he felt himself sink.

How could this have happened? He pictured the recriminations at dinner. It was Thursday night and a whole weekend lay ahead, bringing with it his parents' full-time attention.

Later, he saw Geoff in the hall after class.

"Hey, Geoff."

"Hey. I'm not supposed to talk to you, remember?"

Okay. I deserved that, Charlie acknowledged to himself.

"Is this your weekend with your dad?" Charlie asked casually, ignoring Geoff's rhetorical question.

Geoff perked up. "Yeah, why?"

"Just curious."

They left it there and Charlie retrieved his things from his locker before the long walk home.

He didn't notice the rain that began to pour down just as he turned onto Pleasant Street, and he was soaking wet when he finally reached his house. The walk seemed faster tonight for some reason and he couldn't even remember how he had gotten home.

The sight of the 328i in the driveway snapped him to attention.

He didn't sleep at all that night. There had been no shouting, no threats. His parents had calmly told him that he needed more structure and they were sorry they hadn't provided him with that.

That would change now. He was their first priority. They were going to spend *five-thousand dollars* to send him to Harmony Hills. That's how much they loved him.

No phone, no outside contact except through a shared computer for one e-mail a day. Work, study, fellowship. They told him it was for his own good. *This was not a punishment; he needed to understand that. They were sacrificing for him.*

He wished they would have shouted—it would have been more comfortable.

He felt shunned.

He got out of bed at six thirty the next morning and texted Geoff: *Can I catch a ride with you tonight?*

He had to wait forty minutes for a response: *You sure that's a good idea?*

Yes.

OK, I guess.

He stuffed some things into his backpack and went downstairs just before eight. His mother had already gone to work, and his father was in his office, already working on his laptop.

"Whatcha working on?" Charlie asked.

Don looked up at Charlie and smiled.

"Well, the Atlantic has hired me to write a piece about Donald Trump's announcement," he said, with an air of pride that Charlie hadn't heard in some time.

"The 'You're Fired' guy?" Charlie asked, puzzled.

"Yep, the same," Don said, nodding firmly in Charlie's direction.

"Cool," Charlie said, distracted. Then, "Bye, Dad."

"Bye, Charlie. I'll see you tonight," Don said, as he furiously tapped away at the keys.

Charlie waited a moment, staring at his father, then turned to go.

School seemed to last forever that day, and when the school bell rang at the end of his last class, Charlie was anxious to get going. Geoff had to meet some guys after school, delaying them.

Why today? Charlie had wondered.

He sat on the curb of the parking lot by Geoff's car, waiting. He continued looking around as if his parents might arrive at any moment to catch him—as though they possessed the supernatural ability to predict his crime. In the end, he decided that they were too busy with other things to be that attuned, but that didn't relieve his anxiety. Finally, around four thirty Geoff sauntered over to his car, and they were able to get going. Charlie had preemptively turned his phone off and he feared his dad, when he couldn't reach Charlie, might call the police and put out an alert on Geoff's car.

They made much of the drive in silence, and to Charlie it almost felt they were moving backwards due to the heavy Friday traffic. Geoff insisted on stopping for gas and something to eat in Ann Arbor, adding to Charlie's nervousness. He was beginning to feel as though they would never reach the safety of his grandfather's place and it was just before nine when they finally arrived.

As it was approaching the longest day of the year, there were still some stray sunbeams fighting their way through the clouds in the west and Charlie yearned to be out on the water. Out there in that vast freedom, feeling the breeze in his face; watching the last light of day dancing like diamonds on the water.

Geoff turned to him. "You want some different stuff for the weekend? I just got it."

"Um, sure."

Geoff reached into his pocket and tossed Charlie a small bag, filled with white powder.

"It's some Oxy I got from a guy I know, just snort a pinch in each nostril. And, hey, dude, it's not free." Geoff looked away and Charlie could sense the air shift, like in the moments before the windstorms at the cabin. Charlie loved and feared those brief moments – when the heavy air would go still, and you couldn't hear a thing but the birds calling. Then a terrible wind would come, tearing trees down and blowing around anything lighter than twenty pounds that hadn't been secured. Geoff's voice cut back into Charlie's daydreaming.

"And I'm not an Uber, bro. You're going to have to start paying for gas and shit."

Charlie was taken aback although he had felt this coming ever since the disruption in their friendship.

What am I now, a customer? Charlie wondered, thinking quickly now. *Was it always this way? Maybe Geoff was never a friend to begin with, never felt anything at all.* It had been months since they'd talked about books or movies or the state of the world and Charlie suddenly felt like a sucker.

"Fine. I'll pay you when we get back to school," he said curtly, getting out of the car quickly so Geoff wouldn't see the red bloom he could feel growing on his cheeks. "See you Sunday," he said as he slammed the car door behind himself and opened the back to grab his things.

Charlie walked up to the door and found that it was locked. He retrieved the key from under the black rock in the garden, turning first to watch Geoff's Golf speed away in the growing darkness, and then quietly letting himself in.

It was largely dark in the house, but for a little light that spilled out of the hall bathroom. Charlie wondered if his grandfather was out somewhere, maybe having a drink, but this scenario was soon dispelled by the sound of gentle snoring from the living room.

Charlie quietly closed the front door behind him, locking it and placing the key on the hall table. He made his way back to the living room and saw his grandfather slouched back in his chair. He was sleeping in one of his floral shirts and old jeans, a nearly empty glass of whisky on the table beside him. David's phone buzzed beside the glass and Charlie glanced at it to see his father's number displayed across the screen.

"Whoozat?" Charlie's grandfather mumbled, his eyes still closed.

"It's me, Charlie," Charlie whispered.

"Mmm, Charlie?" his grandfather mumbled, opening one eye. "What are you doing here?"

"Just visiting. Go back to sleep and I'll see you tomorrow."

"G'night."

"Night."

Charlie made his way across to the kitchen and opened the junk drawer where, after some shuffling, he found the key for *Fire Horse*. As he quickly slipped out the back door, he did not stop to grab his lifejacket. He trotted the well-worn path to the marina feeling his heart racing with a mixture of fear and anticipation.

The gate at the roadway was closed, a reminder that this was not the time of day for launching a boat, and he jumped the fence to make his way up the dock, attempting to stay out of the glare of the harbor lights. Charlie had never noticed before if there were any security cameras. He guessed so but didn't care; he wouldn't be here long.

Finding *Fire Horse* in her usual slip, he quickly released the moorings, switched the batteries on, and fired the engine up. He had done this so many times before, but this time it felt different.

He knew he had used up everybody's patience—his parents', Geoff's, even his grandfather's and he thought back to his study of world history earlier this year, to something he'd found interesting. Roman history. He envied the order to society, citizens working together to accomplish greatness, led by the strength and courage of the great emperors. Charlie needed courage now, and he wondered if this was how Julius Caesar had felt crossing the Rubicon, putting on a brave face while searching for it within himself. But Caesar had an army, horses, and a sense of noble purpose.

What did Charlie have?

Just himself; himself and *Fire Horse.*

The open waters of Lake Michigan beckoned, and as he broke free of the harbor and began to cruise westward, Charlie finally turned his phone on to see six missed calls, four missed texts. All from his father. He didn't bother to check them and thought it didn't matter. No one could stop him now and he didn't expect them to try calling anymore.

He hooked his phone up to the boat's stereo and set his music to play Beethoven. Perfect for an evening on the water. The Seventh Symphony. He brought the boat to a standstill at his favorite spot, shutting the engine off. As the boat bobbed up and down in the waves, he looked again at the sky in the last light of dusk, and reached in his pocket for the Oxy Geoff had given him. The stars were still feeble, but Charlie knew their strength would grow until they burned fiercely, uncontested in the night sky.

To Charlie, they were infinite promises of other worlds, other lives.

He loved looking up at them.

CHAPTER THIRTY-FIVE

Don

AUGUST 2019

DON HEARD THE FAMILIAR crunch of gravel as he turned his truck onto the driveway. Although it was growing dark, he could see Diane's blue Impala ahead and he pulled the truck alongside it. He shut the ignition off and paused a moment to prepare himself to greet her. Her text had warned him that she would be here, ready to feed him.

He stepped down from the truck and collected his overnight bag from the back seat, pausing to look up at the roof of the cabin. The top of the stone chimney was obscured from his view, as it was on the rear slope of the roofline, but Don could see gray puffs of smoke rising into the cold air and he could smell the fire.

It struck him that he had not arrived to preexisting signs of life at the cabin since his dad had been alive. It was nearly six o'clock in the evening, and the sun was down over the treetops behind him. Don still had his suit on, but did not have a coat and he felt the chill of the night air as he stepped to the porch.

He had agonized over the memorial for much of the drive home. Don had just left Julia there in the church, standing alone. A black figure in a sea of brown.

Had he run away? Should he have stayed for the lunch, tried to have a real conversation with Julia?

No, he decided, it hadn't been the right time amongst all the strangers, keeping them waiting for their luncheon hostess. He would come back for the interment. *That would be better timing*.

Leaving downtown around noon following the service, he had taken the long way back, down Woodward, and driven through Ferndale past the old rental. It was only a couple of blocks in, and it was easy to spot the house as it was still covered in baby-blue siding.

Their old swing was where it had always been, on the front porch. They'd left it for the new renters, not knowing where they could possibly use it in Birmingham. *Everything* looked as it had before, and Don felt a hopeful moment of time travel. He'd sat with his truck idling at the side of the street, lost in thought, wishing he could go back there, stay there; wishing he could hear Charlie's laughter as he ran through the house, feel his warmth as they sat together on the swing in the late evening, eating ice cream. Feel Julia beneath him in their queen bed in that tiny bedroom upstairs. That had been such a good place for the three of them. A woman had emerged from the front of the house, disturbing his reverie, and looked at him curiously. He realized it was time to move on.

The arrow of time moves relentlessly in one direction, he had thought.

Standing now in front of his dark, mahogany door, he felt a tingle in his spine as he had an image of Julia opening it to greet him. He gave his shoulders a shrug, attempting to shed the day's stress, and he fixed his gaze on the brass handle, its tarnished surface no longer reflecting anything to him. Try as he might, he could not raise his hand to grab it, fearful of what lay beyond.

Don stood frozen, until the door opened, as though of its own will, bathing him in gold.

Diane's brown hair wasn't clipped up today and hung just past her shoulder, and she was dressed for the cabin—a simple white T and faded blue jeans. Her smile was warm and without a trace of pity. He could have just been coming home from work, or the store.

She embraced him.

"I've got some supper on if you're hungry."

"You built a fire," he said, still a little shocked.

"I watched you do it last night. You don't have to show me twice. It takes the chill out of the air and makes the place smell good."

It sure does, Don thought to himself, entering his home feeling a bit like a guest.

They sat down to a dinner of chicken and gravy. Diane had made some homemade biscuits and there was corn and salad to round things out. A half-empty bottle of white wine was on the counter by the sink and Diane swept it up and brought it to the table with a glass for Don.

"Wine?"

"Yes, please."

"You've spent a lot of time on the road today. You must be tired."

"I'm okay."

"How was the memorial?"

"It went okay. David spoke and it was nice and we all got through it. I guess I don't know what I expected," Don said before stuffing some chicken into his mouth. He had not eaten since the gas station muffin he'd had on the way into Detroit that morning, and he was famished.

"This tastes great," he acknowledged.

"Didn't know if I could still cook a real meal," she said as she pulled off a piece of her biscuit with her fingers and popped it into her mouth. "I don't cook like this for myself very often."

"Delicious. You can cook for me anytime." Don had said the words before thinking. He could feel Diane taking control of things. *His* space. She had cleaned the cabin; washed *his* sheets.

She just smiled and chewed her food.

They made small talk as they ate, neither wanting to say much about what today had been. Diane gave a rundown beyond her brief texts to Don about things she'd done during the day—groceries, cleaning, preparing for dinner. She'd cleaned his fridge out and washed the floors. He didn't know what to say.

"Hey," she said, her voice brightening, "I re-read The Little Prince this afternoon, by the fire. I think I understand it better now."

"Really," he replied, wiping the last of the gravy from his plate with a biscuit. "How did you find the time?"

Before giving her a chance to answer, he looked around and continued, "The place looks great, though, thank you.

Now I won't have to worry about accidentally eating dead flies or cobwebs with my next meal."

"You wouldn't let me take you to the memorial and it was something I could do for my friend," she said, smiling and dropping her half-eaten biscuit to the plate. "'Cause that's what we are Don, friends, right?"

"Of course we are, Diane" Don said firmly.

Diane cleared the plates and returned to the table, just the empty bottle between them, their glasses still half-full.

"Did you talk to Julia?" she asked finally, her words heavy with potential.

Don took a sip of his wine to give himself time to think. *Had Julia and I really talked*? It felt more like verbal texting. *Was Diane asking what my intentions were? Today?*

"We spoke briefly. It was better than I expected, I guess. There was a time I was sure I'd never see her again," he replied after swallowing.

Diane listened patiently.

He went to sip again from his glass before realizing that he had already drained it.

"Do you want to go sit by the fire?" she asked.

"Diane, I..." he began, not sure how he was going to complete the sentence.

"Don," she said softly. "I'm too old for games. What did you mean by writing 'Love' on your note?" She didn't wait for him to answer, she had a head of steam and continued, "I think you know that I've had feelings for you ever since we met and it's never been the right time for you. Or maybe you don't feel the same way about me. I don't know. But I'm not going to apologize for it."

Diane's voice was growing softer, in contrast to her face, which was reddening - with anger or shame, or both - and she asked Don a million-dollar question, "I know today was tough but do you think it will ever be the right time?"

"I'm sorry, Diane," he said, struggling to find a better answer for her that was still honest, but the best he could do was, "I can't answer that right now."

Diane looked as upset as he'd seen her in a long time.

"Don, you keep telling me that you're not over Charlie, that the grief is still too fresh. I know that finding out what happened for sure has brought everything back for you and I'm sorry for that, I really am. And I feel selfish for thinking about what that means for me. I'm forty-five years old; I'm not getting any younger."

He hadn't known her age until now.

"I wonder if this isn't just about letting Charlie go. If this is about Julia too. Don, it sure seems like she's moved on. Can you ever accept that?"

I've asked myself that question a million times, Don thought, *why is it so hard to hear it from her lips?* The question he tortured himself over while he rocked on the front porch drinking, or when he'd awake at three in the morning and toss and turn until dawn.

No, I'll never stop loving her, he thought, *who she is...who she was.*

Diane's question prompted him to consider his motivation, yet again. They had both been so badly damaged, surely Julia was a different woman now. He knew that he was a different man. Don looked across the table at this beautiful woman in his kitchen. She had her scars too. Maybe nobody could make it to forty-five without being broken in some way. She was still waiting on him.

"Diane. You saw my note. I signed it the way I felt, so, you know how I feel about you. Why can't things just be like this for now? I'm not ready for more," he finally said, struggling to frame his thoughts, his feelings.

"Don, you've been stuck in neutral since I've known you. Someday, you have to move forward. This is no way to live."

Her tone was almost pleading.

"Hiding out in this cabin day after day. Not working. Occasionally coming into town for some brief touches of humanity, then retreating back to your hermit hole. It's not healthy."

"I know. I know." He paused to carefully consider his words. He looked straight at Diane. "This is all I can give right now. I know that has to change—I *want* it to change. I don't know when it will." Don watched her for clues about whether they could survive this.

She sat back in her chair, looking defeated.

"Don, you say I remind you of the rose, in the story," she said as she stood again from the table, "What made her precious was the time he put into caring for her."

He looked into her eyes and nodded.

"I'd love to feel a little bit of that myself. Care. Love. Life's too short to stay miserable. I'll let myself out," she said softly and without bitterness. "Maybe we can talk tomorrow; you let me know."

She dumped the last of her wine in the sink.

He watched her, frozen in his chair.

"Should you be driving?" he asked, attempting to show the right amount of concern for her, to find a non-committal way to keep her here.

"Don, I've had two glasses of wine since four. I'm fine."

She finished tidying the kitchen, refusing Don's awkward attempts to help, and gathered her things before stopping to hug him in the doorway.

"I hope you get some sleep tonight," she said gently. "Goodbye, Don."

He hugged her back and watched as she drifted over to her car, put her things in the passenger seat, and set herself behind the wheel. The roar of the engine brought the lights to life and his heart skipped a beat. He waved as she backed down the driveway, and he realized that she still carried his gun in her glovebox.

Don closed the door against her retreating car, wishing he could have explained how he felt, how complicated it was. Of course, he loved her, but he couldn't right now, he still loved Julia. Still felt... allegiance to her. Despite the fact that his sentiment had clearly not been reciprocated, his conscience would not allow him to violate that boundary.

How long will I wait? Until Julia finalizes our divorce? Remarries? he wondered.

He went back into the living room, poured himself a drink, and sat alone as the last of the logs turned to ash in the fire.

Chapter Thirty-Six

Julia

August 2019

Julia met her father at his hotel for breakfast. This being a Sunday morning, there were no business travelers, so the dining area was sparsely populated. He sat across from her at a four-top, sipping his coffee and scanning the menu. Julia knew he was going to head back to Saint Joseph shortly and she had wanted to see him off, cement the repairs in the relationship.

She was tired of going backwards. She had talked to Gerrard already today and rehashed the daily platitudes. It was like he had a playbook for the scenario: *How are you today? Did you sleep well? I'm thinking about you, love. I wish I could be there.* She pictured him at the flat, reciting these lines while idling turning pages in some business magazine. Or perhaps sipping his tea across from a young American lover - she, watching him over her coffee, wearing nothing but Julia's bathrobe.

Be careful to be quiet, I'm speaking to my grieving girlfriend, he would whisper to her.

She found that the thought did not incite much rebellion in her, but she also felt slightly guilty at creating this straw man of Gerrard in her mind, making it easier to knock him down. She knew it was unfair and wondered if it betrayed some deeper instinct she had about the man. She had given herself some guilty pleasure during the call by toying with the idea of shocking the shit out of him.

I'm pregnant with your baby and I'm having an abortion. Your voice makes my stomach turn. I don't think I ever loved you. It helped her get through it, the thought of forcing Gerrard, in all his goddamned aloofness, to share in her grief, to feel something up close and personal for once.

She looked up at her father and was still amazed at how much younger he looked than the last time she saw him, wondering how much of it was him, and how much was her, seeing what she wanted, what she needed, to see.

"Dad, thanks again for coming, and for speaking. It was beautiful." She drained the last of her coffee.

"I wanted to be there, for you *and* for Charlie," he said simply. "Will you be okay tomorrow?"

"Yeah. I'll be fine."

"What about Don?"

What about Don? she thought. They hadn't really talked yesterday. He'd seemed anxious to go after the service.

"He'll be there, I think."

"That's not what I meant. Things ended sort of abruptly for you two, didn't they?"

She paused, considering what to share with her father, how to explain things.

"I guess," was all she could manage.

"Do you feel like talking things through with him, maybe working some things out?" David asked over the top of his cup.

Julia opened her mouth to speak but was silent, searching for the answers to her father's questions.

"Dad, when I look at him, I picture Charlie. I think of all the times we weren't good parents," she finally blurted. "I think of how I failed. Things *I* should have done differently." Her father just stared, cup in hand, waiting for her to continue.

"We argued bitterly in the end, Dad," she said finally, searching him for any signs of allegiance. She knew he'd liked Don, even loved him like the son he'd never had, and she sometimes wondered, although he'd never said so, if he had ever wished he'd had a son instead of a daughter.

"He told me that he thought Charlie had committed suicide, that there could be no other explanation," Julia said, suddenly curious about what her *father* thought had happened that evening, realizing that she didn't want to know, didn't want to risk being outnumbered in her hope. "Charlie would have never done that to us," she continued, unable to look her father in the eye, staring at her empty cup while playing with it in her hand. "He would have left a note, something to explain himself. He wouldn't just vanish."

Julia bore a different kind of guilt than Don, choosing to believe that Charlie's death had been an accident, and clinging to those words printed in ink on the final police report. In her mind, she saw Charlie on the boat, looking up at the stars, inspired to take a swim and losing track of the boat in the darkness.

He was fully clothed, Don would whisper from the back of her mind.

No, then, he'd climbed up at the rear of the boat to look at something—a splash in the water, perhaps—a sudden wave causing the boat to lurch and throw him overboard. Or, he had taken some drugs from Geoff, and in a state of disorientation, had simply fallen overboard.

What about the lifejacket? Don would whisper in her brain.

Just shut up! He forgot it! she'd reply.

Oh really? For the first time in eight years?

She'd had this argument with Don countless times in her mind. The living, breathing Don had no idea of the things she'd imagined him saying to her over these past four years, how he'd pummeled at her fantasy with his relentless, dispassionate logic, how much she fucking hated her caricature of him for it.

In her least-plausible scenario, she imagined another boat of boys meeting him out there in a drug deal gone bad. Maybe he'd owed them money, so they'd pushed him into the water, murdering her only son. She hadn't even possessed the courage to raise *this* possibility with the police, instead saving it for her own imagination.

The main source of her guilt, rather, was founded in the contingencies that led to Charlie being on the boat by himself at night, the millions of little branch points in her past. Words and actions that could have changed the course of things. *If only.* She just wanted to go back and change one thing—anything.

Don't make the move from Ferndale—he continues to thrive in his familiar environment, surrounded by good friends and loving parents. *Don't selfishly go off to work. Dedicate your time to him, loving him, understanding him*—he doesn't shut himself off. *Don't send him to writing camp*—he never meets Geoff. *Don't banish him to boot camp*—he doesn't flee that weekend. They would all be home together in Birmingham now.

She'd had a million chances to alter the course of events right up to that weekend. *If only* she had made one different choice. Just one. She'd had the power but hadn't known how to use it when it would have counted, and this, this was the cornerstone of the grief that she'd clung to fiercely for four years. Replaying a multitude of better lives, lives in which Charlie never needed to go out on the lake and die.

When she was being rational, she would tell herself that she couldn't know how these alternate realities would have played out either. Some might have been worse. She would never know, but one thing she knew for sure was that she didn't believe in fate. Charlie had not been destined to die that weekend.

Thinking of alternate realities, *the way things might have been*, led her to the source of her other guilt, a deeper secret she could rarely acknowledge even to herself. The one that crept into her mind against her wishes, in the depths of the long, lonely nights, when she had no distractions to drive it away. The voice in her head that wondered what life would have been like had she gone ahead with an abortion, and that Charlie had never been born. *Could she have been happy then?*

She was lost in her thoughts when her father chose to speak.

"Julia. You and Don were better parents than your mother and I ever were, God rest her soul." She lifted her face to look at him, and she could feel large tears rolling freely down her cheeks.

His face softened and he continued, "Julia, we're all only one chance, one mistake, one coincidence away from tragedy. I'm so sorry that this happened—for all our sakes. But whatever it was, it wasn't your fault. You *have* to forgive yourself." He emphasized this point urgently.

"What if I can't?"

"You have to. I'd be dead now if I hadn't found a way to forgive myself."

"How, Dad? How did you?" Julia hoped her father had some secret source of wisdom she could tap into, her hope a flashback to her childhood, to a time when a father could do anything.

He looked away for a minute, as though searching for the answer somewhere in the hotel lobby.

"Grief becomes a habit if you let it. A companion that, if you feed it, grows in you until you don't know if you can ever live without it. Everyone says *time is the answer*, I don't completely agree. It takes time *and* a decision," he said, staring at her and pressing his index finger down against the tabletop.

"I quit my grief the way I quit smoking and drinking, I decided to. Cold turkey. Oh, it was not easy," David acknowledged, "Some nights all I could think of was how I had taken your mother's love for granted, of what a terrible husband I had been. On those nights I wished I could just curl up and die."

Julia watched him intently, wanting more than anything, to understand. David inhaled silently through parted lips and paused, causing Julia to fear her father had just frozen there.

"We think we're entitled to so much in this world," he finally spoke again, "Four score and ten. A happy marriage, good kids, grandkids. But we're not entitled to any of it, we just *think* we are. So when something terrible happens, we focus on the loss of a thing that was never ours to begin with." He paused as though giving her time to let the words settle in, to filter down through her system.

"I know this may sound like bullshit, but I get past my grief by counting my thanks for the precious time I *did* have with Charlie. I look at those pictures in my mind,

I read our poems. I listen to the memory of his voice." Her father's lip began to tremble. "I think of you and how grateful I am for you."

She came around from the table and hugged him, her eyes refusing to run dry.

"Please try," he said, patting her back.

It was hard seeing him off and she felt protective, her father looking small again as he struggled to sit himself down into the low seat of the rental car. She feared for his drive home and fought the urge to chase after him, to go with him to St. Joseph. She could just forget about Gerrard and move in with her father where they would care for each other for the rest of his days.

As he pulled away from the curb, she realized that reconnecting with her father had been a revelation, a moment of pure truth that she'd found unsettling, causing her to reexamine the life she'd lived these last few years, like a snow globe in her hand.

It had been an artificial construct she now realized, her life after Don and Charlie. The relationship choices she'd made - avoiding the messy entanglements that would have required her to feel deeply, to put herself out there. She'd favored those that permitted superficial engagement, just background noise to fill the room. Reruns of a beloved tv program where everyone said the familiar lines, and there were no uncomfortable surprises. Lisa. Gerrard. They hadn't demanded too much of her, and she hadn't offered much in return.

As she waved goodbye to her father's retreating car, Julia knew this meant she could never go back. The glass on her illusion had been shattered into a million pieces and she would never be able—or even want—to put them back together again.

Chapter Thirty-Seven

Don

August 2019

Don spent most of Sunday busying himself around the cabin. He threw the bait away and disarmed the bear trap. He cut the grass—on a Sunday. He'd never let Charlie do that in Birmingham. But out here it didn't matter because his next neighbor was a quarter mile away. He applied some paint to the trim around the outside of the cabin; it had been damaged that spring by some animal or another chewing on it. Maybe a porcupine, willing to eat anything to survive. He cleaned the windows.

In his darkest moments, he couldn't help but acknowledge to himself that these efforts were ultimately pointless. *Why swim upstream? Mother Nature always wins in the end, she plays the long game.* Today, however, he had managed to imbue these tasks with meaning, and he savored the distraction they offered. It was sunny and warm, and tomorrow would be the last day of August. Summer was over, autumn was coming.

He had actually slept in. It was staying dark longer, and he'd been exhausted from the drain of Charlie's memorial as well as his conversation with Diane, so it was nine before he had taken his first coffee. He'd texted Diane as he'd sat on the front porch with his coffee, staring at the place her car had been.

Morning. Thanks again for everything. I don't know what I'd do without you.

You're welcome. She'd replied after a moment.

This is why he hated texting. He'd had no idea what that had meant. He'd sat pondering her message for a while before deciding to call her.

"Hi, Don," she'd said evenly. "Did you sleep alright?"

"Yes, I did for a change."

"That's good."

Chirping birds had filled the silence.

"What are you up to today?" he'd asked.

"Well, I've got my own things to do today. I've kind of neglected *my* chores the last couple of days. Laundry, shopping, you know, all the fun stuff. I got a full week of shifts at the store starting tomorrow so today's my big chance."

"Yeah. I should let you get to it."

"Okay. Text me after the cemetery tomorrow," she'd said, "If you want to," she had then added, sounding hesitant.

"Will do. Enjoy your day."

"Bye, Don."

So, he'd forced himself to move, needing to fill twenty-four hours before the next meaningful event in his life. He'd gone almost four years with none. Nothing noteworthy to mark the monotonous drumbeat of the days. *Monday, Tuesday, Friday, what day was it again? What difference did it make?* As he reflected on it, he realized Diane had been right; he had lost his drive for work, had no family life, nothing to pull him out of his self-imposed isolation. The news concerning Charlie had been the first shockwave to interrupt the numbing rhythm of the earth's relentless rotation around itself, around the sun.

He put his things away in the shed as the afternoon drew long and checked his phone. No calls or texts. After a shower and some food, he grabbed a beer and returned to the front porch. He drank half the beer on the first swig, and pulled his jacket closed against the cool evening air. He set the bottle down, and grasped the rough wooden arms that surrounded him, holding them tightly.

Chapter Thirty-Eight

Don and Julia

August 2019

Don's GPS had taken him to I-75 and then I-94. He exited at Lonyo, and as he turned right onto Dix, he marveled at the contrasts of the city. To his right was Detroit Iron & Metal, a wasteland of jagged scrap metal piles, only partially concealed by red-stained wooden fencing, leaning and rotting with age. Great excavators roamed the grounds, yellow dinosaurs in search of their prey. It was something out of a dystopian nightmare.

As he drove further down Dix, the iron graveyard yielded to green, lush trees dotting a hilly landscape. It was at a break in the trees that Don found the entrance to the cemetery and pulled in, driving under the red-brick archway and winding his way through the maze of the cemetery until he found plot 'T'. He glanced at the clock on the dash, nervous about the time; it was three fifty-two p.m. He had gotten a late start, agonizing over something he'd wanted to bring for Julia. He had searched the office, not finding it and had to descend again to the depths of the cellar and search through three bins until he could place his hands on it. The traffic had also been bad for some reason on I-75.

As Don arrived at plot 'T', he struggled with the notion of resting in a strange place, a place that held no memories for surviving family members in mourning. His father had left instructions to be buried beside his Cynthia, in Lake Orion. When Reg was alive, Don, Julia, and Charlie would visit, and from time to time they'd all go out to the cemetery. Reg would place flowers at the base of his wife's headstone, and they would all stand there uncomfortably until Reg decided that it was time to leave. Don had no memories of his mother, but he thought for his father it must have felt *unnatural*, heading somewhere strange to remember his wife. Somewhere that held no echoes of their shared time on earth. His father had purchased the plot beside Cynthia, nonetheless, and when he had passed away, Don had respected his wishes and had him buried there. Until Charlie's disappearance, Don, Julia, and Charlie had continued with their annual visits to pay their respects.

Don's views on cemeteries formed the basis for his wish that Charlie be cremated, not buried to spend eternity under strange earth. The subject had not come up with

Julia directly, as they could not bring themselves to contemplate Charlie's burial when he had only been missing, and he was not about to have the argument brokered through Lisa in e-mails. Julia and Don had really only argued the point in concept when they had been together. She favored the traditional approach, and despite her lackluster commitment to the Catholic Church, she had expressed a desire to be buried with her mother and grandmother. The unspoken compromise she'd unilaterally offered of agreeing to cremate Charlie, only to bury his ashes had seemed hollow to Don.

He saw Julia and the priest, through his windshield, up to his left. Two other people in suits he didn't know were lurking at a respectful distance. He parked and hurried to the small gathering, and as he approached, Julia looked up at him and gave a small smile. She was wearing the same black dress from Saturday.

As he approached her, he noticed that the hole in the ground near her feet was not large. It was, however, deep. He didn't know what he expected. Of course it didn't make sense to dig a big hole for a small box. Don's eyes were drawn to the ornate container standing out against the stone and earth around it.

Father Willis invited them to begin. He spoke the words of the invitation and gave a scripture reading, finishing with the blessing: "Almighty God, you created the earth and shaped the vault of heaven; you fixed the stars in their places. When we were caught in the snares of death, you set us free through baptism; in obedience to your will, our Lord Jesus Christ broke the fetters of hell and rose to life, bringing deliverance and resurrection to those who are his by faith. In your mercy, look upon this grave so that your servant may sleep here in peace; and on the day of judgment, raise him up to dwell with your saints in paradise. We ask this through Christ our Lord. Amen."

Don didn't recognize Charlie in these words. They held little meaning for him, and yet he was surprised to find that he took some comfort in the tradition of them; that they had been spoken for countless millions who had lived and died before and found their rest.

Father Willis shook Julia's hand and then came to shake Don's.

"We didn't get to speak the other day. I'm sorry for your loss."

"Thank you, Father."

Soon, Julia and Don were alone at the grave, but for the two men who were still clasping their hands together in front of their belts, waiting to perform their tasks. Don couldn't help but notice the top of a bright, yellow backhoe just over the crest of the hill behind the two men. A lost baby dinosaur from the scrapyard.

"Don, how are you?" Julia asked with genuine concern in her tone.

"I'm okay, Julia. There's so much I want to tell you."

"I know. Me too, in time. I have something for you. In the car."

They walked toward the driveway and Julia grabbed Don's hand, squeezing it once. They came to a black Lincoln with a figure sitting in the front, motionless, and Don wondered why Julia had a driver today. He decided not to ask and watched as Julia opened the rear door, pulled out a small, plain box from the seat, turned and handed it carefully to him.

"What's this?" he asked.

"Charlie's ashes."

"They weren't buried?"

"Some were, but most are in here. I wanted you to have them—if you want."

Don accepted them from her, not knowing what to say.

"Don. I'm sorry," she continued. "I was angry at the world, at you, my father, even Charlie, but most of all, myself." She paused, her green eyes dry as they flicked back and forth between his, and to Don it looked like she was reading him for something. "For what it's worth, I forgive you. Now I need to work on forgiving myself."

She embraced him, holding him tightly while he helplessly held the box with Charlie's ashes in it in his right hand, unable to fully reciprocate.

Her body was so familiar against him and he ached at the feel of it. When she pulled away, they were both crying.

Don switched the box to his left hand and fumbled in his pocket with his right, bringing out a small object.

"Here. This belongs to you." He handed her a silver ring.

She took the ring and examined it as though for the first time. He thought back to the night at the Alley Bar when he'd given it to her.

She smiled and gently put the ring back in his hand.

"Don, it's a beautiful gesture, but I can't accept this." She hesitated, then added, "Right now."

She hugged him once more and set herself down into the rear seat. "Oh," she said, reaching into her purse and pulling out a folded piece of paper. "This is my e-mail address and phone number. Let me know how you're doing, Don."

Don watched the car leave, carrying Julia away, away from this place of death and back to her life. He held the ring in his hand for a time, then put it into his suit pocket. He glanced around, as if just realizing where he was and went to his truck.

The guardians at the grave waited patiently for him to depart.

Chapter Thirty-Nine

Don

August 2019

Don felt a weight lift as he left the confines of Detroit. He called Diane on his cell, his old truck forcing him to commit a misdemeanor every time he needed to talk while driving.

"Hello?"

"Diane. I'm on my way home."

"Are you okay? How did it go?"

"Fine," he said, glancing at the box on the passenger seat beside him. "The GPS says I'll be back to the cabin around nine."

"Would you like me to go over there and make you something to eat for when you get in?"

Don hesitated briefly.

"No thanks, Diane. I think I need to be alone right now."

"Oh, okay. Drive safely, and please let me know when you get there so I don't worry."

He hung up as he pulled onto I-696 with two hundred miles to go.

It was silent in the truck, save for the rhythm of the highway and Don was unable to distract himself from thoughts of Diane.

For some reason, he still had Sirius on his truck radio. He had not bothered or been able to figure out how to cancel it. It was another barnacle that society had attached to him, and he'd not found the energy to free himself of it. He tuned it now to an easy listening, alternative station featuring B-Sides.

Music had been a love of Don's when he was younger and he could remember laying in his room with Julia when they were dating, anxious to play her some CD he had just bought, urging her to listen, *really listen* to the lyrics. He'd always had trouble getting past his logical mind and in touch with his emotions; there were times he'd felt that music was the only medium that could ever really touch him deeply, and that could say the words he didn't have the courage to form. Now, like nearly everything else in his life, it had gradually reduced to background noise.

He wondered if it was something wrong with him or if it was just the human condition. Experiences always seemed the most enjoyable the first time around - sex, music, food, but after countless repetitions, everything begins to fade, becomes less vivid. The memories of the first experience providing the hopeful desire to keep trying. He did know that being with Diane felt different. It felt new.

A man's trembling voice rang out, capturing Don's attention. The lyrics resonated with Don in that moment, causing him to feel, however irrationally, as though the song was written *for him*. The singer sang with such sincerity and emotion that he had to know who it was.

He waited patiently and saw the words scroll in green block letters across the old Ford display. *Gale Song. The Lumineers.* He would remember that. He wanted to find it and maybe play it for Diane. He could feel the tension in his shoulders slipping away, and he realized that he hadn't thought of his gun since Diane had confiscated it three long days ago.

Don rolled his windows down for the last twenty miles, wanting to breathe the fresh air and cleanse himself. He slowed at the drive and heard the familiar crunch of the gravel.

This time, there were no warm lights to invite him up the drive. No smell of smoke coming from the cabin, no Diane opening the door to welcome him in.

Don went straight for the fridge to grab a beer, and he could feel the comfort of his old routine settle in around his heart.

Chapter Forty

Julia

September 2019

THE BLACK CAR PULLED up in front of Gerrard's flat. It had been noon by the time Julia had escaped Heathrow's web and made her way into the city, the driver constantly apologizing for the traffic and blaming construction. She'd hardly heard him, staying focused on what she planned to do, hoping she wouldn't falter.

She didn't bother unpacking her things. A hot shower was in order, and on her way to the bathroom she suddenly felt a desire to do something she hadn't done in years. Without showering she changed into her T-shirt and sports shorts and found her outdoor sneakers in a bin at the rear of the closet.

It was mild, not more than seventy-five, but it was humid. It was hard getting her jet-lagged body going and her legs were stiff and sore before she was a mile in. She began by walking brusquely, and even at that cool sweat started to bead on her arms quickly in the moist air.

As she walked down King's Road past the Saatchi Gallery, she turned right. It felt good to be moving again and her body remembered its rhythm after she had broken it in, then she felt a burst of energy and fought through her jet lag as she began to run. Finally, she ran through Ranelagh Gardens and aimed straight for the river.

Passing through a colorful children's playground, she pulled up at the riverbank to catch her breath. Julia forced herself to stay there for a few minutes confronting the gray water of the Thames as it drifted by her, oblivious to her anxieties. Finally, she extended her two middle fingers toward the river and set back home to the comfort of a hot shower and clean clothing.

Gerrard managed to come home early, around five thirty, to greet her. His warm smile vanished as she said, "Gerrard, we have to talk."

She told him of the baby, and her plan to keep it. She told him that she did not love him and would be leaving him to live near the college using some savings she had from the sale of the house in Birmingham. She would finish her last term, then go to America to have the baby, to find work, and to find herself. She was going back to be near her father—her family, and she didn't expect anything of him, but he could be involved if he wished. It was fine, though, if he didn't.

He sat dumbfounded. It was unfair of her to dump all of this on him at once. She knew that he did not deserve this, but it was the only way she could get through it - headfirst. He wanted to talk about it, work through it, but she had left no openings, no *maybes* in her plan. He oscillated between appeals and anger. *He would get a lawyer if he had to. She could not waltz in here and tell him what to do.*

Julia felt like she was watching an express demonstration of the five stages of grief as Gerrard spun around in confusion, and a part of her wondered where this passion had come from, wishing he had shown some of it during their time together.

He would think about things and let her know. They were going to need to talk about this, he'd said. *He just needed time.*

Fair enough. I have time, she thought.

She slept that night in a separate room in the flat, the room she used to rent from Gerrard. *How funny*, she thought as she lay in bed, her brief amusement replaced by the anxiety of what was ahead for her tomorrow, and beyond.

Finally, she fell into a dreamless sleep.

She awoke early and set to pack, choosing to only take her favorite things, and leaving the rest behind for Gerrard to deal with, suggesting he donate her unwanted things to a local charity. She would start fresh, and anyway, she was going to be needing maternity clothes before long.

She had secured a hotel closer to the college and would begin the search immediately for a small apartment to rest her head in for the next eight months while she finished school. Julia's due date was April twenty-seventh, just when her school term would finish, and this meant that there was a chance that her baby might be born in London before she could make it back. That was okay with her, it was just one more complexity in her already complicated life, and although the uncertainty was at times scary, it was also exhilarating, and she embraced it.

Gerrard took the day off to drive her to the hotel. He continued to try to talk her out of this move on the drive, his enthusiasm gradually fading until it almost felt like a show for her sake; it was as though he knew this was how he *should be feeling* while watching the mother of his child go and losing the love of his life. He seemed focused on demonstrating to her that he had no part in this separation, no responsibility for the state of their relationship and she found that his hollow theatre only strengthened her resolve, and mitigated her guilt.

"I'm sorry for how things turned out. I'll be in touch," he offered, hugging her at the entrance to the building.

"I wish you all the best, Ger," she said as she returned his embrace.

She grabbed her bags, and without any further help from Gerrard, turned and strode through the hotel's glass entryway as it opened automatically to yield a path for her.

CHAPTER FORTY-ONE

Don

SEPTEMBER 2019

DON PULLED UP TO David's house at about eleven in the morning. He exited his truck and made his way to the front door, glancing at the sky and carrying a small canvas bag he'd grabbed from the front seat. Clouds were gathering, but they weren't calling for rain until later in the afternoon and he thought they would be okay.

David greeted him at the door and invited him in, offering a brief macho embrace first. As with Julia at the burial, Don could only reciprocate with one arm as the other continued to hold the bag aloft.

"Don. Sorry we didn't have a chance to talk at the funeral. Come, come," David instructed.

They made their way through to the back of the house where David sat in the lounger and beckoned for Don to sit on the couch. Don complied, setting the bag down beside himself as he perched forward on the edge of the furniture.

"Can I offer you anything to drink?" David asked.

Don did not want to linger here, among the sour memories that hung like smog in this little living room, in this little building. Memories of coming down with Julia and Charlie to visit. Feeling cramped in this dingy room full of stale sweat and smoke; feeling sorry for what David had become. Memories of bringing the boat here, and then the frantic search for Charlie that had anchored itself in this house. Although Don did not feel comfortable, he did believe that whatever eternal spirit Charlie may possess wove threads straight through this room and out to the lake.

"I'm good, thanks." Don inhaled and noticed the air in the house was fresher now, the room a little brighter than he remembered. He took note of the absence of ashtrays around the living room.

"David, thank you for your words at the funeral." *Had it already been two weeks?* Don thought before continuing, "That meant a lot to me, and I'm sure it did to Julia too."

"She's found a little place near the college to rent. She's going to finish her courses and then come back here to America. She couldn't be here today though," David stated, looking at his shoes. "Too hard for her, I think."

Don knew about Julia and Gerrard's separation, as she had e-mailed him the news in a short update a week after her return to England. She had wanted to know how Don was coping, and Don found that he cherished the fragile e-mail link that had now been established. It seemed an acknowledgment of his worth, his humanity. She had also connected him with David again, saying that it would be good for them both.

They sat in silence a little longer, Don worrying about the weather.

"She's ready to go," David finally said. "Shall we?"

They left through the back door, David pausing to grab a couple of lifejackets from the cupboard at the rear of the house.

They processed silently down to the marina, and as they arrived Don recognized the boat immediately, located in the second to last slip on the left near the end of the pier. He stopped briefly.

David paused to consider him.

"You okay with this?" David asked.

Don nodded. They continued down to the boat.

David had cleaned the boat up and it looked like new. Across the hull on the starboard side, David had replaced the word *Fire*. The boat was now *Charlie's Horse*. Don looked at David.

"I thought he'd get a kick out of that," David said with a sheepish smile. Don liked it and told David so, adding his blessing for what it was worth.

David's wit *had* been a good match for Charlie.

They climbed aboard. The wind was picking up a little, rocking the boat gently side to side against the dock. David started the engine, released the lines and they moved out onto the lake.

Don sat in a separate first mate's chair to the left of David, and water from the waves occasionally broke over the bow, misting the windshield in front of them. David was a model of concentration, looking comfortable at the helm, adjusting the throttle and trim of the engine naturally. He wore a blue windbreaker over a thick wool sweater.

He was born to be at sea, all he needs is a big beard and a pipe, Don smiled to himself.

"I'll show you where he liked to go," David said over the noise of the engine and wind.

David held the boat to twenty knots, just fast enough to get it to plane out, and after about ten minutes heading west, he brought the boat to idle. "We're almost four miles out," David said. "Charlie liked to come here. You can barely see the shore—mostly just water. Charlie loved that."

David fiddled with the radio and the calming sounds of Yo Yo Ma playing Bach began to filter through the speakers, the mathematical precision of the music in stark contrast to the wind and waves around them. This resonated with Don. The notion of order amidst chaos; the paradox of nature.

They listened to the music intently, neither seeming to want to disturb the moment.

"We'd listen to his playlists out here while we read poetry." David finally broke the silence, and Don smiled and nodded. He was thankful for the bond his son had shared with this man.

Don reached into the bag he'd brought and pulled out the little box with Charlie's ashes in it. He held it aloft near the side of the boat, balancing it against the gentle rocking of the lake, and it looked like he was about to make an offering to the sky. Don hadn't expected this to be so hard, but he hadn't wanted the ministry of a stranger in black to be the last word for his only son.

David grabbed a worn book out of the glove box and began to read Yeats aloud:

"'We sat grown quiet at the name of love;

We saw the last embers of daylight die,

And in the trembling blue-green of the sky

A moon, worn as if it had been a shell

Washed by time's waters as they rose and fell

About the stars and broke in days and years.

I had a thought for no one's but your ears:

That you were beautiful, and that I strove

To love you in the old high way of love;

That it had all seemed happy, and yet we'd grown

As weary-hearted as that hollow moon.'"

Don emptied the ashes overboard.

"Goodbye, Charlie. Be at peace," was all he could manage. He sat back down amidst the sounds of the cello and the wind for what seemed like an eternity, the rhythm of the waves and the music lulling him into a trance.

David looked up at the sound of thunder in the distance. "Time to head in," he said authoritatively.

Don braced himself for the return to speed as they turned back for shore. As they made their way in, the roar of the engine and the wind made it difficult to converse, and Don could not hear the music anymore. In the chaos of noise and wind, he was left to his own thoughts, and they returned to the power of human will to create, even just sustain, beauty amidst the violence and unpredictability of nature. Today, for the first time in a very long time, he saw that effort as something more than an exercise in futility, more than hopeless swimming against the tide. Even though he knew that all of humankind's achievements would fall before nature in time, and maybe because of that, today the efforts of his fellow human beings and even his own, felt noble. Don thought again of Diane. Her steadfastness, her strength.

They had sustained a fragile interaction by text over these last two weeks and he felt the urge to see her again. Maybe he would call when he got to shore, to see if she would come for dinner tomorrow. He hadn't cooked for anyone for a long time and he found himself growing excited at the prospect, even nervous. He worried over whether she would say yes, hoping he hadn't frightened or hurt her too much.

The wind and waves grew more intense.

David had warned him how quickly things could change out here and Don felt an irrational fear grow in his stomach, awakening senses that had long lay dormant. Reflexively, he looked at the lifejackets under their seats, reassuring himself that they were still close at hand. Water broke over the bow with each wave now as the boat bounced more violently up and down between the swells. Don looked to David, still calm at the helm in the face of the growing storm.

Finally, Don could faintly see the marina ahead. It was mid-afternoon, but the clouds had darkened the skies, and it was the twinkling of lights, the first evidence of life, that Don noticed. He found himself looking forward – to putting his feet safely back on shore, to thanking David, to heading to the comfort of his home.

To Diane.

Chapter Forty-Two

Julia

April 2020

Julia cradled her massive belly with her arms as she sat at her little kitchen table sipping water and looking out at the park, where the trees were becoming silhouettes in the gathering darkness. The world had been turned upside down by a terrifying new virus during her last term in London and her courses were now online, permitting her to take her exams remotely. Julia had seized the opportunity to make her escape back to Michigan before the flights had been shut down, and she had rented a small place in Ann Arbor.

She told herself that she had chosen Ann Arbor because it was safe, because the hospital was close, because it was vibrant and full of opportunity. Secretly, she wondered if its connection with her past had influenced her decision in some way.

Gerrard's threats had evaporated over time, and the contact with him was becoming less frequent and more sterile. She wondered if he even cared about the baby in her belly. He would not be there for the birth, but she would, of course, tell him about it and send a picture. She would not refuse him what she herself had lost - time with his only child, but she would ask nothing of him. She was determined to make it on her own.

She had told Don she was coming, told him about the baby. He said that he *was happy for her, maybe they could meet sometime, when things weren't so crazy, for coffee.* She thought that might be nice, they had a lot to catch up on. She had been pleased to hear that he was working again - on some article concerning the politics of governing through a pandemic. At least he was trying to make some good come out of this misery. He'd also mentioned wanting to introduce her to a new girlfriend, a thought that was initially painful for her, but which had settled into her mind as something *good*, relieving some of her guilt over not being there for Don herself.

Her father had not come to see her yet, each of them concerned about the risk to the other, but they had spoken almost daily since her return. She found herself anxious for their reunion, grateful for something she had nearly denied herself.

She had spent time with a therapist in London and felt that those sessions were what she was missing the most after her abrupt departure. She had maintained contact with her therapist by e-mail, and they had even held a Zoom call, but it wasn't the same. Ultimately, her therapist had informed her that she would not be able to meet remotely as she wasn't licensed outside of the UK, leaving Julia to wonder if she should search for one in Ann Arbor. As she reflected on this, she realized that she was feeling stronger now, the life inside of her demanding more and more of her focus.

She finished her water and made herself some dinner. After clearing the dishes and attempting to read a little, she rose to head up to bed. Julia found that she needed her sleep more than ever now, and her body clock was still struggling to find its way to America. She fell asleep as soon as her head hit the pillow.

That night, she dreamt of Charlie again. They were back at her garden in Birmingham, seated at the table by the rosebushes, and the roses were strangely no longer red, but the brightest yellow Julia had seen. Charlie offered his usual apologies, but this time, Julia was able to hear herself speak to him.

I forgive you, Charlie. For everything.

He stood, approached her, and they embraced.

Good luck... he finally said. *...with the baby.*

She awoke and reoriented herself. She was in her bed in Ann Arbor and it was still the middle of the night. Julia knew it would take time to make it a home—for her, as well as for the baby—and as she lay back, she thought of Don and her father, felt the comfort of knowing they were out there somewhere, supporting her.

She tucked the warm blankets tightly around her neck and fell back into a dreamless slumber.

Epilogue

SUMMER 2022

The old man looked out to the shoreline of Lake Michigan from his chair on the beach, shielding his eyes from the glare of the setting sun with his right hand. The sun's last golden rays cast two figures in silhouette, walking at a distance, along the water's edge.

The pair drew closer, a woman and a little boy clutching a toy shovel in his left hand and holding hers tightly with his right, and they were talking and smiling. They continued that way for a while, their toes being kissed by the gentle tide, causing the little boy to squeal in delight, until the woman turned to look at the old man and smiled, prompting him to smile back and wave.

The woman and boy returned his wave, turning slowly away from him toward the west, and the old man watched with joy as they stepped into the surf.

Acknowledgments

Many thanks are in order.

To my loyal circle of first readers: Susan Goertz, Fiona Miller, Dan Keating, Michelle Norris, Helen Davis, Deanne Goertz, Nicola Goertz, Peter Shaheen, Leslie Immel, Chuck Immel, John Hein, Christine Meath, Jen Johns, Frances Patry and her book club, Kathy Wolfe, Janet Davis, thank you. Some of you provided helpful, gentle criticism, and others quietly read—or endured—both of which were helpful to me in seeing this through. I truly appreciate it. There is a piece of each of you in this book, and through you, I learned how truly collaborative the art of writing can be.

To my editor, Jess McKelden, thank you for your guidance and encouragement, and for catching my sloppy grammar, as well as those pesky typos.

To the voice of the story, Madeline DeCorso, your beautiful voice and immense talent brought this work (and the stories of Don, Julia, David, Charlie, Diane and others) to life in a way that I didn't think possible, and your interpretation helped me greatly in improving the story.

To my sound engineer, Pascal Langdale - a true Renaissance Man if ever there was one - thank you for lending your talent and studio to this project.

To my family: Dorothy and Gary Olney, my daughters, Katie, Robyn and Melissa, and, as always, my wife (and manager) Shirley, your support and tolerance of this project has made all the difference.

Afterword

By way of reference, I have quoted pre-existing works from various sources: *The Little Prince*, by Antoine Saint-Exupéry, selected works of Patrick Kavanagh and W.B. Yeats, as well as certain prayers from the Catholic book of worship and funeral rites. I hold myself as no expert on any of them but have noted the origin when referenced so that it is obvious that these are not my work.

The proverbial last word goes to my archenemy: the typo. I have come to believe that these devils breed when I am away from the keyboard, the most common being "he" instead of "the" and "form" instead of "from" —spell checker being useless for these. I have scrubbed this book ad nauseam and apologize for any remaining typos, although I am confident that my excellent editor, Jess McKelden, has caught my errors. Let's hope the typos don't breed while we sleep.

Magnetawan, Ontario, Canada